"This is cool," Anthony says.

"Yeah."

"The dance floor is empty. Always is this time of night. Nobody admits that they want to dance until a lot later in the evening. It's tradition or something. You see people hanging around the edges of the dance floor. You even see some of them moving in time with the music, a reduced version of what they'll be doing when there are enough people on the dance floor to justify going out themselves. I don't know. I'd probably analyze the situation and try to develop a theory of why that is—self-consciousness? drinks/drugs having yet to kick in?—but I'm too busy staring at Anthony.

"Want to head upstairs?" he asks.

> **Upstairs:** *Upstairs* has connotations. *Upstairs* is the place your friends, if they're sensible, always warn you not to go. Downstairs is where you go if you just want to dance. Downstairs is neutral. Upstairs is not.

"Okay."

Dance REcover rEPEaT

ALASDAIR DUNCAN

books™

POCKET BOOKS

NEW YORK LONDON TORONTO SYDNEY

POCKET BOOKS, a division of Simon & Schuster, Inc.
1230 Avenue of the Americas, New York, NY 10020

First published in 2003 under the title *SUSHI CENTRAL* by University of Queensland Press, PO Box 6024, St Lucia, Queensland 4067, Australia

Published by arrangement with University of Queensland Press

Cover design: Lance Rusoff
Cover photography: Michael Greenberg/TROOPER
Cover design director: Deklah Polansky
Executive design director: Jeffrey Keyton

ISBN: 1-4165-0342-0

First MTV Books/Pocket Books trade paperback printing April 2005

10   9   8   7   6   5   4   3   2   1

Manufactured in the United States of America

For information regarding special discounts for bulk purchases, please contact Simon & Schuster Special Sales at 1-800-456-6798 or business@simonandschuster.com.

Dance REcover rePEaT

0

Pause.

"Give it to me."

"No!"

"Give it to me Jonathan! You always die in this part."

"Do not."

"Yes you do."

"I didn't die last time."

"Yeah you did! Come on, we had to go back after that and it took forever."

"It didn't take that long! And I'll be able to kill the monster this time. I'll do it right."

"No you won't. Come on. I can do it better than you anyway."

Jonathan *always* dies in this part. I just want him to give me the left control pad, just this once so I can do it. There are three characters: a guy, a girl and this little red-haired thing—neither of us can figure out what it's meant to be—but you get to control one of them and the other two follow you around. The boss here—the boss that has just beaten my little brother *again*—is this giant tiger that falls out of the sky and attacks you. All you need to do is hide down the bottom of the screen until he's stopped moving, then you use the girl to hit him with the arrows a couple of times and he's dead. Big deal. He's all scary and stuff and he roars at you a lot, but that's about it. He's one of the easiest bosses to kill in the entire game, but Jonathan never gets it right and we *always* have to start this part over.

> "Jonathan, I'll punch you unless you give it
> to me."
> "Calvin, don't!"

He moves away from me; he slides across the tiles towards the window, but he still won't give me the left controller. He's holding onto it really tight. He wraps his body around it in this kind of ball. He's always scared when I say I'll punch him. Half the time I don't even mean it but he gets so worked up that it makes me *want* to punch him.

He pushes the start button. The guy and the girl and the little whateveritis are locked in the room now; the tiger isn't there yet, but it's about to be. Jonathan starts pushing buttons on the control pad, moves the little guy closer to the center.

> "Stop!" I yell. "Come on, seriously, pause it!"

He's surprised, and he pauses it.

> "Give it to me. Once I kill this boss I'll let you
> play again."
> "No you won't."
> "Yes I will. Promise."
> "You never do. Come on Calvin, just let me
> do it this once."

He has this look on his face. Stares at me. Pleading
with me or something. I don't know why, but I give in.

> "Fine," I tell him. "But you'll die. The tiger's
> gonna kill you then we'll have to start over."
> "No we won't! I won't let it kill me Calvin.
> Swear."

He pushes the start button again. The music goes all
crazy; the tiger falls from the sky and starts attacking.
My eyes kind of go between the screen and Jonathan,
because he has this weird look on his face. He's concentrating really hard or something. I don't know. But
he's doing some damage to the tiger. He's using the
guy, slicing at the tiger with his sword. The tiger's
fighting back. Rolls around in this ball and knocks the
girl over, then casts this spell which makes them all
catch fire.

Jonathan's doing okay. It's weird. Normally he's really

really bad at this—my little brother kind of sucks at anything to do with video games—but now he's doing pretty well. He's doing more damage to the tiger than it's doing to him. He even goes down the bottom like you're supposed to. Suddenly it looks like he's going to beat the tiger. Weird.

I don't know why I do it. I want to, maybe. I can't stop myself. There's no *way* Jonathan could beat this boss. I lean over. Punch him in the arm. Hard. He drops the controller, leaves himself open. The tiger starts ripping into the little guy on the screen. Girl's dead. Guy's standing there not doing anything. The music's going crazy.

> "Calvin!" Jonathan yells. He's rubbing his arm, and he's almost crying. "Calvin, you made me die!"
> "No I didn't. You let the tiger kill you. You never do this right," I say.

Guy's still standing there not doing anything. Music's all weird. Little whateveritis with the red hair is dead too. The tiger keeps swiping at the guy. Guy doesn't even fight back. Controller's just lying there on the tiles.

> "Calvin! You made me die!"
> "Jonathan, you let it kill you. You're dumb.

You never do this right," I say.

Guy's dead.

Message on the screen: *Unfortunately, no trace of the heroes was ever found . . . Play again?*

"You did it!" he yells. He's rubbing his arm and he's almost crying.
"Look," I say. "I'll let you do it again."

I pick up the controller and try to give it to him. He won't take it.

"Jonathan, take it. I said I'd let you do it again. Come on."

Jonathan doesn't say anything. Doesn't look at me. I can't see him crying but I can hear it. He's really dumb sometimes.

"Jonathan, come on, I didn't mean it . . ."

I really *want* him to take the controller now but he won't. He won't take it at all. Keeps crying. Suddenly I feel prickly all over. I didn't mean for the tiger to kill him. I try to touch his arm, see if it's okay, but he won't let me. He slides across the tiles, out of my reach.

"I hate you!" he yells.

Weird, prickly feeling continues. Don't know what it is. I shouldn't have done that. I shouldn't hit my little brother. I don't know why I did it. I should take care of him. It's just . . .

PART 1

A FRIEND WITH WEED IS BETTER

1

Yet another afternoon at school and it's a case of hormones and anxiety running wild, and it's all very teenage and suburban and kind of, you know. Blah. I'm sure you've heard it all before. Chemistry was in third period, and I tried to find the urge to learn ($C^6H^2O^6 - 2CH^3CH^2O + 2CO^2$) but I spaced out completely for most of the second half. Afternoons like this I really don't know what to do with myself. I don't even feel like the stuff happening around me is real. After class I walked around for a while in kind of a daze and eventually met up with my friend and faghag Margot. She had these clips in her hair, pink ones, like a little girl would wear. I think she was making a fashion statement. I hope she was anyway. For some reason— she never explained why exactly—she was carrying this plush raccoon around with her. It was an expensive-looking one with a black smudge over its eyes the way I guess all raccoons have, and this little red tongue that sort of poked out.

"This is Haruki the Raccoon!" she told me. "My dad got it for me when he was in Tokyo." She lifted the tag and started reading it. *"Haruki the Raccoon! are joining you on many adventures!* Oh, and check this out. *Haruki the Raccoon! have many small parts that may causing children under three years to choke!"*

"When did your dad go to Tokyo?"

"He was there last week. Some business thing. I don't know." She waved Haruki the Raccoon! at me and made this *grrrr* noise. "Isn't it fucking cool?"

"It's great," I told her.

She menaced me with the stuffed toy for a while, still laughing. She was making it talk, moving it as she spoke to make it look as though Haruki the Raccoon! was really the one talking to me. It was the kind of thing that I'd normally have found funny, but on this particular afternoon it was way more than I could deal with.

Haruki the Raccoon!: Hello Calvin!

Me: Margot, can you stop that?

Haruki the Raccoon!: But Calvin, I'm your pal! I am joining you on many adventures!

Me: Margot . . . Fucking . . . You're freaking me out with that raccoon thing.

Haruki the Raccoon!: You're making me sad, Calvin . . . And when I get sad, I am causing you to choke!

Margot attacked me with the raccoon. Sort of swiped at my head and chest with it, making this strangled growling noise. That was kind of funny.

> **Haruki the Raccoon!:** Are you going to Edward's tonight?
> **Me:** I don't know. What are the alternatives?
> **Haruki the Raccoon!:** Not much. If you are going, would you like to come around to my place beforehand and get stooo-ooned?
> **Me:** I probably wouldn't object to that.

Margot laughed. Or rather, Haruki the Raccoon! laughed. Both of them did.

> "Cool cool," she said. "Get it together and come over to my house later this afternoon. Think you can get a lift?"
> "With Mum? Not likely. I'll probably have to bus it."
> "She's . . . ?"
> "Don't even ask."

2

The sky this afternoon is gray, almost too gray, like a computer-generated version of a gray sky, which is almost real, like, say about ninety-five percent real, but there's something there, just something on the edges that isn't quite right.

Margot and I decide to head to the library, Margot because there's this book she needs to find—something by Virginia Woolf, because some friend told her she just *had* to read it—and me because I have nothing better to do. The library adds to the air of unreality. It's this huge, vaguely threatening construction—it's all glass and bizarre angles and it looks like that famous museum, whatever it's called, I've seen a picture of it in a coffee table book somewhere, though the memory is pretty much impossible to place. That bothers me a lot for some reason, though I can't really say why.

3

The sky reflecting off the glass panels of the library; the weird, staticky feeling in the air; the clouds. It feels like we're all just characters in some huge, incredibly involved video game. I played too many video games when I was a little kid. Blips of unreality. The sickeningly bright colors—cathode reds and iceberg blues; vast pixellated worlds to be navigated through; tiny pixellated heroes—frogs leaping across ponds when I was a little kid, then dinosaurs and plumbers, then general purpose anime boys armed with strange weapons and unbelievably cool spells, then the next thing, then the next—to navigate them. These things are all a part of my subconscious now.

Those blips of unreality provide my reference points for just about every real-life situation, which, all things considered, probably isn't an entirely bad thing.

4

Something I wrote in my notebook doing chemistry: Some of the time, when the events occurring in real life become too difficult to deal with, you can reduce them to other things, make them seem less significant. If you remove "yourself" from yourself, if you can take a step back and see life as a movie, see you and others around you as characters in that movie, difficult situations become less difficult, painful memories don't hurt anymore because, after all, you're not really there.

5

EXT. LIBRARY. AFTERNOON

It is nearing the end of afternoon break and many STUDENTS are milling around outside the library. The camera lingers on various STUDENTS, including two BOYS who are throwing pretend punches at one another, and a GIRL who is sitting on the ground reading a book. PATRICK is standing by himself on the edge of the crowd. CALVIN and MARGOT approach. MARGOT menaces CALVIN with a stuffed raccoon. As they make their way through the group of STUDENTS, CALVIN notices PATRICK.

CALVIN

(VOICEOVER) That's Patrick. Seriously, I don't know what you'd call him. Boyfriend, maybe, although you'd have to say ex-boyfriend. But he wasn't really. He was never even a friend. Just this gorgeous and kind of screwed-up boy I used to see sometimes. Patrick was fairly unbalanced, but like, *unbelievably* cute. Apologetically cute, or cute in spite of himself. We used to catch the bus home together, which is how we met. He was in the grade below me. For someone so physically perfect, psychologically he was always vaguely disconnected from everything, like he was constantly receiving messages from Jupiter or something. Like I said, we weren't exactly boyfriends or anything. We had this strange kind of arbitrary relationship; I used to go over to his house in the afternoons on the pretext of going for a swim or playing Nintendo or something. His family never seemed to be home. We'd be sitting on his living room floor and he'd be explaining the subtleties of all the games in this deadly earnest tone, who all the characters were, what buttons you had to press in order to do what, and mostly I followed, even though I was checking him out the whole time.

PATRICK looks up. His eyes meet CALVIN's. Both look away, embarrassed, but turn to look at one another again.

CALVIN
(VOICEOVER) It didn't really matter though, because by the time he'd finished explaining whatever game we were playing, he'd always be staring at me with this intense, impossible to ever decode or understand expression on his face, and he'd say something like: "Calvin, I know this is going to sound weird, but like . . . Um . . . If you'd like to, you know, touch me or something, I'll let you."

MARGOT gives PATRICK a suspicious look.

CALVIN
Hey Patrick.

PATRICK
Hey . . . Calvin.

CALVIN and PATRICK look away from each other again.

CALVIN

(VOICEOVER) We'd always end up on his floor touching each other's bodies and then kissing, and then eventually when that wasn't enough we used to fuck, either in his room or his father's office or wherever. It only lasted for a couple of months. Then this one afternoon his father came home and walked in on the two of us . . . in the living room . . . which kind of screwed everything right up. We didn't really talk that much or anything after that. Nobody apart from his dad ever found out about it, but things were awkward afterwards. I stopped going over to his house and eventually we stopped even looking at one another when we met and that was kind of that.

I later found out that I was the only person Patrick had ever really been friends with, which was sort of, you know, weird, or intense, or something. How are you meant to deal with information like that when it's presented to you? I don't know.

MARGOT and CALVIN walk past PATRICK and enter the library. CALVIN shuts his eyes and holds them shut.

6

Seeing Patrick makes me feel strange and uncomfortable and it's like the game has frozen up for a second and I'm having to push the start button a whole bunch of times to get it going again. As the library doors are closing, I look back at him just to see if he's looking at me, but he isn't.

I try to think of the term for my relationship with Patrick, but I can't. The conventional ones don't really fit. I'm thinking:

> a) Friend. But Patrick and I were never "friends." We never had anything to talk about or had anything in common besides attraction or whatever you want to call it.
>
> b) Lover. But it's not like we were ever really boyfriends. We weren't in love or anything, it was just, like, mutual fascination or need or something similar that brought us together.

We were fourteen/fifteen and totally denied an outlet for our fears and desires etc, and we just happened to find each other, at which point we went totally fucking crazy on one another's body, and then we were caught and we stopped altogether and now we can't even talk to each other anymore. What's the word for *that*?

If there is a word to describe the relationship Patrick and I had, I don't know what it is. Is it deliberate or accidental that such a word doesn't exist?

If you don't have a name for something, it's not real.

It doesn't have any power. As far as the world in general is concerned, it means nothing.

7

The Patrick thing is an unexpected variable and the afternoon begins to make even less sense than it did before. I'm in this total *Attack Of The Teen Angst Monsters Part XVIII* state of mind. Agitated, or like . . . Whatever. I don't know what you'd call it. Margot walks off. I tell her I'll see her tonight and she tells me I'd fucking better. I sit down at this desk by the window, pull my notebook out and start to write.

> **Words:** Sometimes words aren't enough. In terms of describing a particular emotion or even thought, most words don't seem . . . *adequate.* For example, the things we refer to as "attraction" or "fear" or "love," we only do so because those words happen to be the most convenient. There are too many colours and textures and subtleties attached to those concepts to call them by their real names, because when it comes down to it I don't think they even *have* real names.
>
> Emotions are like those giant sea creatures you read about—prehistoric squid living miles

and miles below the ocean surface, the kind that no human has ever laid eyes on. We know they're there, even though we don't know what they look like or how to describe them—that's why we don't give them names. We can't.

8

For about an eighth of a second, as I finish writing that, I feel incredibly profound. Then I look up into the glass, the surface of which is more reflective than usual thanks to the overcast sky outside, and it takes me quite a while to make sense of the image I see there, to realise it's my own face.

> **My reflection:** For a second, my features don't fit together at all, then once they do I seem like more than myself, like a hyper-real version of Calvin, and I feel kind of dizzy for a second before it goes back to normal.

I look back down at my notebook and none of it makes sense anymore. It's just words on a page, or whatever—which is obviously *exactly* what it is, but it had meaning before and now it seems like bull-shit. I consider tearing the page out but it's really fucking annoying when the edges get all tatty and

I'm totally anally retentive about my notebook so I just leave it as it is.

9

Patrick returns to my thoughts. I wonder if he's still standing outside, and if he is, if he's still thinking about me. If he ever does. Or if he thinks about nothing at all. Maybe it's better that way. Maybe it would be better if I could think about nothing at all.

I stand up, walk around the library for a while, kind of tense. Try to avoid my reflection in the windows. The thought of being alone is suddenly too much to physically deal with. It would be cool to be with someone right now, right this second—even if it's only to distract me.

10

This guy I sort of know and would kind of like to sleep with, Paul, is standing just near this bank of computers. The computers, and therefore Paul, are in front of a big set of glass windows. When I walk up to him I can see myself reflected in the glass, along with his back, and both of us are reflected again in the glass that's behind me and it's this weird effect that makes us both look like we're going on forever.

My mindset changes completely: As I'm staring at myself and at Paul in the glass, I make myself forget about Patrick. Forget about Patrick and everything that he signifies and forget about everything else that has occurred up to this point and thus affected the flow of the afternoon. My afternoon now begins here, in the library, with Paul, and I erase all the negative stuff that's happened prior to this—it's excess information and it's gone.

I have a crush on Paul. I guess you'd call it a crush. There's a word for that. It's simple. I mean, he's really good-looking, in a boy-next-door sort of a way; I mean, just the fact of looking at him and knowing how cute/uncomplicated he is and the fact that he's almost definitely straight makes my head hurt.

The sex/love dichotomy: It's difficult to explain—and any explanation I could give would have to be a lengthy one—but let's just say the only boys I feel the need to make an effort with are the ones I know I can't have. There's probably some deep psychological explanation for this but I'm not really interested in hearing it. None of the boys I've actually been with have meant anything, not even Patrick. He was cute and everything, but he was just . . . *there*, convenient. Anyway, the real thing is always kind of underwhelming. That's why the *imaginary* thing is so much better.

Paul's cute, and the fact that he's unattainable makes him cuter. That's just the way my mind works. I wouldn't say I was in love with him, because that would just be stupid, but it does raise the question—if sex is the real thing and love the imaginary? I really don't know. Let's just say that the most interesting crushes are usually on straight boys, which is a real fucking drag, and leave it at that.

11

So yeah. Paul and I talk for a while, about school and various things. He asks me if I'm taking Margot to the semi-formal. I tell him we're not going out, and he gives me this look, which might be interpreted as "ohh yeah . . ." or "that's too bad dude" or "so, she's still available?" but I don't have the energy to work it out. The conversation turns to other things.

Paul: My dad's getting stuck into me at the moment. He doesn't think my English is good enough.
Me: That sucks.

I am thinking: It would be nice to have parents who get stuck into you about stuff like that. It would feel more . . . normal or something. My parents don't even ask about school—as long as I'm there and in one piece and I can smile and speak in coherent sentences in front of Dad's doctor friends, my parents are happy. My parents used to show me off, but there's kind of an understanding now that they don't do that any more.

> **Paul:** Dad wants me to get better marks so I can get into law at UQ.
> **Me:** Sounds hardcore.
> **Paul:** I guess. But Dad really wants me to go there. He did law there as well, so he and Mum want me to . . . keep up the family tradition, I guess. Haha.
> **Me:** What do you want to do?

Just by way of clarification—I'm not asking Paul what he really wants to do in any kind of "take the road less travelled/follow your dreams" type of way. Fuck that. I would never want to give that impression because . . . it's bullshit. I'm glad Paul's going into law. I'm just asking him because I'm interested. He might have, you know, hidden artistic leanings or something.

Paul thinks for a while before he answers; chews his bottom lip.

Paul: I don't know. Guess I wouldn't *mind* doing law. Tons of work but the money's good.

Me: You're pretty safe if you can get into it.

Paul: Workload seems pretty scary, but I guess it'll pay off. How about you? Have you thought about it much yet?

Me: About . . . ?

Paul: Uni, dude. About what you'd like to do?

It's something I haven't actually considered at all.

Me: Uni's ages away.

Paul: It's never too early to start thinking about that stuff.

Me: I don't know. I guess I'll probably do IT. There are worse things.

Paul: Thought you'd be into the creative writing or something.

Me: Nah. That's kind of . . . I mean, I doubt if it would get me anywhere.

Paul: Guess not. Man, the whole idea of uni is . . .

12

Sex: As I'm looking at Paul, this fantasy spins off in my head, and it only lasts for like a second and a half but in it I'm pushing him up against the glass and he's kissing me and then we're in his room, or what I imagine his room to be like, because I've never actually seen the inside of it, and he's sucking me off then I'm sucking him off and we're in love and it's all extremely straightforward and cool, but I blink and it dissolves and I'm back in the library again, staring at Paul, and maybe *this* is actually straightforward, and I'm nodding politely as he's telling me whatever it is he's telling me.

13

So yeah. I'm going over all these things in my head as Paul's talking, which is probably part of the reason I'm not listening.

Paul: . . . have you played it?
Me: Have I played . . . ?
Paul: GTA 4, dude, on Sony 2. It's the fucking *best*. Stealing cars, shooting at people, blowing shit up. It's so fucking cool. There's a helicopter in it as well. You sit there for hours and you forget what you're doing. You just want to keep playing, and you can't stop until you get it right. My brother and I were up until

one thirty this morning. Mum cracked the shits. But still . . . it's fucking sweet.
Me: Sounds good.
Paul: You should come over sometime and play it, dude. You'll love it.
Me: That would be cool.

Paul tells me he's going up to the computer labs. Asks me if I want to come. I tell him I can't, tell him I have stuff to do, even though I don't.

14

The rest of the day kind of dragged by. Caught the bus home; still thinking about Paul and how nice it would be to fuck him, or even just get drunk together and mess around. You know what they say—a sixpack and any boy's a faggot. Or maybe not. Thinking about it starts to get to me. I pull out the little notebook I always carry with me, think of everything that's happened so far today and write it all down.

About my notebook. I'm kind of an obsessive notetaker. It's hard to explain—I mean, okay, put it this way. If I could, I'd have a Polaroid camera with me all the time so I could keep a record of everything significant/interesting/pretty/unusual etc that I see. The millions and millions of random things—gray sky reflecting off the sides of buildings, pieces of sushi on display, cute boys,

boys I'd like to sleep with (their profiles, the expressions on their faces), city lights, crowds, neon, posters outside cinemas—which pass most people by. I try to keep a record of the texture of each day, or the color of it, or whatever. Because I can't take photographs of things, I take notes on them instead.

I'm currently using this little spiral notebook. It used to be black but it now has a picture of Stefan Olsdal, the bass player from this band I kind of like, Placebo, stuck on the front. I do whatever with the notes that I make. Use them in stories. Stick them up on my walls— which sounds kind of, you know . . . *gay*—or in boxes, or whatever. But I always take notes on everything. So I won't forget.

15

Written in my notebook on the way home: I always think about ridiculous things. Not even thoughts really, more like fantasies. Stupid things. Totally impractical things— altering my entire life on a whim, things like that. I mean, for instance, I could be watching some stupid movie late at night—like the other night Margot and I saw *Velvet Goldmine*—and I'll think to myself, "Wow, maybe if *I* was hanging out with rock musicians, glamming it up and taking tons of drugs in London in the early seventies, then maybe everything would be okay. Maybe *that*'s what's missing, and if I could somehow travel back in time, somehow wake up tomorrow and be living that fictional life instead of mine, then everything would be great and everything would make sense."

That's the kind of thing I mean. Stupid, impractical stuff, but whenever I'm wrapped up in one of these fantasies, I'm totally into it, to the point of . . .

16

I get checked out on the bus. I look up, out the window, as the bus is slowing towards a stop, and I see this fairly cute guy just about to get on. He distracts me from my notebook. The guy is unassuming, kind of geeky-looking actually, with dark hair and a Radiohead shirt, but he has this, I don't know, this look. Looks older, in his midtwenties or something. I notice him mainly because he looks *exactly* like this Nathaniel guy I was seeing but not really seeing a few months ago.

I look at him and he sees me looking at him and he looks back at me and for a second we make eye contact. I think I know what this is. I know how to play this game. I look away, but a few seconds later I look back, and he's looking at me, he's definitely looking at me, and he doesn't look away and he's definitely, as they say, into it, and I realize right then:

This guy wants to fuck me. If I wanted, I could have this guy. He's not bad looking. He's really kind of okay looking when you think about it. He's interested in me—whether it's for me or for the fact that I'm wearing a school uniform, I'm not entirely sure, but I realize:

This guy and I could fuck this afternoon.

17

Two possible scenarios run parallel in my head:

a) I am standing up, moving towards the front of the bus, and as I'm moving towards him I'm looking in his eyes the whole time, this general purpose slutty look on my face, and he is getting the message, and he is following me. I am walking to this park at the far end of my street and he is still following me. His hands are on my waist. I don't know if they feel warm or not. He's kissing my neck. He's unzipped my pants and I can feel his hand around my cock. I am guiding him down, guiding his head down, and he is so into it it's like an equation solving itself. The familiar warm, wet feel of his mouth. I am closing my eyes. I feel . . . something.

b) I am standing up, ignoring him. My head is bowed towards the floor of the bus. I am hoping he won't follow me, and he doesn't. I am walking home. I am thinking how much it sucks being alone this afternoon, how cool it would have been to feel that closeness to another person. I am going home. I am sixteen and I am walking home all alone.

The two versions fight for supremacy and I wonder which would be better, to try and snag this guy just for the sake of making myself feel alive, or to walk off and spend the rest of the afternoon thinking about how much better the alternative might have been if I'd only been brave enough.

18

It's a split-second decision. The guy is looking at me, I look back at him, we're looking in one another's eyes, and then I lose it. I turn my head and I look out the window and I don't look back.

I'm thinking so hard about him and whether or not I should try again, just to let him know that he can follow me or whatever, that I get distracted and almost miss my stop. Always seems to happen. I close my notebook; hook my pen on the front. I stand up and walk towards the door of the bus. My head is bowed towards the floor. The guy doesn't follow.

19

Standing on the road. The bus is driving off. As I'm slipping my notebook in my bag, I stop for a second and stare at that picture of Stefan Olsdal on the front. He looks extremely European. Aloof. Mysterious. Hot. Etc. I don't know. Whatever. But on the walk home, Stefan starts talking to me.

Stefan Olsdal: What was with that?
Me: With what?
Stefan Olsdal: That guy on the bus, kid. He was cute. You could have had him.
Me: I know. I didn't want to.
Stefan Olsdal: He was into you, kid.
Me: Yeah, but probably only because of how young I look. Lots of guys get off on that.
Stefan Olsdal: Doesn't matter. Think of how

good it would have felt to have that guy sucking you off. To know that you can have that kind of power over a person. That would feel good, Calvin. You know it. That would feel fucking great.

Me: I don't care.

Stefan Olsdal: You should care, kid. You should have let that guy do what he wanted to ya. You know how good it is to feel another person with you. Someone who wants you. Makes you feel alive.

Me: I guess.

Stefan Olsdal: Have you ever thought that maybe that's all you'll ever know about love, kid? What kind of life do you think you're going to lead, Calvin? I hope you're not harboring any illusions that you're going to end up anything more than a sad... old...

Me: Shut the fuck up Stef.

Stefan Olsdal: One day shit's gonna be reversed.

Me: What does that mean? Wait. Fucking... I don't want to talk about this any more.

Stefan Olsdal: Okay then. Porno. See ya, kid.

I really wish figments of my imagination would stop fucking with me. Anyway. Over it.

20

Home. Albany Creek. All of the houses here are big and suburban looking and *safe,* and my parents' doesn't stand out. Neither of my parents' cars is in the driveway, but then that's hardly surprising. When I walk inside, the place is empty. My computer's still on, a bunch of MP3s and other crap I started downloading before I left for school this morning are almost finished. Late afternoon and I have nothing to do and no drugs in the house—except for some pot I'm saving for emergencies, which this definitely isn't—and it's probably a bit too early to head over to Margot's, so I try to come up with some kind of meaningful sexual fantasy involving Paul, or the guy on the bus, or possibly both of them together, but their faces keep getting all messed up and I can never get a clear picture of either, so I get sick of it finally and decide to just listen to some music. I put this album I like on the big stereo in the living room and just lie around listening and spacing out. I wonder where my parents are, and it suddenly occurs to me that I have *no idea* where they are. Dad might be at the hospital, Mum might be *anywhere,* and there's no telling when or if either of them will be back, and the thought of this spins me out even further.

I make the CD skip to track three—"Teardrop," which is this suffocating and weirdly beautiful song with sampled drums that sound like heartbeats—and put it on repeat.

21

Walk around the house for a while not really knowing what to do. I pour myself a coke and then don't drink it. I wonder what it would have been like if I'd brought that guy with me—I mean, you know, I wouldn't have brought him *here*, obviously, but maybe somewhere. Close by, those trees near the end of the street, maybe. That park. There are lots of places to hide. But whatever. He would be sucking me off right now. I'd be feeling his tongue; the warm, wet feel of his mouth. More than that, I'd be feeling another person near me. Someone who was into me, even if it was only for twenty minutes or whatever. I try to make these thoughts dissolve, but I think some trace of them stays with me. Some feeling of emptiness, or regret. I don't know, maybe I'm just in the mood to get fucked. That's probably it actually.

I head into the office. The carpet is white and it feels soft under my feet. I sit on the computer chair and spin around a whole bunch of times. Play with this stress toy thing that's sitting next to the screen—my dad got it from a drug company; and it's green with these big eyes that sort of bug out, so I think it's meant to be a frog or something. You're meant to squeeze it and it relieves your tension. I squeeze the frog thing for a while but I don't really feel any different. I get bored after a while and decide to go on IRC chat, see if any of my friends are online. Break through the boredom or whatever.

22

There are six different windows open on the screen:

1. A page with a whole bunch of photos on it, digital photos that someone took at this rave at Southport last weekend. Margot sent me the link yesterday because there was a photo of her on the page. I scroll through them for a while, up and down, trying to find her. I don't find Margot, but I end up finding the following photos:

a) A boy in glasses—a math geek type, but he's pretty cute—sort of leaning into the camera with this totally blissed-out expression on his face.

b) A blurry shot of a red-haired girl; you can't really make her out because the camera must have been moving too fast when the photo was taken, but there are streaks of light trailing behind her like butterfly wings and she looks strangely beautiful.

c) A DJ, but the photo is more or less ruined because he is too far away and there are too many bright lights behind him so all you really see are smudges of red. There's a huge crowd in front of him, dancing, kissing, sweating, arms thrown in the air. Makes me wish I was there.

d) A pretty if somewhat slutty-looking boy in a "Fuck Me, I'm Famous" shirt. He has blond hair, spiked up, and a dog-collar. He is sticking his tongue out at the camera. There is a pill on it.

2. The homepage of some young guy I met in this fucking chatroom a week or two ago. I think his name is Jeremy. I think he's from Robina. He's been sending me these really, like, bizarre emails. I mean, like, in the very first email he told me that he'd once posed for this porn photographer, and he'd been sucking his father's business partner off for cash ever since he was, like, thirteen or something. But he also sent a pic of himself and he looks pretty cute, if somewhat disturbed. Really tall, bleached blond, though you could still see the dark roots, and he had this, I don't know, dumb kind of look. Dumb, but really hot. His page is impeccably designed. It's almost *too* well designed. It's all white, with icons that highlight and turn a neon blue when you drag the mouse over them. None of the links seem to go

anywhere so I get annoyed and give up altogether.

3. This page that has a whole bunch of Trance MP3s on it. I've been downloading them since this morning, and the little meter thing that shows the download progress says they are 86% done.

4. The IRC chat window. Nobody's online. I always think empty chat windows are weird. I mean, if there's nobody in there, what's the point?

5. A page that is showing an Error404 message, so whatever I was trying to find (I can't remember), it's not there anymore.

6. My email sign-in page. I already checked it once from school today, but I figure I'll do it again, mainly because I'm obsessive about things like that, and I figure someone might have sent me something interesting or cool or whatever over the course of the afternoon, something to grab my attention and hold it for a while. Or whatever. You know.

There is one new message in my inbox. It's from that Jeremy guy. I can't think of anything better to do. The music is still blasting in the other room. Heartbeats. Like being in a big womb. It is still overcast outside. I open the message.

From: Jeremy <jezza99@i-accelerate.com.au>
To: Calvin <hearts_filthy_lesson@hotmail.com>
Subject: i know u don't believe me, but . . .

hey calvin!
how r u?? been ages since we talked, hope things are still good. i liked that photo you sent me—ur pretty cute. i'd ~loVe~ 4 us to get together some-time!!!!!!!!!!!!!!!!!!!!!!!!!!

remember what i told u last time we were on irc chat, about how i'd posed for those photos and stuff? i know u didn't believe me, so here's proof. i can't believe i'm show-ing u this but ha! who carez, besides u seem pretty cool

there's this guy i know and we were at his apartment one night and he got us really drunk and stoned and stuff and started taking pictures and it was heapz of fun, anyway this is his site. he scans the pics n puts them up there, he's kind of fucked up but it doesn't matter. hope u enjoy them but it doesn't matter and even if you don't promise u won't think i'm weird or anything, haha

hahha i'm pretty stoned if u can't tell
we should get together sometime

stay cool calvin dude!!!!!!!!!!!!!!!!!!
see ya soon,
jeremy

24

That email from Jeremy makes me remember something I wrote in my notebook a couple of days ago, after this physics class.

The very act of observing an object will change that object.

We were offered some convoluted explanation, and we were given examples that actually did make a lot of sense, but I've mostly forgotten them now. I know, basically, that as far as real-life objects go, this particular rule holds true. Real-life objects. I'm kind of wondering if pictures on the net count as real-life objects.

25

Real-life objects: I kind of debate whether I should click on the link, and this is why. Jeremy, assuming that's his real name, and assuming the pictures were even of him, is really cute. In spite of my better judgment, I'd like to fuck him. That being the case, seeing pictures of him fucking/being fucked by a third party is possibly the next best thing. In a practical sense, there's no problem with that, but I don't know. I don't know if I want to see pictures of him "drunk and stoned and stuff" in some guy's apartment. I'd feel kind of dirty. I don't know.

But then I start to think about that physics thing. I mean, seriously, the two connect in my mind. I'm kind of fucked up in that respect.

What I'm thinking is: if Jeremy gets drunk and lets some guy take naked photos of him, and then if nobody is there to see the website where said old pervert posts said photos, will the website still be there? If a tree falls in a forest and nobody is there to hear it, does it make a noise?

So really, whether or not I go there and whether or not I look at the photos, they will not be affected. They will not change. So as far as I'm concerned, they're not real-life objects. They're just . . . Well, they're just pictures on a website and who gives a fuck whether or not I look at them?

I forget where I'm going with this train of thought. I'm bored of trying to rationalize it, and courtesy of that guy from the bus I'm still feeling edgy and in need of some method of escape, very quickly.

Fuck it. Whatever.

I click on the link. A new window comes up on the screen.

26

The site is basically just a whole bunch of pictures of these two stoned-looking boy next door types, one of whom must be "Jeremy," sort of goofing around in this apartment: lying on the floor, slumped over the couch, playing a Playstation, sometimes kissing one another. There is this blond guy who I *think* is Jeremy—he looks pretty similar to that picture he sent me of himself, assuming it really *was* a pic of him. I don't know. Still, the same bleached blond hair. He's wearing this hooded top, gray, with no sleeves. Like he's going for a *look* or whatever, like, street, or queerbait, or possibly a combination of the two. In most of the photos he's just sort of standing there, posing or showing off or looking kind of arrogant or something, and the whole thing looks forced. But still, he's definitely cute.

So at first it's just a bunch of shots of him and this other guy, who's brunette, and he has this look about him that's totally fascinating. I mean, it's hard to even describe it unless you saw it for yourself, but he looks about my age and he's really tall, kind of thin; he has this faraway look in his eyes and he's just kind of, I don't know, like, other.

So eventually after a few shots of them messing around and kissing and draped over the couch etc, it's the two of them in front of these red curtains, which are open a little so you can see it's night-time. I'm scrolling down through the photos. They're still standing in the same position by the windows but suddenly they seem a lot friendlier; they're kissing harder and then the brunette guy is no longer standing, he's down on his knees in front of Jeremy and he has Jeremy's cock in his hand; Jeremy's cargoes and his boxer shorts have slid down around his ankles and the brunette guy's sort of kissing Jeremy's cock or whatever, and then he's taking Jeremy in his mouth and there are a few shots of that, quite a few, from all these different angles, and then suddenly they're switching then they've switched and they're both naked and basically just taking turns at blowing one another, you know, and I sort of imagine myself in Jeremy's position, thinking, Yeah, go for it, brunette dude, and kind of getting into it when I go to the next shot and it's one of the brunette guy all on his own.

And this one's weird, because in all the photos before this, both he and Jeremy had their eyes half closed, like they'd just smoked a whole load of pot or they were just like tripping totally on one another's bodies or they'd gone to this whole other place or something, you know, but in this one, the brunette guy's eyes are open. And it's kind of uncomfortable to look at. His eyes are open wide, and it's like being able to see right inside him, into his thoughts, into his soul. Except there doesn't seem to be much of anything in there. His expression is blank. Like he's just there, and he's dazed or something and staring into the camera only because it's there. Which is fucked up when you think about it. And his hair, which has been gelled all perfectly in all the photos up to now, is suddenly kind of messy.

And I don't know why but the blank look on the brunette guy's face is making me feel really uncomfortable. I wish he'd stop staring at the camera, close his eyes or something so I don't have to deal with the look in them. So there are four or five shots of him just like this, just standing there with the traces of a hard-on (like they'd been taken after the blond guy had finished sucking him off), and he just stands there. Looks into the camera. It's disturbing.

Then the next shot there's someone else with him. You can only see the other guy from the shoulders down, but he looks older, or something, and he's wearing boxer shorts. Whoever he is, he's not the blond guy, that's for sure. And then in the next one he's not wearing the boxers anymore, he's sort of pulling them down around his ankles, and the brunette guy is still just standing there with that totally blank look on his face. And then the guy, no longer in boxers, is fucking the brunette kid. There are shots of it from all these different angles, shots of the brunette kid being fucked by this guy, who seems to be really going for it. But the expression on the brunette kid's face doesn't change at all, and his eyes are still wide open, staring. It's like there's nothing in there at all; further along in the sequence there are two guys doing it to him, and he doesn't seem to notice at all. He's just there with that empty look on his face, just taking it, and it's like he's dead.

27

I can't deal with it. I mean I fucking freak out for a few minutes. I head to the living room, turn the music up incredibly loud and just sit there really losing it and I have to sit there for a while to calm down. I'm freaking for two reasons:

a) The fact that the brunette boy is so good-looking. That, I suspect, is the real problem. The idea that someone so fucking cute could be in a position where two guys are fucking him at once while someone else takes photographs to put up on some website. The idea of that really gets to me, a lot. I start thinking about him, wondering who he is, what he must have been thinking.

b) The fact that the brunette boy looks so much like me. Not just on a physical level. I mean, yeah, on a physical level he does kind of look like me. But from that it's possible to extrapolate a whole lot more reasons why we're alike. He looks about my age. He could even be in my grade. He looks fairly healthy. I mean healthy in the sense that he doesn't look too sick, too thin, and he probably comes from a comfortable middle-class family and might even be into the same music and the same video games as I am. From the way he looks, he's the kind of boy you'd see out clubbing, who might easily live in one of the houses along my street.

I put myself in his position, wonder what it would be like. I imagine how it would feel. Doing those things, I mean. Letting myself go like that. It *could* be me. Realistically. It could. But whatever. I don't want to think too much about this.

28

I leave that photo of the brunette boy up there. I go upstairs to shower, change clothes. He's still there when I get back downstairs and he still has exactly the same look on his face.

I click the little x in the corner to close the window.

29

Clothes are important. The way you dress is the best way of projecting the person you are, or the person you want to be. For example, there are art student types, boys who wear skinny T-shirts with ironic slogans on the front. Boys who want to look like they're artists, or in rock bands, or something. These guys cultivate cool, in a fascist sort of a way, and for the most part they pull it off. Then there are gay boys, who put a lot of product in their hair and favor Diesel or Industrie or whatever. Boys who look like they get laid a lot more than you, who look pretty, or slutty or just generally hot. There are girls who dress punk or over the top cute or whatever, who hoard old Cure albums and stuffed toys and wear dresses that are torn in just the right places. They're usually doing it to hide some insecurity or other, but then that's true of pretty much everyone. Dressing in Polo Ralph Lauren says, My parents make more money than yours; dressing all in black says, I think about, y'know, deep and meaning-ful stuff *all the time.* It's all just a big game . . . or something.

Tonight, the look I'm going for is dumb. That is, I'm really fucking hoping to meet someone at this party. I have the kind of personality that tends to put guys off. I've learned this lesson before—using too many big words tends to scare all the cute boys away. That's why it always works better when I switch that part of me off, say as little as possible and just try to appear cute. Shallowness is a lot more fun anyway. I'm bored of not getting laid and that thing on the net has made me feel kind of tense and edgy. I'm in the mood for some brain-less fun tonight.

30

I'm listening to music as I'm getting changed. Brian Molko is urging me over and over to change my taste in men and I'm mouthing the words into the mirror as I get dressed. That image of the brunette boy from the net is still with me. I try not to think of him but I can't help it. And I do what I always do when there's some-thing unpleasant that's bothering me, something I'd rather forget about. Which is to say, I spend all my energy not thinking about it until I don't think about it so hard it gives me a headache.

The sky is still full of big, gray clouds when I leave

the house. It feels as though it's been overcast forever, like the sky will always growl and threaten rain.
It's not like I mind though—I prefer rainy days. When
the sky is gray, it makes everything easier to deal
with.

31

On the way to Margot's a girl got on the bus and she
catches my attention. She has bangs, and she's wearing this black shirt with "HARLOT" written across it in
huge letters, so the word takes up the whole front of
the shirt. She and her boyfriend get on together. He
has bleached blond hair, a dog collar and too much
eyeliner, and they both look kind of industrial or goth
or whatever. Thing is, I was watching them as the bus
was approaching. She was smoking, then when she
saw the bus coming, she took this huge, long, graceful
drag of her cigarette then ground it out, slowly, deliberately, on her boyfriend's arm. He didn't flinch. He
didn't even seem to notice. I was thinking: What the
fuck? They kissed once, then got on the bus.

I have Ladytron on my discman. I turn it up and stare
out the window, trying to look at nothing at all. The
girl's voice is telling me that they only want you when
you're seventeen. When you're twenty-one, it seems
you're no fun.

32

Margot's house is in Ascot, near the top of a hill. It's big and fairly new, the kind of house that says, "We have lots of money but we definitely *haven't* sold out," if you have any idea what I mean.

Margot greets me at the door, wearing a very tight shirt with a picture of Sid Vicious on it. Smiles.

Margot: Calvin!
Me: Hey Margot, how are ya?
Margot: Pretty well . . . Dude, you look fucking *hot* tonight.
Me: You think?
Margot: *Totally* porno. I'd fuck you.
Me: You wish.
Margot: Wishing's for losers.

At this point, she hugs me, or I hug her, or one of us hugs the other—I don't know, it's like this ritual.

Me: Where's Haruki this afternoon?
Margot: The raccoon? Oh yeah. He got rabies. Tragic story . . . Really tragic. Had to be shot.
Me: I can imagine.
Margot: It's for the best really.

Me: It was just a matter of time. So . . . Do you have any drugs?

Margot: Thought you'd never ask. Come in.

33

I ask where her family is. She tells me we have the place to ourselves. Her parents have gone away for the weekend and her older brother is at the Gold Coast with his girlfriend.

> **Margot's older brother:** Nick is pretty much your archetypal boy next door. He's in his second year of an engineering degree or whatever—I don't know, something incredibly normal anyway—and he's been going out with the same girl since grade eleven. They're totally into each other. I've seen them. It's cute. They're probably going to get married and populate the world with incredibly normal children. In a way I kind of envy them that.

Anyway, this is all very . . . blah. Nick, Paul, the way life seems like it's so . . . straightforward for some people, and the moral of the story is that this afternoon I'd rather just smoke a fuckload of weed and not think about it. If that shows a weakness of character on my part, then so be it. That's what being a spoiled teenage brat is all about.

I start thinking about that brunette boy from the net again: I can still see that look in his eyes. I wonder if he's someone's brother. The idea of that gets to me even more.

All of this flashes through my mind in about an eighth of a second, but in that time Margot happens to be looking at me and sees the expression on my face.

Margot: You right tiger?
Calvin: Yeah. Thinking about something else.
Margot: Okay.

So yeah. Let the fun begin.

34

"Hey!" Margot says as we near the top of the staircase. "I nearly forgot—I made you something."
"What is it?" I ask.
She turns back to me, evil grin on her face.
"Wait and see. You'll die."
"I'm intrigued," I tell her as she dashes down the hallway to her bedroom.

Alone in the staircase, the house feels a little surreal. Too . . . empty and modern, like the set of a film whose director was aiming for a hip/contemporary/urban kinda feel. It's not quite right, and I start to feel uncomfortable, closed in.

"It's in here somewhere," she yells. "Wait a minute, it's . . . Fuck!" The sound of something heavy falling to the floor. "Here it is."

Margot dashes back towards me, grinning. There is something small in her hands, and I can't quite see what until she waves it at me, menacing me with it. It's a cassette.

"A mix tape?"
"You bet," she smiles. "Finished it last night."

"Margot, you fucking rule! You made me a mix tape! Thanks!"
I am happy, and I mean it. I take it, to have a closer look.

35

The cover of the cassette box: It's a collage of text and photographs, the kind of intricate, obsessive-compulsive artwork at which Margot is totally brilliant. The words "dOn'T HAte mE beCAUSE i'm BeAuTIfuL" are stuck down one side in these tiny black letters that look like newsprint. Photographs ripped from fashion magazines are pasted all over the front at bizarre angles. The head and torso of a smirking Russian-looking boy in a vaguely pornographic pose sits next to a shot of Madonna circa 1986—she's holding an infected vagina while a banner screaming *Vive La Révolution* covers her mouth. The words "COCAINE" and "ELECTROCLASH," both in bright pink letters, are pasted above them. Amongst the other delights are a howling baboon and a model who looks like Kate Moss, although it's hard to tell because her eyes have been torn out.

36

I turn the tape over to look at the track listing. It's a mixture of spiky, art-punk stuff and 80s pop music, the kind of thing Margot and I are both totally into. Margot and I are both, I don't know, "different," and so we cultivate a sense of isolation from our peers. Taste in music plays a significant part in this, and mix tapes can be coded messages, fashion state-ments, love letters . . . There are certain emotions that are hard to express except in the context of mix tapes.

This one, I have to say, is pretty fucking cool.

37

MARGOT'S MIX TAPE FOR CALVIN
1. "Love My Way"—The Psychedelic Furs
2. "Too Young"—Phoenix
3. "Pray for a Star"—Felix da Housecat
4. "Hungry Like the Wolf"—Duran Duran
5. "Seventeen"—Ladytron
6. "Sexy Boy"—Air
7. "Bang"—Yeah Yeah Yeahs
8. "Say Hello to the Angels"—Interpol
9. "You Can Be Replaced"—Dot Allison
10. "Fade to Grey"—Visage

38

Margot: It's the soundtrack to my own personal hell.
Me: Life in a gilded cage.
Margot: Sophisticated misery—that's where it's at.
Me: . . . Margot, you're the fucking best!

I hug her, or she hugs me, or . . . You know how this works by now.

Margot: Think nothing of it.

39

Margot has pot, just like she promised. She and I sit on her parents' balcony smoking a joint and watching the rain fall on the city. The city is always more beautiful on rainy days. The buildings, tall and dark, reflecting the clouds and almost disappearing into the fog. The ribbons of rain, cold, beautiful, like dancers. The glass of the buildings. The chill in the air. Happy When It Rains. Like the song. Reducing everything to a pop culture reference makes life so much easier to deal with.

40

Margot is playing this Placebo album that we're both obsessed with at the moment, but she's made it skip right to the last track. The whole album is so sad. This song in particular. It's about a boy who dresses in black and cruises the streets of Luxembourg all day, looking for that elusive someone he can fall in love with. He never does. Find them, I mean. He never scores, he just gets an infection, like the song says. Whatever. That's not the part which really gets to me. This boy, he dreams of a face that is pure perfection. I really wonder about this part of the song. I mean, it makes me think, am I ever going to find that particular person? The one I can fall in love with. Or is it always going to be like this—drifting around in this negative image of a city, going from boy to boy but knowing that really none of them will ever match up to the ultimate boy, the perfect, fictional one in my head?

Nobody will ever match up with that. Not really. I'm probably going to spend my whole life chasing him. Writing about him. Trying to catch him in my notebooks and stories and wrapping him up in convoluted sentences until I can lose him in the structure of some book, in the structure of that great novel everyone tells me I'm destined to write. Until then he'll only exist in pop songs like this, and in my head.

41

I'm kind of floating at the moment. I mean in a pleasant way. Sometimes smoking weed gets you in a really bad way, totally unexpectedly, makes you feel horrible. Like the world is closing in on you. Sometimes the opposite happens. You feel perfectly balanced, warm and fuzzy, and you keep waiting for the bad part to come but it doesn't. You feel you can totally drift into anything. You're prepared for everything. You're wrapped in cotton wool.

Margot: What are you thinking about?
Me: I don't know.

I've just taken a drag of the joint. I pass it solemnly back to her. She accepts it; holds it between two fingers. Smiles at me.

Me: I think I'm going to be alone forever.
Margot: Only extremely neurotic people are afraid of being alone forever at sixteen.
Me: I am extremely neurotic.
Margot: Obviously.
Me: I haven't been with a boy in a long time. I really need to feel something. I really need to . . . How to put it—you know, lose myself in someone. Is that bad?

She coughs; passes the joint back to me.

Margot: Is what bad, tiger?

I take a nice long drag; exhale slowly.

Me: The fact that I need to . . . You know, I mean, okay. This guy checked me out on the bus this afternoon. He was pretty good-looking. He looked a couple of years older, but that doesn't matter. I would really have liked to follow him off the bus, or made him follow me. You know. It would have been fucking great to have sex with him. Is that bad?

Margot: . . . You shouldn't.

Me: . . . Shouldn't what?

Margot: You shouldn't feel bad about it.

Me: Oh.

Margot: Fuck. We're young and pretty, Calvin. We might as well have as much fun as we can before we're old and gross and nobody wants to touch us anymore.

I take another drag. I like the way it feels in my hand. I like the way I imagine I look when I'm doing it. I know it's probably not doing good things for me from a health and wellbeing perspective, but, like, do I care? I take a smaller drag. Mainly so I can tell myself, well, I could have taken a bigger one, but I didn't. Because I'm, you know . . . responsible.

Me: I like it better when you put it that way.

Margot: Of course you do.

Me: But, I mean . . . Shouldn't I? Shouldn't I

be worried that I was fully prepared to have sex with a total stranger?

Margot: It's not like you haven't set a precedent. You've done it before. You've . . . Calvin? You okay tiger?

Me: I am. It's just . . . Whatever. I'm sure there'll be plenty of hot guys there tonight.

Margot: Maybe we can share one.

Me: You *wish.*

Margot: Even if there is a nice guy there, he'll probably be more interested in *you.* You dirty fag. Gay boys are nicer than straight ones anyway.

Me: No, we're *not.*

Margot: Yes you fucking are. Gay boys are, like, *totally* porno. You're nicer than any of the straight boys I know. And cuter.

Me: Please.

Margot: And you guys don't get all . . . hung up about giving head.

Me: You dirty bitch.

Margot: You love it.

Me: Shut up.

42

We're at this big house somewhere in New Farm, just near the river. A bunch of young guys who Margot knows "from around" have just moved here, and I think this might be their housewarming or something. I don't really know any of them, though Margot tells me that a friend of hers used to be going out with Edward, one of the guys who lives here, but the two of them broke up because he was on lots of antidepressants and he tried to stab her once, but apparently he's better now.

> **Edward:** Edward, it seems, is not very interesting—all you need to know is he's some guy who dropped out of school to be a model, who might or might not be a drug dealer, who is cute, who is eighteen. Edward, Margot tells me before we arrive, has been photographed everywhere—"like, *everywhere*," she says. I don't ask her what this means, although she tells me that several months ago he played "boy at party" in one of those ad campaigns that are intended to show the dangers of underage drinking. His agent is trying to get him into a deodorant commercial.

The front verandah of the house is level with the street, closed in. When we arrive, Edward is shirtless, walking around in a pair of black three-quarter pants and smoking a cigarette. Margot introduces us—he nods, shakes my hand. His eyes are almost closed and he seems to be extremely stoned. I'm not sure what to say so I mumble something and try to look nonchalant. "This is my bitch," he says of the blonde girl next to him, who laughs nervously and looks away. He leans over to kiss the girl and she goes stiff but lets him do it anyway.

"Edward's famous," she says to me. "Have you seen him?"

43

It's early but already the party is crowded, though I don't recognise anyone, which freaks me out a little bit. Hip-hop beats are blaring from somewhere inside the house, and Eminem is informing us that life would be empty without him, although I am wondering whether this is necessarily true. On the verandah there is an esky with lots of those vodka drinks in it—blueberry and raspberry flavored—and I'm gulping them down way too fast, talking to some girl called Jessica about how much fun it would be to go backpacking around Europe. Margot brought a joint—"for emergencies," she said—so we stand and smoke it with Jessica, under a tree in the back yard. A guy in a Che Guevara shirt is eyeing the joint off but we don't offer him any, and there are noises coming from inside the house. Edward has started a fight with someone. People stop what they're doing and look towards the sounds, interested; and when a friend pulls him out onto the back veran- dah, telling him to "calm down man, calm down," Edward, who is still shirtless and looks a lot more ani- mated now, says, "Stupid fuck. He knows I only *did it* because I needed the money, and it was just that once. Fuck him. What does he fucking know?" and Margot rolls her eyes and passes me the joint.

44

It's much later in the night, and I'm drunk now, like, *very* drunk, and I don't quite know what I'm doing, but fuck it, I'm having fun. The party has become extremely crowded, and Margot and I are both standing on the far side of the living room checking out this boy called Liam, who is standing on the other side of the room talking to a bunch of his friends and looking incredibly attractive/together etc. He has an arrogant look, an "I'm better than you" kind of a look. Like the kind of boy you never get to sleep with, ever, which makes him even better looking, in a vaguely fucked-up way.

Liam. I've never seen him before tonight. But he's cute. I mean, *cute* cute. Tall. Glasses. Wearing this yel- low hoodie. I wonder if he's a model too. He looks like the kind of guy who'd never fuck you. Who'd never even notice you. Liam. I'm pretty sure that's his name. Like, ninety-nine percent sure. I think it suits him.

Liam. The kind of name you never normally hear outside a novel or a movie or whatever.

Liam: If you want to know what Liam looks like, just get a mental picture of every overly-privileged, annoying and really hot private school boy you ever knew and multiply it by, like, one hundred. It's almost too much of a cliché to comprehend . . . Of *course* I'm attracted to this person. But let's stop fucking well obsessing over him and get on with things, shall we?"

45

Margot: He wants to have my children.
Me: Oh yeah . . .
Margot: He was checking you out before.
Me: Really? No he wasn't.
Margot: He completely was. I saw him.
Me: No you fucking didn't.
Margot: I did. Swear to god.
Me: He *wasn't* checking me out. He's not even . . . Come on. You're only saying this to make me feel better about myself because I'll never get to fuck him.
Margot: You're being *dumb.* If you don't do something about this, if you don't at least

talk to him, I mean, you'll be whining about it all night.

Me: He's *not* gay, all right? That would be . . . That would fucking be too easy. When have you ever known *anything* to be that easy?

Margot: Well, whatever. He's really fucking cute.

Me: Yeah. I can totally picture myself pulling his boxer shorts down with my teeth.

Margot: Slut.

46

Slut: The word resonates for a second, more than it should. I mean, Margot was joking, but it's true. I probably am a slut. I get this flashing image of myself down on my knees in front of Liam. I want to suck him off. I want him to totally use me. There's a really vicious thrill in that somewhere. The feeling I get every time I'm with some new boy.

47

While Margot and I are talking, I keep looking over at Liam. I sort of try to make it look casual. I'm not really expecting anything to happen. But the thing is, he looks back. I manage to make eye contact with him—he looks at me, and he doesn't look away. He maintains it for a second, two seconds, I'm not sure. Too long for it to be nothing. Probably not. I don't know. But it happens that once, then he turns back to his friends. He's in the middle of making this joke, I guess, because when he reaches what must be the end, he starts making all these expansive gestures and everyone else starts laughing. He laughs with them, then he turns to look at me again, and there's this whole *other* look in his eyes.

He gestures at them, this "be right back" gesture, and starts to move away. I wonder where he's going, and for an extremely panicked second I think he might be coming over here, but he's not. He's walking towards the CD player. When he gets there, he turns, looks at me again. Right in the eyes. I mean, if that isn't "come over here" I don't know what is. I'm drawn to him, almost mechanically. As I approach, he's leaning down, changing the CD. As he's doing it, I see him clench his teeth once, twice. The muscles in his cheek move a little as he does it. Hard to explain why I'm so fascinated by this minute detail, but anyway. The music starts. He's put on the Strokes album—five rich pretty boys from New York making fashionable and vaguely contrived new wave music for kids with image/self-esteem problems to take home and keep. I own it.

"This is a pretty good album," I say to him.

He turns around, looks up at me.
He says: "I know."

48

I talk to Liam for a long time. We're talking about school—he tells me he's on the rowing team or something, and I remember I'm very impressed by this. Whatever. He tells some stupid joke, and when we've both stopped laughing, he looks right at me and asks me—and you have to understand, he's being really casual about it, as though he's just the coolest guy on the face of the planet—if I would like to get stoned with him. He tells me that his brother, one of the guys who lives here apparently, has some weed and that he was, y'know, going to have some on his own later, but that I seem like a pretty nice guy and all, so he won't feel too bad about sharing it with me. I pretend to consider his offer for longer than I actually do, then I nod my head and tell him okay. He seems pleased that I've said this, suggests that we go somewhere a little quieter.

49

Liam checks to see if anyone is watching, and when he's satisfied they're not, he closes the door. I'm swaying—I'm beginning to realize I'm even more drunk than I thought—and I stagger across to this armchair beside the bed. There are clothes everywhere and I have to push a pile of them out of the way just so there's enough room to sit down. I pick up this book that's lying on the arm of the chair, but I'm too drunk to read what's on the back so I let it drop to the floor.

Liam moves towards the cupboard, opens the door. "This is where he keeps it," he says. "It's always on the top shelf. He won't mind if we smoke in his room. He's not even here."

"Cool," I say.
"He's out. He's down the coast I think. He won't be back tonight."
"Cool."

Liam grins, walks across the bed carrying this *huge* Ziplock bag which is totally bulging with pot. I've never seen that much weed before. "Chris is so predictable," Liam says. "He *always* keeps it on the top shelf."

50

He sits down on the bed, under this huge poster for the movie *Lost Highway,* and begins to chop. A lot of what happens next is a blur. Like I said, I'm very drunk. Eventually he finishes rolling the joint and then looks at me again, gives me this look that's totally beyond any kind of interpretation. He pats the bed next to him. "Come sit next to me so we can smoke this," he says, holding up the joint.

I stand up, taking my time, pretending to be nervous, although maybe I am just a little bit nervous.

"Come on dude," he says.

Still very drunk, I am madly in love with Liam at this point, but I'm trying to cover it because . . . well . . . that's what you do. He lights the joint, takes a nice long drag and then passes it to me. As I'm smoking, he touches my arm, leaves his hand there for a long time. "This is weird," he says. "You're . . ."

"Yeah," I say, and I pass the joint back. My head feels fuzzy and we're suddenly sitting very close together. Everything in here is warm, especially Liam. I look at him—he's staring at the ceiling, this blissed expression on his face, and I stare across the room at a stack of CDs sitting on the desk, although I can't make out what any of them are, though I'm trying really hard, in order to distract myself, in order not to think about what's happening, and I'm feeling almost embarrassed as, once again, Liam says: "This is weird." I ask him a question about his rowing, or his parents, or what he wants to do at uni or something. He doesn't respond. He leans in and sticks his mouth right over mine.

51

Liam's mouth: He's kind of an aggressive kisser. He sticks his tongue right into my mouth, presses into it very hard, and his hand is on the back of my head. It's difficult to describe, but he kisses with his whole body—he moves until he's against me and then he sort of grinds, moves in closer and continues to kiss, and his mouth is extremely warm and wet and all of it, his warmth against mine, is making me incredibly hot for him. He pushes his face into mine. He's making these little noises. I don't know what you'd call them, but they're . . . Cool. It's nice to know that a guy's making noises when he's kissing you.

52

Something about before—before, the way he checked in the hallway before shutting the door—something about that look kind of bugs me. As we're kissing, it suddenly occurs to me that guys like Liam have a reputation to keep up. If we have sex it's going to mean nothing at all to him, and tomorrow morning he'll probably pretend that none of it ever happened. His friends will assume he's, you know, met a *girl* or something, maybe even that Jessica girl, and taken her into his brother's room. That's what brothers' rooms are for. It's different for boys like Liam. Part of me knows. Part of me wants to be upset, but a larger part doesn't even care. Still, I don't want to think about it for too long or it's going to fuck the night right up.

53

He breaks the kiss off. Looks right into me again. This serious kind of look on his face.

> **Liam:** My brother's gone. It's okay if you crash here.
> **Me:** Great.
> **Liam:** Listen.
> **Me:** What?
> **Liam:** I'm not a faggot, okay? I'm just doing this because . . . I don't know. I think you're pretty hot. You know what I mean?

I do.

Me: Okay . . . So are we going to . . . ?

He kisses me again. Longer this time. It feels . . . if not *right,* then nice.

Liam: Okay.
Me: Okay.
Liam: . . . I'm not a faggot, all right?

Got it.

Liam: My brother's not here.

54

The lights are off and he's kissing me, and the whole thing is just like . . . Well, you know. It's really cool, and he's wasted and I'm wasted and the feel of this moment totally wipes out everything that's come before it. Blank. Over. (*He's not a faggot.*) The kind of boy I'd never get to have under normal circumstances. Hell, he probably has a *girlfriend.* But right now, in the fact that I'm so totally hot for him and in the look of hunger that he has in his eyes, we're equals. That feels good. He's sitting on the bed. Unzipped (I think I did that). I'm sort of, well, kneeling close by. You know.

"Okay. Go ahead," he says. I go ahead.

55

. . . random, scattered images of the rest of the night . . .

. . . I'm down on my knees, kind of choking on Liam's cock. It's the old familiar routine, and I keep going, I really don't want to stop, because . . .

. . . Liam's hands in my hair. His fingers kind of rough. He hurts me a bit sometimes, but I really don't care. I'm so hot for him by this point that . . .

. . . he scrambles around in his clothes, finds a condom in one of the pockets, and he's opening it with his teeth, looking me right in the eyes, and his eyebrow sort of . . .

. . . breathing, and he's trying not to breathe too loud, because . . .

. . . blank here . . .

. . . we're both on the bed again, and he looks into my eyes for a second, seems almost like an accident, and it's like . . .

. . . the curve of his cheek, in the dark . . .

. . . we're kissing again . . .

. . . he's going down on me and then suddenly he's not and then I'm sort of lying on my front and . . .

. . . that brunette boy from the net, no, wait, blocking it out, blocking it out, blocking it out . . .

. . . I kind of black out again here . . .

. . . he's saying something to me and maybe it's

because I'm drunk or, I don't know, but I don't hear what it is . . .

. . . his breath, in my ear and on my neck, warm, wet, makes me want to die, and it . . .

. . . and he's sort of biting my shoulder, not really biting but I can feel his teeth, and he's pushing himself in and out and in and out and again . . .

. . . a noise he makes, a breathing noise, and it's almost like he's crying, an almost desperate kind of a noise, and I know it's for me, because of me, and it's impossible to explain but the significance of it, the fact that he made it for me, suddenly hits and it's almost . . .

. . . and for a second I'm not there anymore, because I've lost myself completely in Liam, in how drunk I am, in the hunger, and I'm gone, and it feels . . .

Over.

56

Early morning.

> "That was fun," he says.
> "Yeah . . . I had fun too."
> "We should . . . Get together . . . Sometime . . . I mean . . . Coffee, or . . . see a movie or . . . . Y'know. Um. Whatever."
> "Definitely. I'd like that."

"Look . . . I'm not . . . like . . . gay . . . or any-thing . . . but I've got my mobile here. How about I, umm . . . program your number in?"

"My, um. Number."

"If you don't . . ."

"Cool. Here . . . Let me do it."

"Thanks."

"There you go."

"You want mine?"

"Do I. I mean. Um. Yeah. What is it?"

His phone is very slim, and silver. Almost identical to mine.

"Well. I should go."

"Yeah."

"My car's out on the street. My brother's car, I mean . . . but he lets me drive it, so . . . I can . . . give you a . . . lift if you like."

"I'm fine. Thanks."

"Okay."

"I had . . . fun last night."

"Definitely. It was fun. I had fun too."

"I . . . like you."

"Yeah, totally. You're really hot."

"And last night . . . It was really good. I mean seriously."

"I know. It was great."

"We should . . . see each other . . . again some time."

"Oh, totally."

"Yeah."

"Well . . . I should really . . . go . . ."

"Yeah. Good luck . . . with the rowing . . . or whatever."

"Oh, thanks."

". . . So . . . See ya round."

"Yeah. See ya."

57

Front verandah: I walk out, unsteady, bleary-eyed, hoping to escape as fast as possible. Edward is sitting on a deckchair, barefoot and hunched over a very large bong. A girl—different from the girl last night, prettier—is sitting back against the nearby wall, passed out. Edward's hair is a mess, and as I walk past, he lights up, takes a very big hit and then leans back, exhaling slowly. He doesn't seem to see me, but as I stand looking at him, wondering if he's conscious, he holds up the bong, offering it to me. I shake my head and he shrugs, disappointed almost, setting it down on the floorboards instead. He asks me if I'm Gretchen's friend, asks if I have any more of that speed. I tell him no, sorry. I have no idea who Gretchen is. He mumbles something, runs both hands through his hair, and I leave.

58

Saturday morning: Kind of hung over. I don't really feel like going home, but where else would I be going? My head's vaguely fuzzy. I can still taste Liam.

I head back home. There is a woman on the bus who keeps talking to herself, and she's old and ugly, and I can't even say why but after I've looked at her for a while I can't even breathe. Gives me the feeling that last night was the exception, and this morning—dirty, overcast, crazy woman on the bus, incoherent, dry mouth—is the rule.

59

Big empty house when I get home. My dad said something about being on call this weekend, so I guess he's at the hospital. I don't know where Mum is but I don't really care.

I put on the mix tape Margot gave me, then I collapse onto a big armchair in the living room, the Psychedelic Furs blasting—I find this song really comforting for some reason—and roll this clumsy but adequate joint with what's left of my emergency pot. Within about ten minutes I'm wasted enough to deal with life in general. I eat a grapefruit, which tastes disgusting but I eat it anyway, and I end up spending about four hours playing this stupid video game I used to be into when I was about six or something. Playing it always brings back a bunch of memories of being a little kid. Weird memories. I don't know, of more innocent times or whatever.

60

This particular game that I'm playing is, I have to say, kind of cool. The electronic music on the soundtrack is so much better than it has any right to be that it's almost ethereal or something, like synthesiser lines you might hear on a dance floor with beats thudding underneath, drumbeats, something you can dance to, lose yourself in.

61

I can still taste Liam.

62

This giant tiger thing keeps falling on me, and I keep trying to kill it but I get distracted or lose my focus and it always ends up killing me. It's really annoying, and after a while the game starts getting to me. I start wondering if the little boy who used to love playing this is the same boy who got blasted and let himself be used and fucked comprehensively by Liam from the rowing team last night. Shouldn't think about things like that but I do. Can't help it. For a second the feeling overwhelms me.

Fucking *deal with it,* I tell myself. *Get over it.*

> Message on the screen: *Unfortunately, no trace of the heroes was ever found . . . Play again?*

I return to the game. Try to focus on it. The giant tiger keeps killing me and my head is filling with thoughts of last night and after a while I can't cope with any of it anymore and I switch the thing off and start having this minor freak out.

63

We're young and pretty Calvin. We might as well have as much fun as we can before we're old and gross and nobody wants to touch us anymore/*Unfortunately, no trace of the heroes was ever found . . . Play again?*/ "So . . . See ya round"/the sound of Liam breathing, that one breath he took, for me/that brunette boy from the net/*See ya round/See ya round/See ya round.*

I stand up and breathe deeply until the worst of the panic attack is over. I find myself leaning on the bathroom sink, staring into the mirror. Everything in the bathroom is clean. I stretch the elastic at the neck of my T-shirt, trying to see if Liam has left teeth marks in my shoulder. Turn around and look back at the mirror. I can see a vague red mark there, but it's not really that noticeable.

I stare at my face for a long time; I stare at it until I don't recognize it any more, and I don't even blink and my vision goes all weird and everything turns black then I blink and shake my head a little, and when I look, it's me in the mirror again.

Fuck it. Whatever. I had fun last night. That's all that matters. All the rest of it I can block out.

64

On IRC chat the following night:

    bô¥ KïLlê®™: so . . . .

    sweet*Prince: so?

    bô¥ KïLlê®™: how'd it go? come on, I saw you guys disappearing.

    sweet*Prince: did anyone else see?

    bô¥ KïLlê®™: your secret is safe. I see everything. come on Calvin, fucking *spill* you know you want to tell me. I might as well get fucked vicariously through you.

sweet*Prince: that's a charming thought

bô¥ KïLlê®™:

sweet*Prince: well, y'know. it was fun. he was really fucking hot. that's about it. he told me he was a rower. don't know if it was true. could have been. he had the build for it.

bô¥ KïLlê®™: =)P*

bô¥ KïLlê®™: nice. how far'd you get?

sweet*Prince: far enough

bô¥ KïLlê®™: ooohhhhhhhhh. I'm impressed ;)

bô¥ KïLlê®™: god. why do you always get guys like Liam?

sweet*Prince: cuz I'm so cute and innocent and shit.

bô¥ KïLlê®™: oh yeah, of course

bô¥ KïLlê®™: seeing him again?

sweet*Prince: probably not. it was kind of a one-nighter.

bô¥ KïLlê®™: ah well. it's better that way. boys are boring when they start following you around.

sweet*Prince: I guess. sorry I abandoned you. I mean like seriously. I wouldn't normally run off just for the sake of a guy. I was drunk.

sweet*Prince:

sweet*Prince: doesn't it ever bother you?

bô¥ KïLlê®™: doesn't what?

sweet*Prince: the fact that. I don't know how it is for you. but I mean. I'd like to see a guy for more than just sex. you know. I'd kind of like to have an actual boyfriend. don't you ever think that?

bô¥ KïLlê®™: not really

sweet*Prince: don't you ever get lonely or whatever?

bô¥ KïLlê®™: I don't know

bô¥ KïLlê®™: what are you getting at Calvin?

bô¥ KïLlê®™:

bô¥ KïLlê®™: I don't know.

sweet*Prince: you brought it up

bô¥ KïLlê®™: forget it

sweet*Prince: I had fun. that's all that counts, right? and it's not like I had my heart set on seeing him again or anything.

bô¥ KïLlê®™: yeah. great.

65

I lied before. About the other day, I mean. Before I switched my computer off I saved some of the pictures of the brunette boy. Six pictures in all. I don't know why.

After Margot goes offline I click on the first jpeg to open it. Something about the look in his eyes. I can't work it out. He seems so far gone. It seems wrong that someone so good-looking, healthy-looking, so *pretty* could end up being so far gone. I don't know. He could be anyone. He could be innocent or a slut. This time might have been his first. He might have done it heaps of times before. I don't know. That's the point.

I want to be in love with him; like, love in the most intense sense of the word. Whoever he is. I don't fall in love with the boy himself—not specifically. I fall in love with the idea of him. I fall in love with the fact that he is so beautiful and so fucked up. I fall in love with the fact that I want to save him.

I put the first on full screen then click through the rest of them. Looking at him makes me want to die.

66

Pictures of the brunette boy

1. Sitting on this sofa, which is red and looks expensive. His arm is kind of extended over the back, and it looks like it should be around someone's shoulder, except nobody else is sitting with him. His eyebrow is slightly raised.

2. Still sitting on the sofa, in the same position, but looking to the side, like in profile or whatever. You can see some of Jeremy in this shot. He's sitting on the arm of the sofa, so you can see his legs; they seem kind of weird in that context, I mean, just his legs, disembodied. But

the brunette boy's profile is the most important thing about this one.

3. He's standing now, on his own. His head is sort of cocked to one side, and his hands are behind his back. This is the most complete shot. He's wearing a tight blue shirt with a picture of a bulldog on it; some writing that I can't make out. His brown hair is gelled up in this painstakingly casual way and there's a single earring in his left ear. The whole look could either be deliberate or a total accident, difficult to say. Like the look in his eyes. The look in his eyes is impossible to define. I mean, on the surface it's all "come on, I dare you," really sexy, but there's something underneath that. It's weird.

4. He and Jeremy are both standing, kissing one another. You can only see the back of Jeremy's head and the side of the brunette boy's cheek. His hands are in the small of Jeremy's back. They're long and delicate.

5. He is leaning against a window; his forehead is pressed up against the smooth glass. He looks beautiful. Fragile. It's an arty kind of photograph. He is reflected back at himself. He is looking down; it seems like an unguarded moment, but for all the work and preparation the shot must have taken, I can't be sure

exactly. Maybe the brunette boy is genuinely sad, or maybe he's just a really good actor.

6. He's standing in front of the curtains. His shirt is off. It's this shot that makes me decide he's not acting. The frightened confident guarded calculated innocent fuck-me look in his eyes seems too, I don't know, *real* to be fake.

67

Things written in my notebook: How strangely typical is it that the first person I would pick to get seriously obsessed with is some boy who happens to be on the net? I suppose it's kind of fitting, the reason being that it's safe for me to be into him. Think of it in its most basic terms. He's real enough that he's totally good-looking, but still distant enough that he can be pretty much whoever I want. I can fill in his personality, his background with whatever little details suit me. I can build up stories about him, about the two of us, in my head and have them progress however I want, because as beautiful and tragic etc as he is, we'll never have to deal with each other's bullshit on a one-to-one basis. I'll never discover how fucked up the reality of him is. He'll never get bored of me.

68

It's late at night. I stare at the television, half interested, spacing out. There are breakdancers on the
screen, a movie from the mid-1980s, new wave music
on the soundtrack and a girl in a pink sweater saying,
"I don't want to be reasonable . . . I've been reasonable all my life and it's gotten me nowhere!" Suddenly
a gaping void opens before me and I wonder what it
would be like to die, if it would be painless, and how
I'd do it, but I ignore those thoughts and keep watching the movie instead.

69

Bored. Kind of cold. It's a Friday afternoon, the week
after Liam, and I still don't have a boyfriend. I'm too
young to have a car. I'm still obsessing about the
brunette boy and trying to block him out at the same
time. Consequently I spend most of the afternoon
wandering around the house in a daze, kind of aching
for something to happen.

I comb the place—unsuccessfully—for any drugs I
might have had and forgotten about. There are two
pills in one of those foil wrappers on the floor of my
parents' room. I'm fairly certain my mum's addicted to
Prozac, but these don't look like Prozac. I don't know
what they are, but I figure they're probably not any-

thing exciting. I leave them where they are. Continue to comb the house but come up with nothing. I'm upset at first. Then again, if I'd found anything I probably wouldn't have done it. Whenever I don't have any drugs handy, I get this overwhelming urge to find some, but whenever I take anything I always find myself thinking, Jeez, I wish I hadn't done that. Tricky situation. Well, okay, it's not really.

When I'm done combing the house, I get the urge to put on that particular Strokes album to remind me of Liam, but I can't find it anywhere. I go to the kitchen for some cold water, and as I'm standing by the window drinking it, I stare out at the pool. It looks cool and vaguely inviting; I wonder what it would be like to jump in there with my school uniform and my shoes and socks and everything on, and I actually seriously consider it for about an eighth of a second, then I think better of it. I rinse my glass and go back to the living room. My Strokes CD is sitting on top of the stereo. I don't know why I didn't think to look there. Now I've found it, funnily enough, I don't want to listen to it anymore.

70

Brunette boy: You should have just played that CD.
Me: No I shouldn't.

Brunette boy: You're fucked up. You shouldn't be obsessing over Liam like this. He doesn't care about you. Believe me. He never wants to see you again.

Me: I guess.

Brunette boy: So, fucking, enough with the obsessional neurosis, okay? It's boring. That's the worst thing you can be Calvin. Boring.

Me: What's that, your philosophy?

Brunette boy: Fucking hell yeah.

Me: So what do *you* suggest?

Brunette boy: You're boring Calvin. And you're obsessive. You'd have more fun if you were like me.

Me: You're a figment of my imagination.

Brunette boy: I don't obsess like you Calvin. I just do. I'm young and I'm hot and that's all that matters. Life's much more fun when you don't think about it.

Me: You really think so?

Brunette boy: Just take a look at me Calvin. I'm fun. Guys want me Calvin. *Lots* of guys. Check me out; check out me and Jeremy . . . The shit we got up to. We did that because people wanted us. Because we were fucking *hot*.

Me: So what? I mean, what was it like?

Brunette boy: What was it *like?* Well we were

two hot guys kissing each other and going down on each other and we didn't *care* who was there to see it. We *knew* how good-looking we were. There was some guy with a camera; we were driving him fucking wild. That's all that mattered. That's what it was like.

Me: You make it sound easy.

Brunette boy: You wouldn't know. You wouldn't be *able* to be wanted like that. You're too boring Calvin. Too safe. You don't know how to let go.

Me: Let go of what?

Brunette boy: Let go of yourself.

71

I consider combing the house again, in case there are any drugs around that I might have missed the first time, then decide against it. On the stereo Julian Casablancas is telling me that he wants to steal my innocence. Understandable really. I go online. Maybe one of my friends will be on, hopefully with something interesting to do tonight. Go into IRC. That's where I see Dean.

72

It's not like I know Dean especially well. He's four years older than I am, and he's doing commerce or something at uni. He told me but I don't remember. We met on the net a while ago. Spent a few very late nights chatting about movies and bands and guys we'd like to fuck and the coolest clubs in Brisbane etc, and flirting in a roundabout sort of a way. I sent him a photo of me and though he was surprised at how young I looked, he said I was kind of hot. That shouldn't have made me feel good but it did. It's not as though I'm shallow or anything but, like . . . I need reassurance. When it comes to myself, my looks, abilities, etc, I need things verified for me before I can believe them.

For purposes of continuity, I should perhaps explain what I mean at this point. When I was fourteen or something I had a real *thing* about being, like, wanted, if you have any idea what I mean. I don't know why exactly. Let's just say I'm totally incapable of believing anything worthwhile about myself until I hear it from someone else. Point was that at fourteen I was just this ball of self-doubt, teen angst etc, all the normal fourteen-year-old things, and I needed someone to *prove* to me that I was attractive, that I was wanted.

In the spirit of this, I would seek out quote-unquote "challenging" guys. Dean was a case in point. They'd tell me how good-looking I was, how much they wanted me etc, and it wasn't even what they said that made it worthwhile, it was the fact that I could do it in the first place. The fact that there were people out there who *wanted* to take me and pin their fantasies on me meant I was *worth* pinning fantasies on. I mean, you wouldn't go out of your way to be with someone if you thought they weren't worth the effort, would you? Fuck no. So you can see how this would all make sense.

It made a lot of sense to me at the time anyway.

73

So yeah. Dean and I went out a couple of times. The eighteen-fourteen age difference wasn't really *that* extreme but it was enough to keep me interested and give the whole situation a kind of meaning or context or (for me at least) "literary value" or whatever. Nothing much happened. He told me I was cute, and he wanted to sleep with me, and we almost did it at one point—we'd just finished sucking one another off and he suddenly moved really close to me and I realized what was going to happen, that this would put me in the club, but I had this big freak-out and we didn't. I told him it was nothing to do with him, which it wasn't, it was just that I was really kind of unstable at the time. More so than now. If that's possible. Anyway, Dean and I kept in contact over the net, although I haven't really seen him much over the last couple of months. We're still friends.

I think.

sweet*Prince: hey Dean

pure)(morning: Calvin! how the fuck are you?

sweet*Prince: I'm okay. sort of bored. single. wasting my young life. you know.

pure)(morning: hehhe. I do.

pure)(morning: hey dude, there was a pic of you in one of those street press mags last week! ya see it?

sweet*Prince: shit. no. which magazine?

pure)(morning: oh man. one of them . . . one of the gay ones. I forget. but anyway, it was in the back section. you know where they have all those pictures of people who've been out clubbing.

sweet*Prince: yeah . . .

pure)(morning: it was a pic of you and some girl. you looked pretty cute.

sweet*Prince: fuck. um. I don't even know when that would have been taken. I was out with Margot a couple of fridays ago. might have been then.

sweet*Prince: fuck. I really hope nobody else saw it.

pure)(morning: it was a pretty good pic. you looked hot.

sweet*Prince: yeah, but still. I fucking hate those magazines. I'm too scared to even pick em up any more.

pure)(morning: why? scared of seeing someone you know?

pure)(morning: an *ex* ?

sweet*Prince: probably

sweet*Prince: . . . I'm probably scared to see myself.

pure)(morning: oh

sweet*Prince: shit. I hope nobody I know saw that picture.

pure)(morning: it was only a small one.

sweet*Prince: doesn't matter.

sweet*Prince: so how about you? how's uni going?

pure)(morning: it's okay. I'm still there, put it that way.

pure)(morning: . . . hey Calvin, you doing anything tonight?

sweet*Prince: not really. you have something in mind?

pure)(morning: yeah. well, nothing too exciting. just some friends coming around. we'll probably just get drunk or high or whatever then go out into the Valley or something. want to come?

sweet*Prince: sounds good.

sweet*Prince: who else is going to be there?

pure)(morning: just some uni friends. just whoever's around. rock up to my place anytime soon.

75

After Dean goes offline I click on jpeg number six to open it again. I stare into his eyes for a really long time.

Brunette boy: You're really taking this obsession with me to a whole new level. I'm impressed.

Me: Sorry.

Brunette boy: Don't apologize. I think it's kind of cool.

Me: Okay. Yeah.

Brunette boy: You know I'm just a series of dots on a screen?

Me: Yeah, well, I'm fully aware of that. Sorry if I'm being kind of . . . you know . . . weird about this.

Brunette boy: That's okay. I like weird.

Me: Really?

Brunette boy: Why would I say it if I didn't mean it?

Me: Maybe you're just saying it because you're a figment of my imagination.

Brunette boy: What *is* imaginary?

Me: What do you mean?

Brunette boy: Just because I'm in your head, does that make me any less real? I'm still a part of you.

Me: I guess.

Brunette boy: I *am*. I'm basically just your desires and neuroses reflected back at you.

Me: Well that's great, but can you, you know, stop?

Brunette boy: I can be whatever you want me to be. I'm in *your* head.

Me: Whatever. I'm bored of this.

76

I'm trying to decide what to wear tonight. There's the shirt with "Brain Dead Body Still Rockin'" printed on the front. Margot and I found it in one of those shops in the Valley not so long ago. It looks cool, and it looks good on me, but I was wearing it that night with Liam, so I don't know. The girl singing on the stereo assures me that she is open to falling from grace. I wonder whether or not I believe her.

There's this orange shirt. Button-up. Very tight. I like it.

I try on both the red one and the orange one. Then this white "I LOVE NEW YORK" shirt that my parents bought me when we were over there two years ago. When I was fourteen.

Me: Which one should I wear?

Brunette boy: What are the choices?

Me: This red one here, or the button-up one. Or the "I LOVE NEW YORK" one.

Brunette boy: Don't wear that one. It's stupid.

Me: I guess.

Brunette boy: Unless you're wearing it as some kind of, you know, "ironic" statement or whatever.

Me: I wouldn't be.

Brunette boy: Then don't wear it.

Me: Okay, I guess so. I don't know why I got my parents to buy that shirt for me in the first place.

Brunette boy: I'd go with the red one.

Me: You think? I don't know. I think it's kind of slutty.

Brunette boy: That's the point. I mean, you look hot in it. That's all that matters.

Me: Really?

Brunette boy: Of course. I mean, okay, think about tonight. A hot guy's checking you out from across the room. He's not thinking about how much he wants to sleep with your *personality,* is he?

Me: I guess not. But I mean . . .

Brunette boy: Okay Calvin. Think of it this way. What was it, specifically, that attracted you to me?

Me: The way you looked in those photos. You were hot.

Brunette boy: Exactly. And it was only after you saw how hot I was that you started building a personality for me, wasn't it?

Me: I guess so.

Brunette boy: It was only after *that* I became interesting or worthy of consideration, wasn't it?

Me: I guess so.

Brunette boy: Totally. So you see. You can dress it up as much as you want, but ultimately, in that particular equation, good looks were the most important thing. I was fucking hot, wasn't I?

Me: Okay, yeah, you were.

Brunette boy: There's only so long you can play this "blissfully unaware" role Calvin. Everything's about sex, everything's about good looks, and you fucking know it.

Me: I guess you're right.

Brunette boy: So in the spirit of that, the sluttier the better, you know? Fucking wear the red shirt. You'll be glad you did.

Me: Well, okay. Is it the kind of thing you'd wear?

Brunette boy: Fucking *totally* Calvin.

78

I decide to go with the red shirt.

Brain Dead Body Still Rockin'.

79

I walk to my bedroom window, look at the rooftops of the houses nearby. In the gray afternoon it looks warm, serene. It reminds me of a book I had when I was a little kid—this village, somewhere in Europe, Finland or something, somewhere in the valley, with a bay, and the winters there were freezing cold but nobody cared because they had warm houses and fireplaces, and there was this one little creature, the Snuffkin or something, and he curled up in this boat for the winter, and I remember I always thought that was incredibly cool, I wanted to be like that, and I'd curl up and pretend I was in a boat, under the canvas cover, and it would be cold outside but it wouldn't even matter because I'd be so warm. I try to think what those books were called but I totally can't remember, which starts to bug me in a way I can't even explain, and I walk away from the window.

80

Suburban noir. I don't know what else you'd call it. One of those late afternoons at the beginning of winter, when the familiar takes on this whole different look. Difficult to describe, but it's in the overcast sky, the streetlights as they start to come on; in the way the tree branches hang low over the streets; in the cold air, and the eyes of all the people around you. It's like there's this whole other world just waiting to emerge as soon as night falls. Brisbane, the winter nights are like a whole different country here. You get the feeling that anything at all could happen.

The moon has already risen, too early for night. There's this faint impression of it against sky, like a bleach stain or something. It looks quite beautiful, the kind of thing I'd stop and stare at for ages if I wasn't . . . distracted.

I left a note for my parents telling them I was going out with friends. I don't even know why I bothered doing that. Now I'm on the bus from my parents' big, safe house in Albany Creek to Dean's outpost of sharehouse bohemia in Windsor. The two might as well be on different planets.

I have my headphones on; sitting near the back and staring out the window at the houses and the cars as they go by in the growing dark. I'm thinking about a lot of things at once; my mind is always vaguely scrambled, and my thoughts travel too quickly to ever pin down exactly what it is I'm thinking about at any particular moment. At the moment, I'm thinking about five things at once. They are, in descending order:

5. The brunette boy from the net.
4. Wondering about this couple, a guy and a girl, who were waiting, safe in the faint glow of a streetlight, as the bus slowed to pick them up. It seemed from the expressions on their faces, the way they were staring at each other, that they might as well be the only two people in the world. He whispered something into her ear and he laughed. An honest kind of a laugh. I'm wondering what he said; wondering if I'll ever be able to feel that way with anyone. Really safe, I mean, and contented.
3. Wondering, if I ever do find that guy, whether if he'll feel the same re me.
2. Wondering how tonight will turn out, with the Valley and everything else. I'm not eighteen, and I'm too short and probably too small to pass for eighteen, but you can get into all sorts of places if you want to.
1. Wondering about the music I'm listening to. My discman. Vacant-pretty-sexy-nasty electronic music. I'm wondering what the singer was thinking when she sang about drowning, and forty

days of one-night stands. Wondering if she felt the same as I did, though probably not.

These thoughts circle around and play over in a continuous loop until we're somewhere in Windsor, near Dean's house. The bus stops just near an intersection; I get up and as I'm walking towards the door, I notice the guy who got on earlier. He has his arm around the girl; she's looking out the window and he's looking in my direction. We make eye contact for about an eighth of a second, then he looks away again. His expression is unreadable; I can't help but wonder what he's thinking about, if he's thinking anything at all.

81

Dean's house is at the crest of the hill. I can see the tops of the buildings as I walk towards it, but as I draw closer, the city comes more and more into view. When I reach the top, suddenly the whole of the cityscape has unfolded, and I see the buildings, the cars, the thousands upon thousands of lights glowing and flickering like fireflies. For that fraction of a second, seeing the buildings and the lights stretched out for what seems like forever shuts out all my other thoughts. For that fraction of a second I am five years old again.

It's a night a long long time ago, in a park just near our house, I think it must be a party, though I don't remember exactly. Memory is always elusive, and parts of the night have vanished altogether, but I remember the important things. I remember the music; the cold air. It's so cold I can see my breath, and my father's because I'm sitting on his shoulders, and all around me there are lights, brighter than any I've ever seen before. The lights are in the trees, and every tree in the park is strung with what seems like thousands and thousands of them. To me, at the time, it seemed like the lights could have covered the whole world. It was something magical, something I would never even have dreamed, and I remember the feeling of it was almost more than I could take. I was overwhelmed. Happy.

For a second, as I'm staring, hypnotized, at the lights, I'm a little kid again, and the events of the intervening years have never happened. There is nothing of my parents' coldness, or the gap that has slowly opened between us. Nothing of the secrets. Nothing of the drinks or the pills, nothing of the boys or the "promise to call you" and "promise not to cum in your mouth," the staying out at night or the crawling home in the morning. And as those things which have been buried, half forgotten, begin to come back to me, they bring a sadness with them. The kind of sadness that seems so clear, the *truth* of it can make you double over, suck all the air right out of you. The lights make me remember a time when I was still sheltered from the world. When I could sit on my father's shoulders and I know that while I was there, nothing at all could hurt me.

The image—the trees and the fairy lights and my breath in the cold air—begins to fade. I try to grab hold of it again, but it's like trying to grab hold of a dream once you've started to wake up. I realize that, more than anything, I want some part of that *innocence* back. I want to be overwhelmed as much as I was as a child. I want to be able to be overwhelmed.

82

When I get to Dean's house he's already partially stoned. When he opens the door his eyes are glazed, and he has this incredibly *cute* look about him. I don't know how to describe that look properly—I'd say it's about forty percent the expression on his face, forty percent his figure and the way he carries himself, and then after that a combination of various other factors. But, yeah. Whatever. Dean always manages to look incredibly *together*.

He hugs me when he answers the door. He always hugs everyone.

"Calvin, hey! I haven't seen you in ages."

"No. Dude, it's good to see you," I tell him and we hug one another again. When he's hugging me he feels warm, and I can smell the scent that surrounds him, which is a mix of pot smoke and what I suspect might be LYNX or some other kind of fairly aggressive deodorant. His hands are in the small of my back this time. For a moment I start to become kind of vaguely turned on by this, but then he breaks the hug off.

"I haven't seen you since the play," he tells me.

Dean's referring to *Long Day's Journey Into Night,* this incredibly depressing Irish play he was in last year. He does something acting at uni. He's pretty good. Convincing, anyway. In *Long Day's Journey* he was playing someone's son. Things were tense, and everyone in the family was depressive or an alcoholic or both. Mostly both, actually. So, you know, it did have a pretty fair basis in reality. Anyway. The play was really good. Dean was fantastic. But my whole memory of that night is kind of dampened by what happened afterwards.

83

Adam, this dark-eyed and slightly canine guy from the outer orbit of my circle of friends, was at the play as well. Afterwards we all went out for drinks. By that I mean Dean and his friends went out for drinks and I tagged along with them. I obviously couldn't buy my own because I was fifteen or something at the time, but Adam plied me with rum and Cokes all night, and after a lot of flirting and telling me how good-looking I was—which I'm fairly certain he didn't mean—he leaned over and kissed me on the mouth. I let him do it. He told me he wanted to take me home. I let him do that as well.

We ended up at his house, sitting on the sofa, watching some movie in the dark with the sound turned off. I don't remember what we were watching. I was kissing him all over and blah blah blah, and then either he pulled his cock out or I pulled his cock out, I don't remember, but I know at that point I wanted to suck it, like more than anything, partly because I was hot for Adam, and partly because I knew he was an *older* guy, a *uni* guy, so I went down on him and I remember how big it felt in my mouth and kind of uncomfortable, and the taste of it, like, you know . . . I remember I made this really tragic attempt at a blow job that lasted several minutes and then that was that. Adam started acting all weird afterwards and dropped me off at home the next morning. It wasn't bad. I mean, I've had worse, but you know. Anyway.

I try to avoid thinking about that.

84

Dean and I talk for a little longer, just mindless catch-up bullshit, and eventually he invites me in. There are a few other people here. Adam is here. He looks sinewy tonight—vaguely predatory and very good-looking. Totally porno, as Margot would say. Immediately I begin to dread the prospect of having to talk to him, but for the time being at least, he is locked in an intense conversation with the girl sitting next to him. She has black bangs, too much eyeliner and a Hello Kitty shirt on; she is pretty in a slightly dishevelled way. They are both on a futon in the corner, and I think they're both stoned too. Looking around, I start to suspect that everyone here—seven or eight people—is on some kind of drug except for me. I can't decide whether this is a good thing or not.

The stereo is pouring out guitar noise with repetitive dance beats underneath and a man's voice, extremely sexy/detached/cool, over the top. I think it might be the new New Order—matter of fact, I'm about ninety-nine percent sure of it. But that's not important right now.

85

The brunette boy from the net is standing beside the stereo.

86

It can't be, but it is, but it can't be, but I'm pretty sure it is. Looking at him, I'm almost positive, but it can't be, but it has to be, and I mean, it is, it's him.

I spent so long staring at those jpegs. I memorized the angles of his face. The details. His hair—the color of it and the way it sat. His eyes. And I'm certain that this is the same boy. I'm sure. It has to be. I have no frame of reference for how to deal with this situation.

87

You know how there are some people you can just look at, you can see them only once and know that you want them so much it just about kills you? This boy is like that, only worse. Like that times about a thousand or so. He's tall, thin, with chocolate brown hair. His features all line up with perfect symmetry. I can't think, and I don't have to think, because right now I have no memory, I have no past; all I have is right now, and I am so into this particular person that it's like a wave breaking over me, and it makes me sick. I think of that look in his eyes—blank, like he'd been emptied out completely.

88

In my mind I'm going over all the ways this could be possible. This particular situation, with the boy, with everything, makes sense, if you think about it. Jeremy's from the Gold Coast. It's not that far away. Brisbane's a small city, and if you're a gay boy, it's a very small city. Within a couple of degrees, everyone has slept with everyone else.

> **Everyone has slept with everyone else:** This thought embeds itself in my mind. Jeremy has been with this guy. This guy knows Dean, obviously, even if they're just friends, it's probably in the same way that Dean and I are just friends, and the whole thing makes my head spin.

89

He has a bottle in his hand. He looks across at me, gives me a look that could be described as a half-smile, before returning to the conversation he's having with a dark-haired girl whose back is facing me. All of this happens in the space of a few seconds, but in that time, something in me understands that it's definitely him.

90

Movie: There is a big television set on the other side of the room, and the sound is turned right down but that doesn't really matter because the movie has subtitles anyway. I think it might be Spanish or something. A boy who looks about my age is sitting at someone's dining room table, cutting up what looks like lines of speed. A plane is taking off against a gray sky. An old woman is picking a lizard up off the ground. I try to get some sense of what might be going on from these fragments but I can't. Nobody seems to be paying any attention to it but me. I don't even know why it's on. I guess it's an arty kind of wallpaper. Maybe it's meant to be distracting or something.

91

The thing is, on the net he was basically just a series of pixels on a screen. Yeah, he was beautiful, yeah, he was the kind of boy I'd willingly obsess over, but he wasn't real. He was . . . safe. Despite how he looked in the pictures, despite how cute/vulnerable/wasted/desperate he appeared, he wasn't a real person. There was a membrane that separated him from the real world.

In a sense he'd become a fictional character. He was beautiful and fucked up but you'd never have to get close enough to actually deal with or experience any of those things for yourself. But now he's a flesh and blood person standing across a party from me, it's way too much to deal with.

92

The two—the imaginary and the real—collide. The gap between beautiful vacant boy on the net and actual boy standing across the room closes so rapidly it makes me seasick.

> **Across the room:** The brunette boy has finished telling whatever story it is he's telling. He and the girl he's talking to both laugh. For a fraction of a second he looks across at me, and then looks back at the girl again. In that moment I get to look right at him. His eyes, the color of them, and the way they turn down at the corners. The angles of his face, the geometry of his cheeks and his lips, and I know, it's him.

My mind goes elsewhere.

93

I sort of retreat to this other place: I begin to build a personality for this new version of the brunette boy. He's wearing a little silver cross around his neck; I'm sure he's wearing it as a fashion statement rather than a religious one, to give himself that alluring lapsed-Catholic air or whatever. Maybe he actually *is* a lapsed Catholic. Maybe he's not lapsed at all, but he *looks* lapsed, in more ways than one. When Catholic boys go off the rails, they really go off the rails. Something to do with original sin; all the dogma they're fed from the time they're little kids. I don't know. Whatever. But he's beautiful. He's wearing a black shirt with a picture of a paperclip on it. A single piercing near the top of his left ear. He's taller than I am, and he has this strange wide-eyed, frightened look that makes him all the more interesting. The look on his face really throws me. It gives him a kind of mystery. Depth even. I don't know. It's a problem of mine that I always equate good looks with depth. The boy fascinates me; he has that slightly damaged look which always makes guys enigmatic, and about ten times more interesting. I start to wonder about him, like, seeing him now, as a boy across a party, and seeing him as he was, as the boy in the photographs—it's a pretty big gap.

I always spin these elaborate fictions around guys I

find attractive, imbue them with a kind of depth that probably just isn't there. That's why when I meet someone, I'm almost always let down, because the truth of them is always a lot less interesting than the fiction I've created in my head.

94

Fiction: Adam, for instance, was a case in point. That night I met him, I became more or less obsessed. I mean, from the way he looked, all dark and intense, I thought maybe he was some kind of artist; like, if I could find my way inside his mind, decipher him, I could become his muse and it would all be beautiful and dark and sexy and interesting. Turns out, of course, he was only into me because I was underage. The sheer superficiality of it all gets to me sometimes. But, y'know. I'm just getting distracted now.

95

Dean's arm is around my waist. I want him to keep it there. It feels nice, reassuring. "So Calvin," he says. "Feel like a jay?"

Suddenly I do.

I shrug in a noncommittal way and allow Dean to

lead me across the room. I look over at the brunette boy again. He's looking back at me; grins and narrows his eyes a bit, an expression that could mean any of a number of things, none of which I feel like thinking about right now.

Suddenly Dean and I are standing over by the futon, and Adam is looking up at me. Dammit. He's smiling at me, an alligator smile, and I know straightaway that he remembers everything. Jesus, this is going to be awkward. I wish he'd stop giving me that smarmy look, like he's aware of some weakness deep within me.

"This is Adam," says Dean. "I think you guys have met already."

Adam doesn't stand up.

". . . and this is Jodie," Dean continues, unaware of the excruciating current of superiority/inferiority that is passing between Adam and me.

The Hello Kitty girl—Jodie—waves at me and offers me one of the jellybeans she's eating. I smile and tell her no thanks. "Cool shirt," she says. The tone of her voice doesn't give much away, but I choose not to interpret the comment as sarcastic.

"Thanks," I say.

At this point in time I'm only too eager to take Dean up on his offer. He moves towards the coffee table; there is a wooden box sitting on it. I stare at him, attempting to look nonchalant as he produces three pre-rolled joints. So, you know. Blah blah, etc. Once Dean has everyone's attention, they all sort of drift to this side of the room, and everyone ends up on or around the futon.

Various things happen. Dean puts the New Order album on repeat, turns it up; the music comes at a volume that could rot your teeth. He lights the first of the three joints, and within about fifteen minutes "Vicious Streak" is blasting and we are all stoned out of our minds and the singer is telling me I have a vicious streak for someone so young. The music is so loud it is almost a physical presence in the room. It flows around our stationary bodies like water; it is difficult not to sway with the currents of it, difficult not to dissolve right into it.

The brunette boy is sitting beside me on the floor. He and the girl he was talking to seem to have drifted apart. She's now on the futon, next to the Hello Kitty girl. The Hello Kitty girl giggles, then she says something that sounds like, "I love Winona Ryder. I mean, she's like, the queen of indie movies." I have no idea what prompted that comment or what it means, so I ignore it.

Somebody says (presumably in response to the Winona Ryder comment): "There's a thesis in that."

Everyone laughs. I don't get it.

The boy is still beside me.

I try not to get obsessive about it, but like, that's not the way things work when I'm high. I'm *way* obsessive most of the time, but whenever I'm high, whether or not I want to, I always take it to new and not always comfortable places. I trance out on things, fixate on them. It's usually just lights in the distance, or video games or music or just, you know, anything pretty and uncomplicated, anything that can connect me to a sense of unreality. Unreality is pleasant. At present the idea of ever sleeping with this boy is unreality. I can stare at him and fill in the blanks with whatever details I want. It's a dream. Enough to float away on. And right now, I'm kind of in the thick of it and I'm trancing out totally and completely on him.

Floating: The boy is just a little taller than I am, with thin, birdlike shoulders jutting out just slightly underneath the fabric of his shirt. I can't stop staring at his hands—they're so long and graceful, almost feminine. Everything about him is beautiful. He takes a hit from the joint, slow and careful, then puffs out a cloud of misty white smoke. I love the way he holds it, in between two fingers, with his thumb extended slightly at the side. When he takes another drag, the underneath of his fingers press against his lips, and he holds the smoke in his mouth for a long time before letting it out.

music from the stereo: a frightening sexy compelling vacant drum loop that seems to be echoing in every corner of the room.

He breathes out, and I breathe in. If I move in close I can smell the thin clouds of smoke which drift lazily from his parted lips. This feeling, or an idea of a feeling, or whatever it is, totally overwhelms me like a physical force, and I realize I'd really love to stand, walk into one of the other rooms and have him follow me. Like, let it happen; feel him kissing me, against me—our two thin bodies grinding perfectly against one another. To go down on him, taste every inch of him, as he stands, head back; groaning as his warmth flows down my throat. When I kiss him, my mouth will fill with smoke.

I am so absorbed in these thoughts that I don't even notice when he passes the joint to me. I snap back into the moment, take it from him with a hint of a smile, which he returns. As I stare, the urge to take him, absorb every part of his body into mine, becomes more acute. The force of his beauty gives me a headswim, and I realize that I will die if he never tells me his name, if I never explore his body, if I never find out what his mouth tastes like.

He's still looking at me, like he's expecting me to say something. I'm not sure quite *what*. I give him a smile that could be interpreted in any of about a hundred different ways. He sort of cocks his head to the side, still looking at me.

> "Hey," he says. Just that. Hey. Not even any inflection, but still, there are so many different ways that "hey" could be interpreted; it has so many possible meanings that it makes my head hurt just thinking about it. Why did he say hey to me? Why is he talking to me? Is he just trying to be polite, make conversation? Is he into me? There's no way he can find me attractive. No way at all. It's against the laws of physics.
> "Hey."

He doesn't break eye contact. "Anthony," he says.

> **Lust:** Sometimes it's so intense it's a color. It's red; I mean, it's hard to explain, but when he introduces himself to me, all I see and all I feel is *red.* Red like desire. Red like an exotic violence.

This is my life now, and everything else that's ever happened to me is like a movie I once saw. "Calvin," I tell him, and reach out my hand so he can take it, which he does. His skin feels cold. It seems strange that someone so beautiful should have such cold skin. I try to focus on the feel of his hand in mine; his grip is tight, his skin is fleshy, maybe a bit dry; I try and imagine the feel of this hand all over my body. I imagine what this hand would feel like as Anthony dragged it across the skin of my belly, my neck, my face.

"So how do you know Dean?" A totally expected question. He happens to have asked me.
"Met him on the net," I say.

I kind of wonder if the word "net" will produce any kind of reaction from him, but it doesn't, and then I start to wonder why I even thought it might—it's kind of stupid, on reflection.

"So you've never been out with him or anything?" he asks.
"Not really. Have you?"
"I don't really know him at all. Friend of a friend."
"Cool."
"I came with Jodie. I think you met."

"Oh, cool. We did."

This is not real.

96

The group has splintered. Anthony and I now occupy our own space underneath this poster for a foreign movie. We take solemn turns with the joint, say nothing.

> "So Calvin," he asks after a while. "Do you smoke like this all the time?"
> "I smoke it a little."
> "I like being stoned," he says. He takes another drag, holds it in for a long time. I watch as the smoke curls out of his lips. "I forget who said this, but of all the modes of consciousness, sobriety is the most highly overrated."

I smile. We both laugh at that, though for a second I forget exactly why I'm laughing. Though it doesn't matter. I'm hopelessly caught up in Anthony, and at this point that's enough. He hands me the joint, offers it to me slowly.
It's him.
For a second our fingers touch. He keeps his on

mine, and before he pulls away, he rotates his hand a little so the surfaces of his fingers and mine rub against one another. His fingers contain an electric current. This is not real.

"I agree."
"With what?"
"I don't know."

97

Cut ahead about an hour. The Valley. We're making our way down the mall. To the left of us is a line of cafes and bars, and to the right is an ocean of tables, people. Too much to take in, too many faces, too much conversation, too many looks, so my mind assimilates most of it into a big drunken noisy sweaty Friday night out in the Valley kind of a blur.

I take in the occasional, vague detail of people at the tables we pass.

1. **A waitress:** Her long red hair is tied into two loose twists. She's carrying a tray of drinks, and gives me this distracted smile as we narrowly avoid walking into each other. Her lipstick is really dark. Purple. Almost black. The color of it stays with me for a few seconds after she's walked away. It's so deep. Her lips were

so deep. The kind of color you could sink into.

2. **These three guys at a table:** One of them is young, about my age. Haircutted and dyed to a certain level of alternative/cool. One of those boring Valley faggots who *knows* he's cooler than you because his hair sticks out at a certain angle, because he holds his cigarette in a certain way. He looks bored. The two guys with him are a lot older. They have the same cropped blond hair. They're both dressed in black. They're making the same kinds of gestures, facial expressions. They're both staring really hard at the boy. He blows smoke at them as though he doesn't care. The whole tableau is rather creepy and I'm wishing now that I hadn't seen any of it.

3. **Princess Peach:** She has long, golden hair. A pink dress. She's pretty, you know, in a pixellated sort of a way. But she's always getting kidnapped by the Koopa family, who are these giant turtles, and Mario's always having to rescue her. She's kind of defenseless, you know. But still. She's pretty. I blink. It's just some girl in a pink dress. Vinyl, aggressively pink. It clings to her body. Her hair is cropped short. She looks nothing like Princess Peach. I shake my head, look at her

again, to make sure I'm only staring at a girl in a pink dress, which I am. Which is a good thing.

98

Dean, who is walking ahead of me, waves at someone—a boy in an FCUK shirt, smoking a cigarette and floating at the edge of a conversation. The boy sees him, waves back, this look on his face that's kind of . . . slutty. This makes me feel tense for some reason and I walk on, ignoring them, trying to keep my balance.

99

We walk through a big group, and people are passing us by too quickly to take in any of their details. The other sensory information I'm receiving by way of lights and noises is all bleeding together. Every cafe we pass has different music playing—hip-hop beats, icy new-wave synths, a woman singing, then a man, rapping, jazz, then breakbeats, then the two mixed together—and it's impossible to differentiate individual songs, so the elements of all of them come together like some weird new composition. Something that would probably sound incredibly scary if it didn't sound so cool.

I'm almost totally out of it, following the line of my friends—I hope they're my friends—ahead of me. We might have been split up. I might be following a totally different group of people. I couldn't tell in this crowd. The one certain thing is Anthony. He's following me. His hand is in mine. For some reason this feels like an incredible amount of responsibility. Or something. I don't know. But I really don't want to let go of his hand.

I turn around just to make sure he's still there. Still following. He is.

100

Anthony smiles at me. I think it's a smile. Hard to tell.

Looking at him triggers a weird memory. He's down on his knees, sucking Jeremy's cock. Jeremy's doing the same to him. Now he's with two guys. His eyes are dead. It's hard to reconcile the look that was in his eyes in the photos with the look that he's now giving me. Maybe it's not.

I turn back around. Try to forget all about it.

101

We're at the end of the mall, approaching our destination. We're standing around in this loose kind of a group. Anthony is no longer holding my hand. I keep giving him significant looks, making sure he's still interested. If he was ever interested.

We're getting into formation, approaching our familiar outpost of clubland. This place is, at various times, a gay club, a meat market, a *scene,* a place to hang out, dance, to leave your body behind or get messed up with someone else's.

The sign: At the moment, the B is broken, so the sign hanging high up on the facade says "EAT" in glowing blue neon. This seems weirdly appropriate.

"Right guys," says Dean. "Everyone know what to do?"

102

How to sneak into a gay club when underage and without ID: Pretend to be someone's boyfriend. It helps, of course, if the people you're with happen to be regulars, if the bouncers are familiar with them already. Choose a friend who is over eighteen and can blend in well. When you're heading into the club, have him hold your hand, or put his arm around your waist. Put your head on his shoulder. It helps to appear wasted. Or lovestruck. Both of these are pretty easy to fake. Look like you're in your element. Look as though you have *every fucking right* to be walking into the club. You'll get through without them even giving you a second look. Nine times out of ten, this trick will work. Try it.

103

As we walk towards the entrance, Dean takes my hand. I lean into him, as though we're together, as though I'm his lover. The two of us sort of become one. I take hold of his hand and don't let go. The bouncer recognizes him. A little conversation is made. They let us both in. Anthony came prepared with a fake ID. It seems stupid to think he might *not* have come prepared. He seems like the type who would be prepared for more or less any situation.

104

Music: As we enter the club, noise swallows everything. The music hits me, assaults my body, and it's a pounding force. Narcotic. Suffocating. Beautiful. It's hard to explain, but it's like being inside some great, pulsating womb. I close my eyes for a second and let my body dissolve into it, and it's like being a little kid again. I spent so much of my childhood sitting in front of my Nintendo, and what I seem to remember most about old video games is the music, synthesized, repetitive; I could sit for hours on end and just listen to it build then fade away, sequences of tiny artificial notes endlessly repeating themselves. The thing of it was that although the ambient soundscapes that accompanied the big-eyed anime boys as they went to rescue their princesses, or find their magic crystals, or avenge their dead brothers or save faraway worlds from forces too evil to imagine, were meant to be heard and then forgotten, they somehow transcended that, and anyone who ever played those games as a kid now has some small part of that embedded in their consciousness. Electronic music was the sound of my childhood, and as I stand here now and close my eyes and let the ethereal synthesized keyboard lines swirl around me and the beats pummel and assault my body, it's like being there again, like childhood, somewhere I can be safe and warm, and I'm not even kidding about any of this. And I stand there and sway for the longest time, because the DJ is playing this one particular song, a high, swirling keyboard line, and it doesn't seem as though it can go any higher, and it swells and then fades away again then comes back and it swells and fades and swells and fades and I'm hypnotized by it. I stand there and sway, lost in the purity and the beauty of it, and for a second it's like I'm not even there anymore. It's like I've disappeared completely into the music.

105

For a while I'm lost in the flood of memories. It's a good feeling. When I open my eyes I see Anthony just near me. He turns. Smiles at me.

"This is cool," he says.
"Yeah."

The dance floor is empty. Always is this time of night. Nobody admits that they want to dance until a lot later in the evening. It's tradition or something. You see people hanging around the edges of the dance floor. You even see some of them moving in time with the music, a reduced version of what they'll be doing when there are enough people on the dance floor to justify going out themselves. I don't know. I'd probably analyze the situation and try to develop a theory of why that is—self-consciousness? drinks/drugs having yet to kick in?—but I'm too busy staring at Anthony.

"Want to head upstairs?" he asks.

Upstairs: *Upstairs* has connotations. *Upstairs* is the place your friends, if they're sensible, always warn you not to go. Downstairs is where you go if you just want to dance. Downstairs is neutral. Upstairs is not.

"Okay."

106

The staircase is narrow. Dark. Kind of suffocating. The carpet is nearly purple, like the grape juice I spilled once when I was a kid.

Grape juice: I remember, it was our old house in Melbourne, this white, *white* carpet, so clean, like everything else in the house, and when I spilled it, I remember I felt so guilty, terrified, in that way you can only get when you're a little kid, and I tried to clean it up, which only made it spread and look ten times worse, and there was this hot, prickly feeling on the back of my neck, and I felt so bad for what I'd done that I *wanted* my parents to yell at me, punish me, but when Mum came downstairs, she did nothing at all, she kissed me on the forehead, told me she would clean it up, and the fact that she *wasn't* angry with me, that she barely even noticed, was worse, because then I realized—as far as you can when you're that age—that something really *was* wrong, missing, and that Mum was this way because of what happened to Jonathan, and she poured me another glass of grape juice and sat me in front of my Nintendo while she went to do something about the mess.

There are patches on the carpet that look like bruises, they are so dark. It's hard to tell what color they are. It's hard to tell what color anything is. The carpet might be black. I don't know. Too dark to tell. There is loud, tacky pop music echoing from the top of the stairs and suddenly I get the urge to be up there. I follow Anthony's shadow to the top.

107

When we get upstairs, it's already kind of crowded. Dean is leaning over the bar, talking to the boy who is behind it. The bartenders here all seem to be these tall, bleached vicious/pretty and vacant-looking types who roughly resemble cyborgs. The boy that Dean is talking to is no exception. Adam and Jodie are nearby, talking to a girl in an Astro Boy shirt, and all three of them disappear to a far corner of the room.

Anthony puts his hand on my shoulder. Leans in. "Want a drink?" he yells. His nose brushes up against my ear. It feels warm. Really good.

I nod. He asks me what I want and I tell him whatever, because I really don't care at this point. While he's gone I stand still, swaying, trying to get a focus on the room. There are strobe lights above the dance floor, shifting too fast to see. I stare up into them—it's almost as though they're flashing on the surface of the water. This guy with glasses looks at me like he recognizes me, and I look back at him, but he turns and walks away, towards the dance floor, so I guess I'm not whoever he thought I was.

108

Anthony comes back holding two beers. He hands one to me and I smile, chug about half of it and then thank him. He mouths a word that I think might be "anytime."

We don't head out onto the dance floor. You don't. Not this early.

He sort of motions towards the tables; asks me if I feel like sitting down. I nod, let him lead the way. We sit at one of the tables about halfway back, on the borderline between the bright lights of the dance floor and the darker space at the back of the club. The table is high, kind of perilous, and our drinks are balanced on it. There are four chairs around it; I sit down first. Anthony follows. He chooses to sit next to me as opposed to across from me. I take this to be incredibly significant. Every now and then I look across at his profile. He makes me want to die. Somehow—we both shuffle in until we're right next to one another. Not touching. Not quite.

109

Girl: There is a single figure on the dance floor, a girl. She has the whole space to herself. She dances slowly, like a ghost. Every few seconds the strobes flash; in the pure white light—flashes of light/dark light/dark light/dark—she moves backwards, forwards, sometimes with her arms in the air, sometimes touching her face, her hair, her breasts. She glides across the dance floor like she's suspended on the lights. Like she's fragile; she might break at any minute. She doesn't seem real. Her whole appearance; she seems too beautiful. Like an illusion. It's hard to tell what's illusion and what isn't.

110

The music is incredibly loud. I let it wash over me in waves. This kind of saccharine and clingy but extremely danceable song is playing; the beats are pumped up to the point where they're practically distorted; a female voice, candy sweet, pink, singing over the top.

Anthony turns; says something to me: "— he's b—— ful —s—sh—?" His voice is kind of obliterated by the music.

The music goes quiet for a second. The girl/cyborg's voice echoes; the keyboards begin to build and build and a massive break follows and the strobes go wild and the beats seem to be coming harder than ever.

We have to shout to be heard over the song.

"What was that?" I ask Anthony.

He leans in closer. "I said she's beautiful isn't she?"

"I guess."
"Are you still stoned?" he asks.
"I think."
"Me too."

Silence. A silence and a half. The air is heavy; one of us has to say it.

"Do you have a boyfriend?" he asks.

"No."

"Cool," he says.

"Do you?" I ask.

"No."

I can't say how exactly it happens, but there comes a point when suddenly our shoulders are touching.

The song continues. Endless. Don't know who the singer is, but it doesn't matter. I mean, none of what's happening here means anything, in the grand scheme of things. Anthony and I are two underage boys sitting at a table in a club. Some highNRG anthem is playing over the sound system. He's just flirted with me, at least I think he has, and if he has, if things progress like they usually do, we're probably going to have sex sometime later. Take the Anthony and the Calvin out of it and this scene could be playing itself out at any club in the world. In Bristol. In Luxembourg. In Tokyo. The specifics are insignificant—so from here on it really doesn't matter what we do.

If we sleep together. If we don't. Whatever happens. This scene is not unique. We're young and good-looking and that's all that matters.

Thinking about all this makes me feel better. I can't say why exactly. The girl is still dancing by herself. Moving through the strobes as though they're the only things holding her up. As though she might come crashing down at any second.

His cheek brushes mine. We are kissing. Just like that; a fluid motion. Hard to explain. The way it just happens. We close our eyes. His mouth is warm. Slippery. It tastes of lollipops and pot and something else I can't identify. His tongue forces its way into my mouth. I don't resist. Mine is on his teeth. Smooth. His hand. On my side. It's warm. Mine on the back of his neck. The skin there is smooth. Warm. His hair. He forces me deeper into the kiss. His mouth. Electricity. These noises he makes. Noises I'm making. Pushing forward and back against one another. Suck.

He breaks off the kiss. I'm kind of flushed. Kind of stoned. Kind of drunk. And I want Anthony. Totally and completely, and I'm going to die if I don't get to kiss him again, dance with him, sleep with him, absorb his body into mine.

111

Moments like these I forget about everything else. Moments like these, nothing matters. With Anthony, with whoever. I can forget who I am. Forget anything else exists. No future. No past. Just this.

112

This moment of uncertainty. I'm not quite sure what he's going to say next.

"Do you take pills?" Anthony asks me. Just like that.

"I sometimes sneak my mum's Prozac," I tell him, and smile coyly, even though I figure that's probably not what he means.

"That's not really what I'm getting at."

"I know," I tell him. "I do." I've taken ecstasy before. One time was with Margot—we just sort of floated around her house all night listening to her Björk albums and eating jellybeans and hugging one another an awful lot, playing with her stuffed toys, including this rabbit called Mr. Rabbit that I became weirdly obsessed with. The only other time I've done it was actually the first night I ever went out to a club, and I was also with Margot. That was good.

"How come?" I ask.

He produces this little folded-over piece of paper from his pocket. "You want to?" he asks. He looks right into my eyes; I swear to God there's like, this, *otherness* in his face. I hesitate for a second. I really shouldn't do this. I'm, like, a different person on ecstasy. There's no accounting for what might happen if I take it. This is both a good thing and a bad thing. In this case, it's probably mostly bad.

"Yeah, well," I say, trying to sound cool. "Sobriety is the most overrated option."

"I go crazy on this stuff." He smiles. "We *have* to dance later . . . When it gets a bit more crowded," he adds hastily as a qualifier.

"Absolutely. Sounds like a fucking blast."

"You sure you want to?"

I nod, go to take one of the pills from him, but he shakes his head, motions towards the side of the room.

113

We're standing in one of the bathroom stalls together, and it's kind of gross, but I suppose that's beside the point. The echo coming from outside is strange and sinister, a distant thumping, as though the music is playing through cotton wool. Anthony takes one of the pills, lays it gently in my hand. I go to lay the pill down on my tongue, but Anthony stops me. He puts his between two fingers, moves it towards my mouth. He grins at me. Evil grin. I realize I'm expected to do the same. I do. His fingers taste salty. When we kiss, his lips on mine feel cold.

114

A weird moment: A thought occurs to me. That gesture was so simple it was deceptive.

Feeding me his pill; getting me to feed him mine. Kind of intimate, you know. Sexy. It was cute because he did it. Fun. But how many guys have done it before; I mean, where did Anthony learn that move?

It's like me. I think of myself as not one, but like, the culmination or the accumulation or whatever of all the guys I've been with since the first time. Sebastian. However long ago that was. There were little things he taught me, with or without his being aware of it. When we kissed, Sebastian sort of bit my bottom lip. Not really bit, but kind of nibbled it. You know what I mean. It felt good.

After Sebastian, I started doing that too. I tried it on the next boy I kissed; this guy called Trent, someone's cousin. He was blond and cute and he told me he liked me and stuff but he could never go out with me because I was too weird. I think that's what he said. Anyway, that bit's not important. What's important is I tried that little trick of biting Trent's bottom lip—not really biting it—and it worked, and I think he liked it.

I'm sure he went on to use it on other guys. I used it on Patrick. Patrick probably uses it on whatever guy he's with now.

Anyway. They probably teach him things too. And so the cycle continues.

The point is that nobody's moves are really their own. Everyone has to learn them from somewhere. So I mean, when Anthony fed me that pill before, was it really Anthony feeding me the pill, or was it the boy before me or the boy before that boy or the boy before him?

Thinking about it makes my head spin. I don't want to think about the guys before me. I'm not in the mood for that. I try to block it out.

I think way too much. I shouldn't think. I should just do. I let myself slip back into the moment.

115

"How long's it going to take . . . To come on?" I ask him.

"A little while." He motions outside. "Hour maybe. Want to wait outside until then?"

The two of us get a few looks as we emerge from the stall together, especially from an Asian-looking guy who is standing by one of the sinks, but . . . fuck him. I follow Anthony out. There's a balcony, where you can sit and talk or chill out or whatever if you don't feel like dancing. There are trees around the edges, these little topiary-style ones, in big terracotta pots. There are fairy lights strung up in the branches and out here in the night they look lush, beautiful.

Adam and Jodie are already out here, sitting at a table with two other guys I don't recognize. One of them is wearing a sleeveless shirt and the other isn't wearing a shirt at all, they're both young and good-looking. Everyone out here is young and good-looking. Anthony and I pull up two more chairs and sit down. We're introduced but it all kind of goes over my head. The boy in the sleeveless shirt, who has dark hair and is really cute, is Lawrence, I think, and the boy he's with, who is less cute but still pretty hot, is Ben, and Adam tells me Ben—I think it's Ben, though it might have been Lawrence, I'm not sure—is an ex-boyfriend of his, and Ben rolls his eyes when Adam says that, then they both laugh and Ben says something I guess must be a private joke and the two of them laugh again and Lawrence, who I assume must be Ben's boyfriend, doesn't laugh either, and when Ben leans over and kisses him on the mouth I figure I'm probably right about the boyfriend thing and then when Jodie starts talking, sends the conversation off on a new tangent, something to do with Winona Ryder, I try to piece it all together.

116

Six Degrees of Fornication: The theory that within a particular control group, every person can be traced back to every other person by virtue of who they've slept with. This works especially well in a small city like Brisbane. Here it's more like one or two degrees.

(Note: Faggots are the *ultimate* control group for this kind of experiment. The Brisbane gay community is basically a petri dish, but with a danceable soundtrack and bacteria that happen to be cute and have names like Ben and Lawrence.)

117

Trying to work this one out: Lawrence is sleeping with Ben. If Adam is to be believed, then he has slept with Ben. Adam has also slept with me. So really, I might as well have slept with Lawrence. Or with Ben. With both of them, I guess, but Ben more than Lawrence. I think. Things start to go fuzzy. They're still talking but it's all going over my head. I catch about one word in every ten, and I lean in, get this look of very deliberate concentration on my face, as though I'm hanging on every word they're saying, but it's all flowing over me like so much water.

118

Something appears in my peripheral vision and it's demanding attention. I turn and realize it's Lawrence. He is asking me a question but I can't quite make out what he's saying, partly because of the noise of the music and the conversation out here, and partly because everything I've taken so far tonight is leading me towards a kind of crescendo that makes it difficult to focus on anything. Lawrence has this look on his face like he's waiting for an answer. I shake my head, look sort of quizzical and cute at the same time. Maybe about sixty percent quizzical, forty percent cute. I don't want to appear as if I've misunderstood; I don't want to look dumb in front of him, because he's really good-looking. (If he were not good-looking, would I mind appearing dumb in front of him? I file this one away for further examination and then forget all about it.)

I lean in farther. "Sorry?" I say. "Didn't hear you."

"I asked how you know Adam."

I hesitate a bit before I answer. "He's just . . . Um . . . A friend."

Lawrence smiles at me. "Yeah. Ben's fucked him too." We both laugh at this. I think we each laugh because the other does. Because we have to laugh.

Anthony puts his arm around my shoulder.

"You haven't fucked Adam, have you?" Lawrence asks him. Lawrence is drunk.

"No." He might or might not be lying.

"Everyone's fucked Adam," Lawrence says. "*Everyone.*" He's smiling but there's something not at all humorous about his tone. The look in his eyes. Something. I don't know. But whatever it was that Anthony gave me is starting to take hold and I'm reading way too much significance into everything and it's disturbing me and I don't want to be here anymore, and there's a drink sitting near Lawrence, fizzy, cathode red, and he ignores the straw sticking out of it and takes a huge chug from the glass even though I don't think it's his, and Adam and Ben are still talking, and Adam's fucked everyone, *everyone,* and I don't want to be around this just now. I want to be dancing. I want to be with Anthony. Suddenly that's the only thing that matters.

119

Anthony's arm is still on my shoulder. I turn and look right into his eyes. "Feel like dancing?" I ask.

He nods. "Definitely."

He takes my hand or I take his hand or we both

take each other's hand, I'm not sure entirely, but after a few seconds of fluid motion we're both standing up. I sort of lean, fall into him. His T-shirt feels soft. The flesh below it is warm. He's warm. I put my hand on the small of his back. I really really want to dance with him now, right away.

The trees and the lights have suddenly taken on a whole new level of beauty, intrigue. I feel like I could get lost in them just by staring at them. Lush. Glowing. A thousand fireflies. Being a little kid. On my father's shoulders. There are so many lights it's all I can do not to trance out on them completely.

Things are beginning to blur. Anthony is saying something: "We're going inside." I look down at the table, at Adam and Jodie and Lawrence and Ben, and suddenly I wonder whether Lawrence has fucked Adam. Adam has fucked everyone. Everyone.

120

Inside. On the dance floor. It's crowded. I don't know how long we've been here. How long we've been here doesn't even matter. He's kissing me again, and he's all over me, and it's hard to tell through all the noise and interference of the huge speakers all around us and the noise and interference inside my head from everything I've drunk/smoked/swallowed so far tonight, but I think I'm as happy in this moment as I've ever been.

Overwhelmed. He's beautiful, and I can taste his sweat and feel the skin of his back—because my hands are way under his shirt—and I'm so breathless I can't think but I know he's kissing me and he's all over me and everything else in the world is hateful apart from how desperately we feel for each other. I'm pleading for him to fuck me; like, seriously, right here on the dance floor, I wouldn't even care.

121

The beats are huge, thick, like candy-coated razor blades. A woman's voice above layers of keyboards and samples.

> **Female voice:** I want to be a porno star/
> I want to be a porno star

122

I move with him, and we grind against one another, sharing warmth and sweat, and my eyes are sort of closed, open, closed, open, but when I feel his lips touch mine again and we sink into the rhythm of another kiss, it makes me want to die. He tastes of sweat and lollipops and pot and the night. Bodies undulate around us. My hands are in the small of his back. I'm kissing him as deeply, wanting him as badly as I had ever wanted any boy. In this moment, everything is perfect.

After that it becomes difficult to focus on just what's happening. I'm coming and going, sort of like scenes from a half-remembered movie, although it's all happening in the present tense. A violent and dizzying montage. Lost inside him. We kiss for a long time; sway against one another.

He breaks off the kiss; looks right into my eyes and asks if I want to go somewhere else. "Do you want to go somewhere quieter or something?" At least I think that's what he says. It's so loud in here that I have to read his lips, but he's motioning away from the dance floor, and when he moves, I follow. ". . . or something." I'm sure that's what he said. There's an ocean of anticipation in that "or something." I follow him out; we push our way through the crowd, through the flashing orange and red lights, the thundering beats and sinuous bass line, through the throng of girls with butterflies in their hair, boys in T-shirts, girls kissing boys, boys kissing boys . . .

123

Quiet: For a second, everything goes quiet, and I'm removed from all of this. Everything is blank. Silent. Reality is totally gone. You know, erased, or whatever. It's just the two of us in the moment, and it's all white noise, thoroughly.

I'm happy.

124

Taxi. My mind is all over the place, and lights are passing by the taxi in waves of ladybird reds and candy-apple greens, and I want someone to save me. We're sitting in the back of the taxi, and even though my hearing is kind of fucked up thanks to the club, the silence in here is throbbing, alive, and I'm out of it at this point, thanks mostly to the drugs, I think, and I'm sweating, sort of, swaying all over the place, and I can feel Anthony's hand on my leg, my head is on his shoulder, and I'm really hoping he hasn't lost the urge to fuck me or whatever it is he'll do when we get to where we're going, because, I mean, the trip seems to be taking so long, and he won't tell me where we're heading, he told me he wanted it to be a surprise and maybe I should have been cautious, but I am so hot for Anthony I would pretty much follow him anywhere, and like, the driver's a Pakistani or something, and somewhere in the back of my mind I'm freaking out because Anthony kissed me before, after we got in, and I know the driver was watching and I'm wondering what he must be thinking and it's all, you know, too much, although I'm so wiped out at this point it really doesn't matter.

"Are we getting close?"
"Really close," he says to me. "We'll be there soon."

Anthony feels warm next to me and he's squeezing my hand or maybe I'm squeezing his hand and he looks across at me and smiles this dumb smile, and I realize we're in this together, which is a good feeling, which calms me down a lot, and he says, "It will be cool, seriously," he's being all mysterious but the smile on his face tells me nothing bad's going to happen. The lights of the city pass by in a blur, and every now and then an incredibly bright one fills up the whole taxi and I have to shut my eyes against it. I hang on to Anthony's hand and hope we get where we're going soon.

125

My memories of the next part are kind of scattered, but like, I know enough of what happened to get the general drift. Basically:

1. Blacking out in the taxi, but the feel of Anthony beside me keeping me grounded.
2. Having this weird and incredibly meaningful train of thought about Anthony and I, how we

are two particles drifting through space and the fact that we've managed to find each other, that I've found him, is incredibly significant, because . . . I don't know. Losing that thought altogether. Being stoned makes you come up with the most unbelievable bullshit.

3. Anthony's suburb: Windsor. Large, expensive houses set back from the road. Older houses and newer ones. The city below us. Fragile. Ghostly. Anthony's house is one of the newer ones.

4. Getting out of the taxi. Cold air. Walking up this very long driveway, in the dark. These tights that come on as we walk past them. Thinking they were magic or something.

5. Holding Anthony's hand, kind of stumbling into him. His hand is warm.

6. Dark. In my current chemically altered state, his house is huge and threatening except for Anthony.

7. The sound of his key in the lock.

8. Sneaking through the entranceway. Whispering:

126

Me: Aren't we going to . . . wake your parents or something?

Anthony: They're not here.

Me: Where are they?

Anthony: At this . . . Like, this . . . thing. I don't know.

Me: Where?

Anthony: Fucking . . . I don't *know*. They're not here though. Trust me.

127

Anthony and I are standing against the wall, kissing. His hands are all over me. Something about the act of kissing Anthony brings me back down towards reality. We're going to fuck very soon, but I realize I am suddenly incredibly thirsty. I need a drink. Like, really. I really need a drink of water immediately.

Me: Can I have, like . . .

Anthony: What?

Me: Can I have a drink of water . . . or something?

Anthony: Sure. Come on. I think I need one too.

Me: It's probably the pill. They always make me thirsty.

Anthony: You should always drink lots of water after you've taken one.

Me: It's the responsible thing to do.

I'm not sure if I was trying to be funny or not but Anthony laughs.

128

Anthony leads me into the kitchen. I vault up onto one of the counter tops, sit there and sort of nod my head waiting for everything to slow down, but it doesn't. Anthony grabs a tall glass, pushes it against a little ice lever on the fridge. The ice cubes clink into the glass. It sounds cooler and more meaningful than it should. He pushes the glass against the other little lever and it fills with water. Hands it to me, and it's so cold, cold, I suck it down in one huge gulp and it makes my head spin and I try to put it down on the counter but I miss and it falls to the floor and shatters, and I have no idea how Anthony will respond to this, but he's laughing when I look at him.

Me: Sorry, I think I . . .
Anthony: Fuck it.
Me: But I broke the . . .
Anthony: We can clean it up later. Come on.

He motions for me to get down. I slide off the counter. Kind of unsteady on my feet. Swaying a little. He grabs me around the waist. Warm. My mouth still feels cold from the water. Broken glass all over the tiles. I hear some of it crunching under my shoe.

129

The living room is huge and white even in the half-darkness. I collapse onto a sofa. Anthony sits down with me. We don't make any pretense at conversation. He puts his arm clumsily around my chest and then we're kissing, and his mouth seems hotter and wetter and more, like, immediate than it did before, and we're both pushing against one another, and he feels so incredibly warm. I forgot that another person could feel this warm. How warm he is, that feels almost as good as the kiss. It's like I can feel him all over me.

Our cocks are incredibly hard. His fingers are digging very hard into my back. We're still kissing and his tongue is going totally crazy and he makes this kind of *mff* sound, or maybe I make it, I really don't know. He breaks the kiss off and we're looking right at one another. He's looking sweaty and sleepy-eyed but incredibly turned on at the same time, and his face is very close to mine and he kind of breathes on me, and I move up to kiss him again and he shakes his head, like, no, and I know what he means.

130

Anthony pulls his cock out, or I pull his cock out, I don't know, but I feel myself fumbling with his zipper and he's breathing really hard, and there's something else there, I don't know, and he slides back on the couch, kind of slides down so he's lying across it, so I can lower myself into position. I lean in to kiss him again, but I don't, I slide down him, his body—his neck, his T-shirt—feel his flesh against my nose, my cheek, feel his stomach, kiss it, and I've moved almost all the way down his body now and I'm on the floor, kind of, and Anthony's above me. I take hold of his cock and he says my name, "Calvin," not even says it, sort of whispers it, and lean down and kiss Anthony's cock and he whispers it again, "Calvin," but this is different now, closer, but further away, and I look up at him, look up his body and see him, his eyes half closed, his mouth half open, his top teeth, just the way he looks, I mean . . . I want him to own every part of me, I want him to consume me, I want to be his property, I want him to take me over and consume me, so I close my eyes, move down towards his cock, and the feeling totally takes me over . . .

131

what this means: It's not even the act of going down on a guy, not as such. If you break it down, analyze the act in itself, the physicality of it, it's not particularly significant. On its own, Anthony's cock in my mouth doesn't really feel like anything much, it's just a piece of meat, warm, and it tastes of sweat, salt and something else I can't quite describe, and that's it, period. In a purely physical sense it means nothing. It could be any boy's. What it means, really, is that it's *his,* that I can do this to him, make him feel good, that I can make him say my name in the dark. That's half of it.

The other half, I know, is when I'm sucking him off, I belong to him. I'm just here because he wants someone to make him cum. I could be nothing at all. I'm only here to suck Anthony's cock; he can do whatever he wants with me and I'll let him. That's the other half. It's this kind of submission that's so intense it's like a drug, and while I'm doing this, I feel like nothing at all, I disappear, I'm totally erased. Gone. I like that.

132

"Calvin," he says again, and I respond by going faster. I lick the head of his cock, lick all the way around it, and I'm suddenly aware of his hand on the back of my head. I'm kind of flushed, my cheeks feel hot but I keep going, and Anthony pushes himself further into my mouth, all the way in, and I gag for second but it makes me want to keep going. I lick it, suck it, let him keep pushing himself in. I swallow a couple of times and almost choke but I keep going, and one of my hands is on the arm of the couch, I think, the other in the small of Anthony's back, and I've been doing this for a long time, it's getting hard to breathe, but I keep going because Anthony is so hot and I want to make him feel good, and as I move backwards and forwards on his cock I tell myself, it's more than just a piece of meat, it's Anthony, he's so hot, he's so hot, I have to do this to him, I have to make him . . .

133

. . . Anthony's grip tightens, his whole body bucks upwards. "Calvin." He's breathing out, hard, and I can feel him start to cum. I hold my mouth around his cock, and he bucks upwards again once twice, and then it starts to fill my mouth, the hot taste of it. I feel it behind my teeth, filling my mouth, and Anthony cums in three short bursts. He totally fills my mouth now, and I hear him breathe out again, very heavy; his whole body relaxes and he lets go of my hair and I let his cock slide out of my mouth. Before I can decide what to do—I'm still there, kneeling on the floor, kind of flushed, kind of disoriented, before I can swallow, or anything, he pulls my body up, and we're in this awkward position, it would normally be uncomfortable but considering the circumstances it's not, and he leans in and kisses me, and his cum is still in my mouth, but it mixes with his saliva, and warmth, the warmth of our two mouths together, and he's kissing me very hard, we're moving against each other, in opposite directions, and I feel like I'm about ready to melt, and he keeps kissing me and eventually I can't tell what's cum and what's saliva but it doesn't matter because . . .

134

Did he feel anything?: I'm thinking of those pictures on the net. Of Jeremy. Did he feel the same as I did when he was with Anthony? Did he feel anything?

135

The sex/love dichotomy, once again: Sex without love. Love without sex. The two concepts have never really connected in my mind. I mean, I've never wanted to stick around with a guy after I've cum. I don't mean in a malicious way or anything. I mean that afterwards, after we've fucked, or he's sucked my dick or I've sucked his or whatever, it's like there's nothing there at all. I know it and I'm pretty sure the guy knows it. It's just like, we've made each other cum, we've lost ourselves in each other's bodies for a few minutes, and that's, you know, that's pretty much all there is. When I'm with a guy I've just fucked, there's usually no use pretending. No use hanging around—we've both got what we wanted, we should just move on. It's almost embarrassing to face a guy after I've fucked him. I've never wanted anyone to hold me, stay with me. Seriously. It's easier if the two of us just go our separate ways.

With Anthony it's not like that.

136

Early morning: We somehow made our way to his room last night. I remember the look in his eyes. I remember us being inside one another. The sound of his breathing, and mine, and the two merging so it didn't really matter *who* was breathing at all. I can't sleep anymore. Waking up in an unfamiliar bed always does that to me. I'm lying here, half awake, staring out the window. Something in me wants to stay, with Anthony. I don't know what you'd call it. Probably not love. I don't know. I think it's too complicated an emotion for that. It's difficult to say exactly what I'm feeling. But I don't want to leave. He's still asleep and I look across at him. With his eyes closed, he looks almost . . . peaceful. Younger, more innocent. I want him to hold me. I want to stay with him.

I am thinking: I want to be his boyfriend.

He murmurs, shakes his head a little. He coughs, just once, and then he breathes out. The smell of his breath is a surprise—it's nasty, sour almost, probably from all the smoking he did last night, but it's hard to reconcile with the peaceful expression on his face. For some reason, I see a momentary flash of the photos, of the way he looked *then,* and in that space of a second, part of me wonders if maybe his breath is the result of some kind of corruption somewhere much deeper inside him. I try to push this idea away, dismiss it as paranoia or a bad comedown or something, but it doesn't work.

PART 2

YOUNG, DUMB, AND FULL OF CUM

137

Four of us at this cafe in the city. The place is, like, trendy or whatever at the moment, the kind of cafe you go to if you want to be seen. And I guess most of the people here—most of my friends, for that matter—fall into that category.

At the table next to ours there is a woman in an orange Japanese style top. Her hair is cut short and she is wearing a pair of those glasses with the fashionably thick frames. She's talking to an older guy. He's bald and dressed all in black and he keeps looking over at our table like he's checking one of us out. I hope it's me. I mean, it's not that he's good-looking or anything—he's really old and kind of creepy—but it's just like, I hope I'm the one he's checking out. If that makes any sense. But yeah. Whatever. I'm fucked up.

An album of extremely sultry trip-hop is playing through a set of invisible speakers—Portishead's "Dummy." It drifts through the cafe like perfume, heavy on the bass, the singer insinuating the lyrics from somewhere way down in the mix. This music is thick enough to drown in.

I'm still coming down from last night, and the place feels vaguely suffocating. But something feels different. I'm still thinking about Anthony. A feeling not unlike . . . happiness?

There are four of us at the table, which is to say, I'm here with:

1. **Margot:** Margot looks completely sexy today, as usual. She wears a jacket with fur around the collar, lipstick that seems a little too dark, her hair done up in pink hairclips like a little girl's.

Concerning Margot: About a year ago I was having this big freak-out, one of those "I'm fucked up and everything sucks and I might as well kill myself now" kind of things. You know what I mean. I was over at Margot's house at the time. I spent ages staring into this mirror and sort of grimacing at it, and after a while I asked her very casually if she thought I was good-looking. "Of course you are," she said. "I wouldn't be your friend if you weren't." That probably shouldn't have cheered me up, but it did. It's just an example of the same vague fascism that informs all my friendships.

2. **Mykal:** Mykal is tall and blond and a little foreign-looking. I think his family might be from Russia or something. He goes to school with me; we've been out to a few of the same parties and clubs together, and I guess what we have more or less approximates a friendship.

Mykal's really hot, and he knows it, but pretty as he might be, any compliment you could give him would have to be qualified with the words ". . . but dumb." He's on antidepressants. His big ambition is to become a composer—"An electronic musician," he told me one night after he'd dragged me into the corner at one of the said parties. "I love keyboards, you know, and computers. That's real beauty. So pure. I want to create music with meaning, you know, that makes people . . . feel things deep inside of them." I guess I admire his sentiments and everything, but let's just say that nobody, as far as I know, has ever *seen* him anywhere near a keyboard, or a computer. As far as I know, all he ever does is take antidepressants and sit around in cafes bragging offhandedly about whichever new guy he's managed to fuck the weekend before.

3. **Jamie:** I don't know him, he's with Mykal. An acquaintance of some kind. I don't bother to ask.

The afternoon started out at Margot's house in Ascot. I went there to hang out—I was still feeling the effects of the pill from last night and I needed something to keep me active. I really needed to be around people, so Margot inviting me over seemed like the coolest thing in the world at that point. Mykal was there too, along with Jamie, who I just assumed must have been his latest boyfriend. For Margot to have invited Mykal over, I guess he must be a friend of hers too, or maybe she's a friend of Jamie's, I don't know. This is a group that would never normally mix, put it that way. Mykal spent a lot of time talking about his antidepressants and his ambition to make electronic music. Jamie spent most of it ignoring me. Margot ransacked her older brother's room for drugs—she found this little baggie of white powder which we were all way too scared to experiment with, and in a stack of sweaters she found a much more promising bag of weed, a moderate portion of which we consumed. She put on some music and we all sat around in the living room listening to that and watching a foreign movie with the sound turned down.

I think I must have said something unintentionally insightful about one of the actors in the movie because after I said it, Jamie turned to me and smiled. "You're such a writer," he said. That stuck with me. I mean, a) because it was, you know, a weird thing coming from a stranger; and b) because Jamie had been ignoring me so comprehensively all afternoon. I could have analyzed that comment to death, but I drifted off into the music for a while instead.

Music: The girl on the stereo tells me that tonight she's going to hunt me down. I think I might believe her.

Long story short: We decide to go out into the city. Mykal is the least fucked of all of us, not to mention the only one with a car, so he drives us in. We sort of drift for a while; someone suggests we get sushi, then we have this big argument over which sushi place is the best and we narrow it down to Sushi Central and Omekaido Avenue.

Eventually we wind up here, in the cafe with the woman in the orange shirt and the guy in the glasses who I kind of hope is checking me out even though he's really kind of gross. Anyway. Sushi. Fairly mindless conversation. Anthony in the back of my mind the whole time. The weird but certainly not unpleasant mix of the pot and the after-effects of the pill from last night. I'm in a better mood than usual.

Mykal sits opposite me. He stares off into the distance for a while, then back at the table. He leans in conspiratorially. "So . . . Heard you got with a guy last night."

I don't know how he could *possibly* have gained this information, but it doesn't bother me at this point. A likely scenario is that he was also at the club last night, or one of those scene queens he hangs around with (or maybe even an ex-boyfriend of mine) told him about it. Anyway. Not important. ". . . Yeah," I tell him. I look to Margot for help but she's staring out the window and looks as though she's drifted away somewhere else.

"So . . . ?" Mykal asks.

I mean, okay, one way or the other, it's not really that important to me. I might as well just tell Mykal the story, a) because it will give me a chance to process what happened—I'm still having trouble with that; and b) because hopefully it will make him shut the fuck up and I can turn the conversation elsewhere.

"We were at a party," I tell Mykal. "In Windsor. At my friend Dean's house. I think you met Dean."
"I think," Mykal says.
"So I saw this guy and thought I recognized him, and it turns out I . . ."

Saw him having sex with a friend of mine on this website?

". . . kind of *did* know him, so we proceeded to get very fucked, went to the Valley and ended up at the Beat, blah blah blah, where everyone always goes, so we took some pills and we got even more fucked, basically, and I went home with him. You know?"

By the time I get all this out, I have to take a breath. Mykal raises an eyebrow. Grins. "So was he hot?"

What I want to say: He was so beautiful that just looking at him made me want to die. I would have, like, killed myself if he'd asked me to. I've never been so into a guy. Ever. It was scary.
What I actually say: Yeah.

"Yeah," I tell Mykal. "He was pretty cute." I look over at Mykal's friend. "Kind of like Jamie," I add, even though it's a lie, just to see if it provokes a reaction.

It does. Jamie grins at me and Mykal sort of flinches. I smile.

"So," Mykal asks quickly, "what was his name? You catch it?" He says this with a wink which is both conspiratorial and kind of nasty at the same time. Whatever. This has put Mykal on my list of "People Who Are Not Worth The Effort." He may have been on there already, come to think of it. It's kind of a long list, but anyway, y'know . . . Over it. Mykal sucks.

"Yeah, his name was Anthony."

Mykal narrows his eyes for a second.

"I don't think you'd know him," I continue.

Before I can start to pick Mykal's reaction apart, the waitress approaches the table and we all look up at the same time, distracted. Her hair is black, streaked with this incredibly bright, almost alien shade of red and tied up into two loose twists behind her head. Her name tag says "Isabel." She's wearing a lot of eyeliner. Isabel kind of resembles a raccoon from Venus, but in a weirdly cute way. If you'd seen her you'd know what I mean.

"How are you guys doing?" she asks, looking down at me. "Can I get you anything else?"

"Could I have another long black?"

Isabel seems to find this funny. "Yeah, sure." She pulls a pencil from her black apron, and as she's writing it down, she asks, "You're going hardcore, are you?"

"Didn't get much sleep," I tell her.

She smiles knowingly at me. I tell her that the Portishead album they're playing is extremely cool. She looks at me like she has no idea what I've just said. Oh well. Over it. She asks if my friends want anything else. Mykal has long since eaten all the chocolate sprinkles off the top of his coffee. He asks Isabel if she could bring him any more of those. She laughs and tells him sure, okay, whatever, then leaves.

"So," he says. "Anthony."

"Yeah," I tell him. "Anthony. I don't think you'd know him."

"No," he says. His expression says otherwise.

A number of possible scenarios are forming in my head:

a) Mykal has gone out with and possibly slept with Anthony.

b) Mykal has gone out with and possibly slept with Anthony.

c) Mykal has gone out with and possibly slept with Anthony.

For the next few minutes I am thinking about this. I am not listening to the conversation. I am not able to.

Isabel is back with my coffee and Mykal's chocolate sprinkles. She tries to pour them over his coffee, but Jamie stops her, motions with his hand like he wants her to put them there instead. He and Mykal grin at one another as he holds his hand out. Mykal takes the cue and leans forward to lick the chocolate sprinkles out of Jamie's hand.

Jamie purrs. Mykal continues to lick his hand long after all the sprinkles are gone. We're drawing looks from the people at the next table.

Adorable. Jamie is kind of cute actually. On any other day I could probably be forced to try it on with him. Of course, the way things are now, with Anthony . . .

"So," Mykal asks. "Anthony. You think you're going to see this Anthony guy again?"
"Seeing him tonight."

Which is true. I *am* seeing Anthony tonight.

138

Flashback to this morning: I'm sitting at my computer. My phone is sitting next to me. I'm swivelling around, playing with that little squishy frog thing that's meant to relieve stress. I'm not stressed. It's hard to say exactly what I am. I'm still buzzing totally. I only got back from Anthony's house, like, an hour ago. It's weird—whenever I'm sleeping over at someone's house, I always get the urge to leave as soon as I wake up. It's like I physically can't make myself stay. Not even this morning, not even when it was Anthony. So yeah. I woke up. Then he did. We kissed once. I left and as I was leaving he promised to call me.

It's that indeterminate phase. That "what the fuck happens from here?" phase. Does he want to see me again? Was it just a one-nighter? Did I tell him I loved him or just think it? I don't know. It doesn't matter. I'm still tripping in any case. I know it's too soon for Anthony to call but I'm hoping that he will. I'm staring at my phone, which is slim and silver and saying nothing at all, and I stare away and hope that it will think I'm ignoring it or whatever and start to ring.

I'm looking at those pictures of Anthony. The ones I saved. It's kind of giving me a headache. I scroll through the pics; bring up this one:

Picture of Anthony on the screen: His forehead is pressed onto the glass window—he's reflected back at himself. He's so beautiful it makes me want to stop breathing.

I stare at him for a long time. Run my finger down his profile—try to remember the feel of his skin. Touch his mouth—try to recall what it tasted like, its warmth. Anthony.

My phone beeps twice. Someone has sent me a message. I look across; lurch towards it.

Screen of my phone:
1 message received.
Read?

My stomach falls away for a second. I was prepared for this, but not really. You know what I mean. There's no question of my not reading it. I go into my inbox.

Screen of my phone:
1 new message:
"Anthony"

Fuck. Fuck fuck fuck.

SMS from Anthony:
Hey calvin—wuz very
cool to meet you last
night. u free tonight?
feel like going out or
something?

I sit for a while and let that one sink in. Feel like going out or something? Fucking, of course I feel like going out or something. Fucking . . . I'm still scrolling through the pictures, trying to connect the boy from last night, the boy who slept with me and who possibly wants to see me again, with whatever that is on the screen.

> **Picture of Anthony on the screen:** He's standing by the window, shirtless, with the frightened-confident-guarded etc look in his eyes. He stares at me. I stare back at him. We have a competition to see which one of us blinks first. I do.

I don't want to reply too soon? Or do I? Fuck it. I click reply.

> **Reply to Anthony:**
> Heya dude. Last night
> was very fucking cool.
> love to see u again—
> where do u want to
> meet?

I click the button, stare at the screen for what seems like several hours until it says "message sent."

Picture of Anthony on the screen: He and Jeremy are kissing. You can see only the curve of Anthony's cheek in this one. I make my eyes go blurry; put myself in Jeremy's position. It actually works. The picture is now of me kissing Anthony.

SMS from Anthony:
City sound good? by
the information booth
on the mall at about
six?

The whole night begins to unfold in my head. Saturday. City lights. Anthony. His smell. His taste. I want him very badly and I want this to work, very very badly.

Very hurried reply:
Cool. cya then
=)P

I consider whether or not to put that little smiley face thing in; it does look kind of lame. I delete it then put it in again, then delete it then I put it in once again and click send before I can change my mind.

Anthony wants to see me again.

Shortly after that, Margot calls and instructs me to come over to her house. I tell her I met a boy last night and I'm seeing him again tonight, and ask her whether or not that's fucking cool, and she agrees that it's extremely fucking cool and adds that she's jealous, and using her Haruki the Raccoon! voice, tells me I'm a slut, and we both laugh and I tell her I'll be at her house soon.

139

We're still in the flashback at this point: I head up to my room to change clothes.

After various attempts, putting things on and then discarding them, dismissing items of clothing as "too emo," "too gay" and "I've already worn this fucking thing in front of Anthony," I manage to come up with something I like.

The girl singing on the stereo is asking me whether or not I am human. I'm thinking about it.

I am thinking: Anthony. Not human. Not at all.

Then I head off to Margot's. So yeah.

140

It's nearly five by the time we leave the cafe. Mykal and Jamie have their own thing to do. There's supposedly this party at some guy's house. This guy is an ex-boyfriend of Mykal's and he's supposedly older, a doctor of some kind, who lives in Toowong. Jamie doesn't want to go but Mykal keeps insisting that it will be really cool and even if it's not they don't have to stay very long. Margot is going to a rave or something. Margot's always going to a rave or something.

I tell them to have fun at their party. Jamie pouts and says he doesn't want to go. He wants to go to the rave with Margot. Mykal insists that the party is going to be cool. Jamie asks if this supposed ex-boyfriend of Mykal's is going to try anything on with him/with the two of them, and Mykal insists that this supposed ex is *not* going to try anything on with *either* of them, but Jamie doesn't believe him. Mykal says maybe they can go to the rave with Margot if Jamie really wants but Jamie's not sure if he wants to go to the rave or not and he says maybe they can go clubbing instead, and Mykal says . . .

141

I'm standing at the Citycat stop at North Quay. I'm not waiting for the Citycat or anything, I just come here sometimes because the place calms me down. I like to stare at the buildings, the river. I'm thinking about Anthony and how tonight will turn out.

According to him it was very cool to meet me last night. What did that mean? I shouldn't be thinking so hard about this but I am. I want Anthony to like me. I don't want to fuck this up. I *really* don't want to fuck this up. I'm obsessing. That's why I'm here—like I said, staring at the river always calms me down.

I'm leaning on the railing, staring down into the water at the strange configuration of ripples.

A bee is floating on the surface of the water—I guess it must be drowning. A way off in the distance, near the buildings and the bridges, the water reflects the sunlight; it seems sparkling and clear, but close to me it's brown and murky. The bee is just floating with the current; every few seconds it beats its wings, sending out a small circle of ripples. The farther out it floats, the weaker its wings beat and the smaller the ripples get. Eventually it will disappear altogether.

If you went out to the middle of the river, would you find hundreds of drowned insects just floating on the surface of the water? I guess the Citycats would sweep them all away. But still.

I stare up at the buildings in the distance—several huge apartment blocks by the river, the boats moored nearby, and beyond that, the city. The moon has already risen, too early for night. I can see it between two buildings. I look up at them, huge, unreal, and at the moon above, and then back down at the bee. It's hardly even beating its wings now. Every now and then a frantic burst of activity and then nothing.

It's nearly six. I'm meeting Anthony soon. I hope I'm hot enough. I hope he wants to fuck me again. I suddenly wish I was more stoned. I can deal with things when I'm on drugs. Otherwise everything is so intense. Everything. Like Anthony.

This cold breeze comes up from the river. I am the shallowest person on the face of the earth.

142

It's six and it's dark now and I'm standing at the information booth at the Queen Street Mall and there are *lots* of people standing around near the information booth at the Queen Street Mall and I'm scanning the crowd but I can't see Anthony at all.

People in the crowd:

1. **Skaters:** A group of boys who are all about my age, standing around with their boards, smoking and ignoring everybody. They're all going for a look, which seems to be cool/hardcore/aloof/etc, and for the most part it seems to be working.

2. **Girl in a black dress:** She's standing by herself, smoking a cigarette and looking around nervously like she's waiting for someone to arrive. She looks kind of like Winona Ryder, but only because I've had her on my mind since the other night. The queen of indie movies. *There's a thesis in that.*

3. **These three immaculate looking boys:** Who are all total Valley types, and all of them too cute for rational explanation.

Rough-cross section of my thoughts at this exact moment: Knowing that these are the kind of guys who'd never even look at me, no matter what, and this being Saturday afternoon, they would all be happily caught up in the slipstream of parties and clubs and youthful indulgence that is the Valley by nightfall. They'll all end up going home with boys a lot better looking and more sure of themselves than I am, because I know that I don't even occur to boys like that. And in a way I envy them; envy their good looks, and the fact that they seem to know exactly what they want, where they're going. Anthony's one of those boys. That's his world, and I still can't quite believe I'm caught up in it. Boys like that can do whatever they want, have whomever they want, and the best thing about it all is that none of this even occurs to them.

4. **Girl in a Paul Frank shirt:** Her shirt has a picture of a pig with "We are your friends! Please don't eat us!" written on the front.

143

EXT. CITY STREET. EVENING

CALVIN waits nervously. He bites his bottom lip. ANTHONY approaches, passing a group of three BOYS and nodding at one of them. CALVIN sees

ANTHONY and starts walking towards him but then holds back. One of the BOYS says something to ANTHONY. ANTHONY moves on past the BOYS and sees CALVIN. For a second neither of them moves. ANTHONY approaches.

144

Anthony: Hey dude.
Me: Hey.
Anthony: Good to see you again.

For a second I'm not sure if Anthony is going to reach forward and touch me or if I'm meant to touch him, but he doesn't and I obviously don't and neither of us touches the other and I'm left to stare at him for a second.

Expression on his face: It's weirdly blank. I don't even know how to describe it. But it's blank in an extremely sexy way. You know what I mean.

145

Anthony: What do you want to do?
Me: I don't know. Whatever.
Anthony: Sushi sound good?
Me: Sushi sounds great.

I don't mention that I've already eaten it today.

Me: There's this one just near here. Omekaido Avenue.

Anthony: I know that one . . . We shouldn't go there.

Me: Why not?

Anthony: This friend of mine got food poisoning there. Plus, there's this dude who works there. One of the chefs. I see him out all the time and he was going out with this guy I know a while back. He's really fucked in the head.

Me: How do you mean?

Anthony: How do I mean what?

Me: How is this guy fucked in the head?

Anthony: I don't know. Just is.

Me: So we should go somewhere else.

Anthony: I guess so.

Beat of silence.

Anthony: It's a pity we're not stoned. I always like being stoned before I go out to sushi. That way you can eat heaps more. Makes it better.

For some reason I decide not to mention that I'm still partially stoned.

Me: I've never tried sushi stoned.
Anthony: You have to. It's the best. It's really fucking cool. Too bad I don't have any pot with me.
Me: Me either.

Well *obviously*. I mean, we're in the city, so even if either of us *did* have any, it's not like we could just do it right here on the mall. I consider raising the point, but I don't. I probably wouldn't be able to articulate it anyway.

Anthony: I have some at my house. We can go back there later if ya like.

When Anthony says that thing about going back to his house, he looks right across at me and sort of smiles. It's not exactly a smile. It's like he knows what he's really suggesting and he already knows I'm going to say yes and he's giving me this sort of but not exactly triumphant "I'm going to fuck you later and you're going to be *totally* into it . . . How cool is that?" kind of a look.

Me: That would be cool.
Anthony: Cool.

146

Anthony's walking beside me, almost close enough that he could be holding my hand. There's this weird coldness about him. I don't know. On the way to sushi we walk past a souvenir shop, the kind that sells expensive and useless toys and stationery, most of it from Japan. Things you'd never need, no matter what the situation. But they're cute. The window of the shop kind of reflects my state of mind at the moment. Crazy.

Transparent wall at the front of the souvenir shop: The wall is backlit, made up of what seems like thousands upon thousands of glass boxes. A whole galaxy of them, and each one holds some bizarre toy or other with crazy bug-eyes or industrial hair, razor-candy red or phosphorescent yellow or sea-sick blue; frogs and fireflies and creatures whose names no-one knows, all moving or staring or croaking or chirruping and blending together in a dizzying zoo.

147

Hot by association: We're walking down Albert Street, away from the mall, and this other guy is approaching from just near Starbucks. He's tall, older looking. Dressed in a black sleeveless top, with his bleached hair all spiked up. He has a tattoo and a piercing through one ear and he seriously could not look any queenier if he tried. The point is that as this guy is approaching, I see him check the two of us out. I meet his eyes and he doesn't look away, then he glances at Anthony, and as he's passing us I realize he's checking Anthony out. Every fag we pass in every cafe and standing on every street corner is probably checking Anthony out. Anthony is really young and really hot and I'm really young and the fact that I'm with this person makes me hot by association. From the moment the guy in the sleeveless shirt passes I'm looking in all directions—suddenly I'm seeing guys everywhere and they're *all* checking us out and it's this incredible feeling, like seriously, I can just tell they're imagining Anthony and me, the two of us together, imagining what the two of us must look like when we're fucking, imagining who knows what, and we're just two young, anonymous, attractive guys, and it makes me feel really good. I can never *remember* feeling this good. It's like being drunk.

148

Me: Did you see that guy?
Anthony: What?
Me: Nothing. Don't worry.

149

We're at a sushi train café, the one on Elizabeth Street in the city. You step down from this little wooden platform into the main part of the restaurant. The place is full of business suits and incredibly pretty girls with their law-student boyfriends. There is this saccharine highNRG pop music blasting out of the speakers and it's kind of cool but the lyrics aren't in English so I can't understand them.

Anthony and I are sitting near the back. The waitress brings us tea, which we didn't ask for but the waitresses here always bring you tea and it's kind of cool.

The sushi itself goes around on an actual train, which is cute, if somewhat anal. The train is moving annoyingly fast. You see something coming and it looks good and you almost reach out to grab it and then you don't and then you decide that maybe you might but by that time it's already passed and you have to wait for ages until it comes back. If it ever comes back.

150

I don't even know what we're talking about. I mean, we're talking about everything, and I think I'm actually holding Anthony's attention, but through a combination of factors.

> a) The fact that there are still drugs actively circulating in my system.
> b) The fact that Anthony is so incredibly hot.
> c) The fact that I keep nervously looking around the restaurant to make sure nobody I know is here.

. . . I don't really know what I'm saying. I'm aware of making conversation but that's about it. I know I'm trying not to embarrass myself but I'm also aware of saying incredibly stupid things on a regular basis. I know we talk about the Valley for a while—he asks me where I like to go, the people I know who he might know, boys that maybe we've both been out with. I talk about school for a while, all the usual bullshit—how it's difficult to fit in, how you can only go out with boys from outside your school, how it's hard because nobody's out of the closet yet, how *fake* it all is and how cool it is that *someone else thinks exactly the same thing!* All the usual bullshit.

I eat one of those little rolls with orange roe on the outside. I never know what they're called but they taste really cool, plus, they're orange! Anthony asks me if I had much of a comedown from the pill, and I tell him a bit but not too bad, that I'm feeling a lot better now, and he says the same. He tells me about the first bad comedown he had, which involved sitting around watching talk shows all day at the house of his then boyfriend, who was "a total loser—he was psychologically damaged." I don't bother asking for any more details. I offer him the plate with the orange rolls on it and he takes one.

We sit at the sushi train for half an hour or so. Anthony grabs two pieces with squid on them. The squid is fleshy and white, with blue around the edges, and the tentacles are still attached. I stare at it and trance out for a while. Anthony offers me a piece. I tell him it would be cool but no thanks.

I'm making these faux-nervous and extremely obvious gestures. I'm looking down a lot and we're talking about music. He thinks Craig Nicholls from the Vines is okay-looking. I nod my head and tell him I sort of agree but not really and I think he understands. Sometimes, what you say really isn't . . . adequate to express what you're actually thinking. It's not even a conscious thing, but . . . you know. We both like Ladytron. A plate of tuna salad comes around. We both reach for it at the same time. Our hands touch.

The tuna salad goes past and neither of us tries to grab it.

151

> **Me:** I really like you.
> **Anthony:** I really like you too.
> **Me:** It would be cool to keep seeing you . . . I mean, if you'd be into that. I don't know.
> **Anthony:** It might be.

152

Anthony looks at me for a few seconds then. In those few seconds I look back at him, at the angles of his face, at the way his features line up, and his expression is totally blank. In those few seconds I'm looking at him as he was in the photos. I realize that throughout tonight, throughout this conversation, and before that, last night, when we were at his house, and the club before that—the whole time Anthony has been like a blank page. He hasn't told me anything about himself. Hasn't even let anything slip. Hasn't showed any emotion at all beyond . . .

153

> **Memory from last night:** Anthony is saying my name. "Calvin."

154

Anthony looks away and asks me if I'm ready to go, which I am, and it's not until we're standing on the street outside and we're ducking into a side street and he's kissing me that I think of it again, how blank he seems, how cold, not like a real person at all, but then there are more pressing things on my mind and I forget all about it.

155

Anthony and I have finished kissing for the time being. Even though his face is still very close to mine and I can feel his breath on me, smell him, and even though his hand is on the small of my back, the other in my hair, and mine are both around his waist, it is accepted that *this* is as far as it's going to go for the time being. Which is cool. It's fair enough. But it's also disturbing, because say this *hadn't* been far enough, say Anthony had wanted to go further, I would have let him, despite the fact that we're in the city, in, like, a *side street* for fuck's sake, where anyone at all could walk in on us, I would have let him do whatever he wanted to me.

156

It's only eight. Eight on a Saturday night, way too early to do anything else. I follow Anthony into an arcade on the mall, a staircase leading down and down. It's almost overwhelming in here, claustrophobic. The pulsing neon-bright lights and the laughing and the curses and the swell of electronic music all peak and subside and blend together and the result is a sensory assault. It's really cool, in other words. Hundreds of young bodies, sweating, breathing together. Even with the air conditioning, which is pumping full blast, making this low-pitched sort of hum you can hear over the top of all the other noises, it's hot in here.

The arcade is incredibly crowded. Groups of boys drift around between the machines, looking or trying to look threatening. An Asian guy dressed all in black is playing a game where you have to travel back in time and shoot at these samurai who attack you; I'm watching him from the corner of my eye, and he has this look on his face like he knows what he's doing, except he keeps missing the samurai and they swarm and start to kill him and chop at him with their swords and the blood that comes out of his man looks pretty realistic. Two girls are standing by one of those machines with the claw that grabs the stuffed toys; they're not playing it, and one of the girls, who is wearing a red dress and who looks kind of familiar, keeps looking across the room at a tall boy with a smirk on his face: He says something to his friends and they all laugh.

Anthony is playing one of those *Dance Dance Revolution!!!* machines. The ones you feed money into and the whole thing lights up and music starts playing, a hundred-plus bpm, or so it seems, and there's always a woman singing with an incredibly high, artificial voice and she's always singing about love or butterflies or dancing or whatever. It's incredibly loud, thundering, overwhelming, and you have to dance to it, which is to say, there are four little sensors and you're meant to follow the directions the game gives you and jump on each one at a certain time. Forward/back/left/right, and various combinations of all four. The more you get right, the harder the dance steps and the more you have to jump around and the more people gather around you to watch.

anthony's feet: thump / thump / thump / thump / (silence) thump / thump

Anthony has a look of intense concentration on his face. He's been dancing virtually nonstop for twenty minutes. He's breathing deeply. His dark eyes narrow as he stares at the screen. I hear the sound of his breaths, the thudding of his feet as he dances. A droplet of sweat will run down the curve of his nose. It will stay there for a few seconds, shimmering, the blue and red and purple lights from all around refracting through it, and then it will fall, hit the floor, disappear. Every now and then another droplet of sweat will form and I'll stare at it, hypnotized.

157

We're still in the arcade. The song that's playing is loud and trashy. The kind you want to crawl inside. Saccharine. For the three and a half minutes that it plays—three and a half minutes of deceptively simple chord progression and bang bang bang—everything is going to be okay. Anthony and I are standing in a corner. It's dark. His hand is on my waist. He is sweating a lot from that dance thing. He looks really hot, and . . .

158

Anthony: What do you want to do?
Me: I don't know.
Anthony: Do you want to go out?
Me: Not really.
Anthony: Do you want to go back to my place?

He's been waiting to say that all night, and I've been waiting for him to say that all night, and he's been waiting to hear my answer, which he already knows will be:

Me: Okay.

159

Anthony: In a realistic sense, I know nothing about Anthony at this point. I know he's good-looking. I know he's a very good fuck. I suspect he might have let some guy take pictures of him while he was naked and on drugs and with Jeremy. That's about it. I don't know anything about *him.* He has told me nothing. He's still more or less a blank canvas at this point. Which bothers me a little. It bothers me a lot, come to think of it.

In the past when I've been with guys, it hasn't really mattered how much I've known about them. Sometimes it's actually better when you *don't* know the guy that well. You don't have to deal with his hopes/fears/anxieties etc, you deal with him strictly on a physical level, and the rest you can make up.

Which is why the fact that Anthony is such a *blank* makes me so tense. His physical presence is still only as real to me as those pictures. I can hardly tell the two apart. Maybe he's incredibly complex. Maybe there's nothing there at all. But the fact remains, I don't know who he is. Pretty, unattainable, pixellated boy on the net. Pretty, unattainable boy in real life. Figment of my imagination.

I want to know something about Anthony. Anything at all—some detail that will make him human. Maybe that's why I have been so obsessed by that one particular picture, the profile shot. Because it seemed to make him real. Showed signs of vulnerability or . . . something. Is this going to bother me? Yes. Is this going to stop me from going home with him?

160

Anthony's room: Anthony stands by his bedroom window, staring out at the city lights, wearing only a pair of boxer shorts. I'm sitting on the floor, leaning against his bed with a joint in my hand, and the silence in here is weirdly suffocating. Anthony looks at me and I offer him the joint and I'm about to stand, to give it to him, but he shakes his head, no, and walks over to me, takes it from my hand. He takes several long, slow drags while I stand and begin pulling at his boxer shorts, clumsily, trying to slide them down his legs. I can't quite manage it but he ends up doing it for me and then we're kissing, so I guess it doesn't matter that for the whole time leading up to this moment the look in his eyes hasn't changed at all.

161

Cut ahead: It's Monday morning. Early. I'm waking up in my own room and everything is gray and my head feels as though it's stuffed with cotton wool. I'm not ready to deal with any of this. A weekend spent with

Anthony and I'm not sure when I'll be seeing him again or if he's going to call me or if when we fucked on Saturday night it meant anything, or any more than it did when we fucked on Friday night. But more than anything I'm thinking of what happened *after* we fucked on Saturday night, but no, I don't want to think about that.

It was raining earlier and feels like it's just about to rain again. Some leaves from a big tree outside my window have stuck to the glass. The colors in here are too bright and my Placebo poster seems to be melting off the wall. The sheets are twisted around my legs and I have to fight to get them off. When I stand up, the floorboards are cold and I shake a little as I make my way to the mirror. I'm wearing only boxer shorts, and my hair still looks okay, and I stare at myself for a long time and eventually I decide that I look pretty good. I'd probably fuck me. My school uniform is hanging on the door. It starts to rain outside.

After a shower/change of clothes, I go downstairs to the kitchen. My mother is there. She's sitting at the counter, wearing a white bathrobe. There is a glass of orange juice next to her, untouched. She hears me come in and she looks up. When she sees me her expression doesn't change.

"Calvin," she says.
"Hey Mum."

"Would you like some breakfast?"

"Not really."

"I could . . . make you something."

"I'm fine."

"Okay."

Mum's still looking at me. I look back at her. I'm not really sure what to say.

"So . . . Where's Dad today."

"He's on call . . . At the hospital."

"Oh . . . Cool."

I start to fidget a bit. Mum offers to drive me to school. I thank her. Then without warning, she asks me if I'm seeing anyone, and it seems like a weird question for her to have come up with—and I fidget even more and tell her no.

She has yesterday's social pages open in front of her and there are all these pictures of people I don't recognize at a benefit for childhood cancer or the launch of some new book or a book on childhood cancer or something. Mum points to a picture of a blonde girl and tells me that the girl is Caroline, the Harveys' daughter, and I don't know who the Harveys are and I've never seen this girl before in my life but I just nod and say oh, cool. Mum asks me if I remember Caroline and I tell her no and she tells me I must because Caroline's mother is a friend of hers and I tell her I don't know who this Caroline person is and she tells me I *must*, like I'd be *lying* about whether or not I know Caroline, and eventually I figure it's not worth the effort so I nod and tell her that oh yeah, I do remember Caroline now (even though I've never fucking met anyone named Caroline). Mum asks me again if I have a girlfriend and I tell her no, then she asks me what about that Margot girl and I tell her I was never going out with Margot and she smiles at me conspiratorially and I really wish she'd stop. I'm tempted to tell her that Margot is the world's biggest faghag, just to see the look on her face, but I don't. Then Mum tells me I should be seeing a girl like Caroline and she points to the picture again and I take another look and that Caroline person, whoever she is, is holding a champagne glass and there's a young guy standing with his arm around her, and he looks vaguely like someone I know but it doesn't matter, and they're both young and good-looking and wealthy, which is all that counts really, and they both have these dumb smiles. I start to wonder whether it would make Mum happy if she could have a picture of me with my arm around some girl, dumb smiles on both our faces, and the idea of it starts to depress me, and then Mum tells me that she and Dad were there too, at that particular benefit, but they didn't get their photo taken, and she seems a little upset by this but she's slurring her words so I think she's probably taken a tranquilizer already this morning. She picks up her orange juice but doesn't drink any of it. I decide to leave her to it.

162

I grab a pear from the fruit bowl and head to the living room. The carpet feels soft underfoot. I slump on one of the chairs and it feels comfortable and warm and I want to fall asleep again but I don't. There are newspapers spread all over the coffee table. I choose one at random and flip through it, hoping there will be something at least partially interesting in there. I find an article about this certain British pop star who joined a boyband at sixteen and was exploited by his managers and then these naked photos of him from when he was, like, fourteen or something came out and he ended up a "teenage alcoholic who suffered from drug and sex addiction" before returning with several hugely successful solo albums; apparently he still has feelings of confusion and isolation even though he's young and good-looking and makes, like, *heaps* of money and probably gets to exploit lots of groupies himself. For a few seconds I entertain the idea of joining a boyband and being exploited and then turning into a teenage alcoholic who suffers from drug and sex addiction before returning with my *own* hugely successful solo albums, and it kind of appeals but I figure, well, I'm already a teenage alcoholic but the chances of my joining a boyband are pretty slim. Alongside the article there are several pictures of the certain British pop star—one of him on stage and one of him where, if you squint, it looks like he's naked even though he's really not—and I decide that if the situation were ever to arise, I'd *definitely* let him exploit me. I read the article through three times and I'm really tense and rocking back and forth by the end, though I'm not sure why exactly.

163

Flashback to Saturday night: Just before we smoked that joint, before we fucked. Anthony has left the room, assured me he'll be right back. His house is in Windsor, way up on a hill, and I can walk to the window and see an ocean of lights, and beyond that, not far away, the city, rising up like something out of a dream. The lights all run together and then apart again and it's beautiful, like, really beautiful, but the more I look at it, the colder I start to feel and the more I wish he'd get back already so I wouldn't be here all alone. I walk away from the window, sit down on his bed, which is unmade and smells kind of sweaty, although not in a bad way, not exactly, and it seems as though he's been gone for a *really* long time, and I'm aching for him to get back.

I want him so badly at this point it's like I physically *can't* wait for him to get back. I get up from the bed and walk around, looking at Anthony's things, trying to, I don't know, learn more about him from the things in here—a poster on the wall for a movie I haven't seen; a computer, switched on; a stereo, switched off, with some CDs scattered beside it. I take a quick look through the CDs: Massive Attack, a bunch of trance and trip-hop compilations—I guess that pretty much sums up his taste in music—and seeing them makes me feel better in a weird sort of a way.

164

I'm drawn back to the computer. The dull glow of the screen is the only light in the room, and there's something tantalizing about it. Other people's computers are always interesting. There is an IRC chat window open; must be from earlier today, one that Anthony obviously didn't bother to close before he went out.

I shouldn't read it. But, y'know.

I walk over to the door, listen very carefully to make sure he's not coming. I hear a tap turning on and off in a distant part of the house. Hear the pipes. Seems so much louder in the dark. I figure I'm safe.

I reach for the mouse; scroll back up to the top. Hope he doesn't come back. Read what's on the screen. And it's like . . .

Ši©k b₀ÿ: tony . . . haven't seen you online in a while.

toNy: I've had you on invisible. I was avoiding you.

Ši©k b₀ÿ: very funny.

toNy: I'm not kidding.

Ši©k b₀ÿ: fuck you

toNy: already done it

Ši©k b₀ÿ: you offering to do it again?

toNy: haha

Ši©k b₀ÿ: . . . so. I saw you out last night.

toNy: where at?

Ši©k b₀ÿ: where do you always go?

toNy: right

Ši©k b₀ÿ: saw you out on the terrace.

toNy: right. I didn't see you there.

Ši©k b₀ÿ: . . . I was avoiding you.

toNy: haha

Ši©k b₀ÿ: I was only there for a little bit. there's this guy I used to go out with who was obsessed with me . . . he was stalking me practically. he showed up and I was with my boyfriend and neither of us felt like sticking around after that.

toNy: who was the guy?

Ši©k b₀ÿ: you remember Laurent?

toNy: not really

Ši©k bºÿ: he was this uni student from france or something. he used to do the weirdest shit. follow me around. anyway, doesn't matter.

Ši©k bºÿ: anyway, I was going to talk to you, but you seemed kind of . . . preoccupied.

toNy: occupied. yeah.

Ši©k bºÿ: . . . so who—was—that guy you were with?

toNy: I don't know. some guy. met him at a party.

Ši©k bºÿ: he was pretty cute.

toNy: I guess

Ši©k bºÿ: so are you seeing him or something?

toNy: nah.

Ši©k bºÿ: . . . mmm, interesting. you hook up with him?

toNy: might have

Ši©k bºÿ: I was just interested.

Ši©k bºÿ: so "might have" means . . .

toNy: yeah, we did.

Ši©k bºÿ: . . . and?

toNy: and yeah. we went back to my place. he was a pretty decent fuck.

Ši©k bºÿ: cute

toNy: I think he's the clingy type though. I

mean. he seemed to be getting kind of attached. you know. it's always kind of boring when that happens.

ši©k bºÿ: you seeing him again?

toNy: seeing him tonight

ši©k bºÿ: boyfriend?

toNy: probably not

ši©k bºÿ: so . . . well . . .

toNy: well

toNy: are you . . . stocked up at the moment?

ši©k bºÿ: yeah

ši©k bºÿ: how many do you want?

toNy: probably just four. how much?

ši©k bºÿ: . . . umm, normally they'd be thirty each

ši©k bºÿ: but . . .

ši©k bºÿ: twenty-five for you.

toNy: sounds good. can we meet in the city on Monday afternoon? that cafe?

ši©k bºÿ: kay

toNy: four o'clock?

ši©k bºÿ: can we make it later? I've got this thing for school.

toNy: it's good you've got your priorities sorted out.

ši©k bºÿ: you want it or not?

toNy: yeah

Ši©k b°ÿ: let's make it five. table in the corner.

toNy: cool. I'd better go soon. Jamie and I are going to this friend's house today. I'm meeting him later.

Ši©k b°ÿ: okay

toNy: see ya monday

Ši©k b°ÿ: okay

toNy: see ya Mykal

Ši©k b°ÿ: see ya

166

Information I draw from this:

a) Ši©k b°ÿ is Mykal.

b) Anthony has fucked Mykal.

c) If Anthony has fucked Mykal and I have fucked Anthony, vicariously I have fucked Mykal.

d) Mykal is a drug dealer.

e) Anthony thinks I'm the clingy type.

f) Anthony has *told* Mykal, and therefore probably a bunch of other people, that he thinks I'm the clingy type. This should bother me a lot. I don't *want* Mykal to have that kind of information.

g) All this explains a lot. It explains a lot about what was *really* going on at the cafe the other day.

h) All of this should get to me, but it doesn't, because:

i) Anthony thinks I'm a pretty decent fuck.

167

There are actually two windows open on the screen. One is the IRC chat. I'm not sure what the other is, but the text down the bottom identifies it as gc864_12.jpg. So it's a picture file. I don't know whether I should open it or not.

Part of me doesn't want to see it. Part of me's afraid. But opening it could clear a lot of things up. I weigh up whether or not to do it.

Case for opening the picture file: Whatever this picture is might be proof that it really *was* Anthony in those photos.

Case against opening the picture file: Whatever this picture is might be proof that it really *was* Anthony in those photos.

My hands are shaking. I don't know. Whatever. I click on the window to maximize it.

168

gc864_12.jpg: Two people fucking. Two boys. One of them is blond, kind of feline-looking. The other is Anthony. They are on the floor, on what looks like a futon. It's red. The futon. The blond boy is flat on his back. Anthony is above him, arching, kind of. The blond boy's mouth is open, as though he's just said something, or is just about to; if he is even able to form words, he might be saying Anthony's name. If he knows Anthony's name. The blond boy's hands are balled up into fists. Anthony's teeth are clenched. Their eyes are closed.

169

I don't know if it's, like, adrenaline or what, but as I'm looking at that photo, some body chemical is released which makes my head swim and for a second I don't even know where I am. It's definitely Anthony in that picture.

It's him. It's Anthony. I try to construct a list of possible scenarios/consequences in my head—with the basic question of whether or not I should ask him about this photo, about all the photos, in mind—but there are too many to grasp and my thoughts are moving too

fast to make any kind of rational connections anyway.
I mean . . .

170

The fact that Anthony left his computer on: I wonder if this was entirely an accident. I guess there are two alternatives: either he was lazy and didn't bother to shut the chat window before he left home tonight, or he left it on deliberately, knowing that I'd read it when we got back here. What that says is "I want you to read it." Either that, or "I don't trust you not to look." Probably both. Either way, it doesn't matter.

Whatever his motivation, Anthony, this secretive and possibly extremely damaged but still incredibly hot person who never seems to show any expression at all and lets himself be photographed having sex with other boys and the pictures be displayed on the internet thinks *I'm* a good fuck.

Porno. Totally.

171

Cut ahead: Anthony returns. We kiss, say nothing. He is standing by the window in his boxer shorts and I am sitting on the floor with the joint. He comes over to me. I try to pull his boxers off, fail, he pulls them off himself and we collapse on the bed and we're kissing and we're both naked and I'm holding his hips, he's sighing, groaning, and the whole time I'm thinking about those photos, wondering how many boys Anthony has been with, how many times he has done it, wondering what it must *feel* like, and I continue, faster and faster, trying to make him cum, and the whole time my mind is on those photos, and I'm thinking, I could be one of those boys, in the photos, I'm thinking, I'm just the same as they are, I might as well be one of those boys, and I'm wondering what they would look like, photos of me with Anthony.

172

I am thinking: Pictures of the two of us. Pictures of Anthony and Calvin. Thinking about what they would look like.

> 1. Calvin is sitting on the floor, leaning on the bed. His arm is extended across it, and it looks as though it should be around someone's shoulder, except nobody else is sitting with him. He is holding a joint and staring into the camera with a mysterious/purposeful/slutty look on his face.
> 2. Calvin and Anthony are standing together,

by the bed. Anthony is wearing only boxer shorts, and the two of them are kissing. It's hard to tell whether the kiss has just begun or just ended, whether their mouths are about to connect or whether they are pulling away from one another, but it doesn't matter because they are totally lost in one another and it's totally hot. Their eyes are closed.

3. Anthony is leaning down, pulling his boxer shorts off. Looks almost delicate. Calvin is on the point of collapsing on the bed.

4. Calvin is going down on Anthony. Anthony is holding Calvin's head, his eyes closed, his expression still largely blank, but something else is creeping in there. Hard to say. Anthony's head is thrown back. The expression on Calvin's face seems to suggest that Anthony's cock is, like, the *coolest* thing in the world. And to him, at this point, it probably is.

5. Calvin and Anthony are fucking. Totally lost in one another. Calvin is flat on his back. Anthony is above him, arching, kind of. Calvin's mouth is open, as though he's just said something, or is just about to; if he is even able to form words, he might be saying Anthony's name. If he knows Anthony's name. Calvin's hands are balled up into fists. Anthony's teeth are clenched. Their eyes are closed.

173

Cut ahead: Yesterday afternoon. It's still overcast outside, threatening to rain. I'm back at my house, sitting in the office and staring at my computer screen. I pull those pictures of Anthony up again and stare at them for a long time.

My whole body feels like it's going to just float away or whatever. It's weird, difficult to describe. I check my hotmail for the fourth time this afternoon, just to see if something's there. There is one new message. It's from Margot.

174

From: Margot <boy_killer@net-power.com.au>
To: Calvin< hearts_filthy_lesson@hotmail.com>
Subject: Survey!!!!

Heyya Calvin

How are ewe? I know how much you love these fucking annoying email survey things. Here's one someone sent me. It's kind of amusing, I think. Anyway. Do it and forward your answers to all your friends and get them to fill it out and stuff. My answers are below.

Stay cool,

You are the lubbliest dude in the world,
Margot

>>name: Margot
>>nicknames: magoo, faghag, fucking cunt, or even
   just hey bitch
>>describe yourself in five words: Faster, pussy-cat. Kill,
   kill!
>>interests: obsessing over cute boys, playing bass
>>role model: Bjork, Betty Page
>>drug of choice: crystal meth, baby, all the way!!!!!
   (hahha)
>>in five years I'd like to be: a member of an anarchist/
   dadaist art collective somewhere in Berlin
>>quote a line from a song: "If you complain one more
   time you'll meet an army of me."
>>I most resemble: the mind of Dorothy Parker in the
   body of Angelina Jolie. except it's probably the other
   way around. hahhahhahha

175

From: Calvin <hearts_filthy_lesson@hotmail.com>
To: Margot <boy_killer@net-power.com.au>
Subject: re: Survey!!!!

hey Margot
I got that survey thing you sent. It was cool. These are

my answers. They kind of suck but then again I didn't think very hard about them.

Things are weird lately. I guess I'll talk to you about it at school tomorrow.

>>name: Calvin

>>nicknames: I don't think I have one, not that I know of . . .

>>describe yourself in five words: hyperactive. synthetic. nancy boy. liar.

>>interests: living in my head

>>role model: (this one I left blank. I couldn't come up with anybody)

>>drug of choice: cute guys

>>in five years I'd like to be: waking up somewhere with a hell of a hangover

>>quote a line from a song: "a friend with weed is better"

>>I most resemble: a porn star

So there you go. Hope that was enlightening.

Talk to ya soon,

Calvin

176

I am sitting in front of my old Nintendo. Kid Icarus is on the screen and he's jumping from platform to platform, higher and higher, in search of something, I guess, but I don't know what, and he's in this environment that's meant to resemble, like, Ancient Greece or something, except it really doesn't, and the soundtrack is this absolutely perfect late eighties synthesized video-game music, and Kid Icarus is being chased by Eggplant Wizards and ghosts and these weird eyeball kind of things that fly around and it's really insane the more you think about it, so I try not to think about it too hard.

Mykal and Anthony: It's late in the afternoon. Overcast outside. Anthony must be meeting Mykal in the city about now. I think of the two of them sitting in that cafe together, wonder if it's the same one from the other day. I wonder if the two of them really have fucked—wouldn't surprise me—and if they have, whether they'd ever consider doing it again. I think of Anthony, and of Mykal, and of the two of them together, of Anthony like he was in those photos, I think of Anthony sucking Mykal off, Mykal sucking Anthony, of the two of them lying together, naked. And even though Anthony's not even my boyfriend, not really, and even though the chances of him actually fucking Mykal are probably pretty remote, the thought of it is driving me insane.

Kid Icarus falls off one of the platforms. Dies. The weird eyeball things continue flying around the screen. When I was a little kid, when I played this, I used to have nightmares that the eyeballs were following me around. I don't know what made me think of that. A message on the screen asks me if I want to play again. I don't.

177

The venetian blinds in my bedroom are open. A cold half-light is shining through them. My room is white and the outside world is gray. My phone is on my bed, where I tossed it when I got home this afternoon. The urge to send a message to Anthony is overwhelming.

SMS to Anthony:
Hey Anthony—the weekend was very cool—I really like you. can we do something tonight?

I wait for it to send, staring at the little moving lines on the screen, wondering what the hell those little moving line things are meant to *resemble;* I mean, what the hell could it possibly be that they're supposed to represent? I stare out the window at the overcast afternoon, at the houses up the hill, a few drops of water sliding down the glass. I start to freak out, waiting for Anthony to reply.

I go over to the stereo, put on a Placebo album then skip straight to track eight and put it on repeat. I really need music to calm me down at the moment.

I don't know what to do. I walk down to the fridge to pour myself a Coke then I don't drink it. I head back up to my room. When I get there, my phone is still lying on my bed.

Screen of my phone:
1 message received.
Read?

I pick it up. Stare at it for a few seconds, debate whether to open it or not. "Read?" Of course I fucking pick "read." What else would I do, leave it to sit there? The idea actually crosses my mind for about an eighth of a second, but I dismiss it. I pick up the phone and see what Anthony has sent me.

SMS from Anthony:
Hey calvin. I like you
too—saturday night was

fucking cool. I'm busy
this afternoon—feel like
maybe doing something
tomorrow?

"Feel like maybe doing something tomorrow?"
I do, but that's beside the point.

Anthony and I are fucking. Does that mean we're together? What *does* that mean? I like him. I'm pretty sure I do, although it's possible that I'm only attracted to him on a physical level and in love with the fictional version of him I've created in my head.

It was probably only a one-nighter anyway. I have no right to be analyzing it to such a great extent.

It means nothing. Get over it.

. . . So why does it sting so much that he's busy this afternoon and won't tell me where he is? *Should* he even tell me? I mean, if we're not, like, boyfriends or anything, and if we really are just fucking, then . . .

Fuck this. Fuck this *right* off. I don't want to think about it any more. I click reply.

SMS to Anthony: Love to dude. I'll
call ya then.

Substituting "ya" for "you" was very deliberate. The "love to" says "I care." The "ya" says "but not too much."

At least, this is the way it seems in my head. I hope it has come across this way to Anthony.

178

I'm in the office, kind of freaking out, swivelling around on the chair a whole bunch of times. I'm still playing that Placebo CD but it's now on the big stereo in the living room so Bryan Molko's paint-stripper sexy voice fills the whole house. I go to the hotmail page, check my email for, like, the eighteenth time today.

Which is when I find it.

179

Before I went offline yesterday, I took that survey thing and forwarded it to various people in my address book, just to see what would happen, whether anyone would respond.

I sent one to Jeremy. I'm not sure why I did this. I mean, like, maybe I just wanted to see if he'd respond, and if he did, to see the kind of stuff he'd come up with. Maybe it was something more than that. As I'm reading his reply, I start to suspect that it might have been.

From: Jeremy <jezza99@i-accelarate.com.au>
To: Calvin <hearts_filthy_lesson@hotmail.com>
Subject: how to be a porn star

heyyya calvin!!!!!

wuz very cool to hear from you again. love those survey things!! yur answers were very cool. hehhe. these are mine:

>>name: jeremy
>>nicknames: jezza, the virgin (loooong story), slut
>>describe yourself in five words: hahha. I don't know. it would take more than five
>>interests: going out clubbing, raves, meeting cute boyz
>>role model: kylie or something—aren't gay guys meant to say that?!?!?!
>>drug of choice: I've only taken eccies a couple of times but they're heaps fun!!
>>in five years I'd like to be: a model or travelling in europe or making my own music or something
>>quote a line from a song: hahha, I don't know, hit me baby one more time
>>I most resemble: someone cute hopefully

so yeah, that's me, hehhe

email me back dude, it would be cooool to get together
sometime
luv your work,
jeremy

181

I pull up another of the pictures on the screen. This is the one of Anthony and Jeremy, the one where they are standing, kissing. You can only see the back of Jeremy's head and the side of Anthony's cheek . . . That one. I look at the position the two of them are in, Anthony's hands in the small of Jeremy's back.

I wonder how close they were. I mean how close they really were. I wonder if Anthony and Jeremy knew each other before those pictures were taken. I consider the idea that they might have been strangers, but that's too much to deal with, so I put it aside. They had to have known each other. Had they been together? Had they kissed, or had they tasted one another? Were they boyfriends?

> **Boyfriends:** I don't know if that would make it better or worse. It's too much to think about.

It's crazy. I mean, seriously, it's one of those fucking insane things you do and you can't even really explain why you do it, beyond the fact that you have to. It's almost a force stronger than me that makes me do it. Something devious.

Some plot that's forming in my mind: I click reply.

182

From: Calvin <hearts_filthy_lesson@hotmail.com>
To: Jeremy <jezza99@i-accelerate.com.au>
Subject: re: how to be a porn star

Hey Jeremy

It was very cool to hear from you again. I've been think-ing about you a fair bit. It would be totally cool if we could meet sometime.

Are u free next weekend? Cuz if you are we could meet in the city or something. Just get together and have coffee or something like that. Might turn out to be really cool.

Saturday good for you?

Stay cool dude,
Talk to you soon,
Calvin

183

From: Jeremy <jezza99@i-accelerate.com.au>
To: Calvin <hearts_filthy_lesson@hotmail.com>
Subject: meeting would be cooool

heyyyyyyya calvin!

knew u couldn't resist me, hehhe. meeting would be totally sweet. saturdayz totally sweet with me. ummmm . . . there's this coffee shop I always go to just near the eagle street pier. u probably know the one. would u like to meet there on saturday morning, ten or so?

it will be *coooooooooooooooooooooooooooool* to finally meet u, hahha!
I'd better go . . . stuff to do. love yur work dude
cu then?
jeremy.

184

From: Calvin <hearts_filthy_lesson@hotmail.com>
To: Jeremy <jezza99@i-accelerate.com.au>
Subject: saturday

Hey hey Jeremy

Saturday morning will be sweet. I'm looking forward to it, hehhe.

I'll see ya then,
Calvin

185

Wednesday afternoon. It's overcast, and I meet Anthony in the city. I see him and immediately my stomach starts to hurt. He looks blank, as always. I can't read him. I don't know what he's thinking. But I want him. Insanely. Completely. We just kind of walk around for a while, directionless. Stop at this cafe, still in our school uniforms, and we both order long blacks. Sit at this table near the window. He pours two sugars into his coffee but only drinks half of it. I watch the raindrops as they slide down the glass, the people as they hurry by outside.

I turn, look right at Anthony. He's looking right at me.

186

Anthony: This sucks.
Me: I guess.
Anthony: I have some pot at my house. You want to go back there?
Me: Okay.

187

Blur: Getting stoned and watching a DVD *The Fifth Element.* Anthony and I kissing as though we're both incredibly hungry, as though we'd both die if it weren't for this one kiss. Sinking further and further into it. Knowing that at this point, right now, Anthony is the only thing that matters to me in the world. I want him so badly it's like a physical pain. Kissing. He is leading me upstairs. Still kissing, and I'm sucking him off, now he's sucking me off, and we're both totally lost in one another, and he asks me if I want to, and I know what he means, and I do, and he's inside me, and we go from kissing to just, I don't know, staring at each other, eyes closed, eyes open, and it's like this red wave of desire and I can't even explain it, he is consuming me and I'm consuming him and we're kissing and we're consuming each other's body, but that same blank look is on his face the whole time.

188

Cut ahead: Saturday morning. I am meeting Jeremy in the city this morning, but it's cold, foggy, and I don't feel like walking anywhere.

Cold days: I only really feel right on days when it's overcast like this. I feet safe, insular, like being in a cocoon or something. When the sky's gray and the whole world looks as though it's underwater, this incredibly calm, warm feeling comes over me. It makes me want to be all by myself, warm, forever; it makes me want to move to, you know, a lighthouse or something on a small island at the end of the world, and hear the waves roaring, the cold air on my skin. Look up and see nothing but gray clouds in the sky. Always. The idea of disappearing forever, nobody knowing where I am except for the seagulls, the ocean roaring at me and me roaring back at the ocean. The idea of that just seems so . . . peaceful.

189

Dad's going into the city, to one of the hospitals; I swallow my pride and ask him if he'll give me a ride.

Luckily Dad's in a bad mood, so we don't talk a lot on the way. I am in the front seat of his Saab, staring out at the houses shut up against the cold.

We stop, waiting to turn onto the main road, and Dad looks across at me, as though he has something on his mind, as though he's planning to ask me a significant question or something. I really wish he wouldn't.

> **Dad:** I know I haven't asked you this in a while, but . . . how are you Calvin?
> **Me:** I'm fine.
> **Dad:** Are you really?
> **Me:** I really am. I'm fine.
> **Dad:** There's nothing that you'd like to . . .
> **Me:** No, there isn't.
> **Dad:** Because if ever . . . I mean . . . I'm always . . . there, for you to . . . if you ever . . .
> **Me:** I'll keep that in mind.
> **Dad:** Please do . . . Because if there is something on your mind . . .
> **Me:** I will.

We never talk about my brother anymore, ever. We never mention him. It's as though he never existed. Since Jonathan, all Dad ever does is work. He's let himself be subsumed by it, to escape or something, which is fine. I don't have a problem with that, it doesn't *bother* me, because everyone has their own way of dealing with things. Mum takes her pills, and Dad works, and we never talk about it, ever. Which is fine. It *bothers* me, however, when Dad tries to reach out to me, tries to relate, or whatever. It seems deliberate, forced. It seems *false*, and I won't play along with it. We get along just fine when we leave one another alone, and I refuse to let him make *me* feel like the bad person, feel like *I'm* the one who doesn't care.

190

I'm meeting Jeremy at this cafe just near Eagle Street. As I'm stepping out of Dad's Saab, saying goodbye, as I'm stepping into the overcast morning, as I'm walking down George Street, people passing either side of me, I'm wondering about the terms of this meeting. I mean, are we just meeting as friends, or is he assuming that I asked him out because I was *interested* in him? It doesn't really matter though—Jeremy knows Anthony; therefore he has the information I need.

191

Riverside: The morning has grown progressively denser and colder. The city is wrapped, choking almost, in cloud and smog. The pinpricks of light that occasionally cut through the clouds seem too intense; they hurt my eyes and make the familiar sights of skyline and river into hyper-real versions of themselves.

192

Jeremy is sitting at a table out on the cafe terrace, overlooking the river. There is a cup of coffee in front of him, an espresso, and he sips it and occasionally looks up, like he's looking for me. He is wearing a tight red T-shirt; his hair is bleached, messy, but an intentional kind of messy, and he is too fucking cute for words.

Jeremy grabs a sugar packet, rips it open, pours the whole thing into his coffee.

This guy walks past, older guy, about forty or so, graying hair but fairly good-looking, charcoal suit, you know. Not so strange for around here. He walks right past Jeremy; Jeremy looks up. It's almost impossible to describe, but it's like:

193

Interplay between Jeremy and the man in the suit: The man turns his head to look at Jeremy. Jeremy looks up, meets his glance, doesn't look away. The man hesitates for a fraction of a second. To an observer, it's almost as though Jeremy is daring him. Jeremy still doesn't look away. The man turns, keeps walking, walks faster.

I wonder what the man must be thinking as he hurries away. Maybe: My life could have changed forever. If I'd stayed, if I'd stopped. If I hadn't kept going on my way to work, if I'd stopped and sat down with this kid. Bought him a coffee, talked to him. I could have done things with him, if he'd let me. I could have . . .

194

The man keeps walking. Walks away. Jeremy smiles. Looks back down at his coffee.

I consider turning around.

Fuck it.

Jeremy looks up, spots me. Smiles, sort of. Animal smile. You know, I'm young and hot and what the fuck are you going to do about it? kind of a smile.

"Calvin," he says.

"Jeremy. Hey."

His gaze stays locked on me. "Dude, it's *fucking cool* to meet you finally."

"Been looking forward to it," I say.

He's still sitting down, but he offers me his hand to

shake and I take it. His palm feels kind of, I don't know. Dry. Strange. It doesn't feel like Anthony's hand. It makes me feel weird for a fraction of a second. Uncomfortable or something. When we stop shaking hands, I sit down.

"You feel like a drink?" he asks. "Feel like a coffee?"
"Sounds good. I could use a strong coffee."

He laughs. "Hahaha, yeah. Fucking *caffeine!* It's all good."

195

Jeremy: Caffeine . . . I need as much of it as I can get.
Me: Did you go out last night?
Jeremy: Ohh yeah.
Me: Was it good?
Jeremy: Fuck. I'm wiped out. Fucking trashed, totally. Last night was massive. Like, completely. Big night. Fucking *huge* night. It was a blast.
Me: What happened?

Jeremy looks at me, smiles kind of. Then he launches into his story.

Jeremy: Well, okay, like, there's this friend of mine, Joe. He's a few years older than me. Kind of an ex-boyfriend but not really. I don't know what you'd call him really. He's a lawyer, and he's like thirty. We still get together and fuck sometimes, like, when he's bored. I guess I'm his fuck buddy. Haha, I never really thought of myself as a fuck buddy before, but anyway . . .

The waiter—"Stephen"—interrupts. I order a long black; Jeremy asks for one too, even though he hasn't finished the one he's drinking. Stephen pulls this little pad out of his apron, writes it down. Like it's such a difficult order to remember. Two long blacks.

Jeremy: Yeah, so we were out in the city, Joe and me and a couple of other friends of ours, just getting trashed and stuff, and he was wearing this shirt, like, it was *totally* revealing, you fucking had to see it, and yeah. And we went to Fridays. Can you believe it? Fucking *Fridays*. I *hate* those city clubs . . .
Me: They suck.
Jeremy: Hehhe. Fucking, totally. So yeah. We were at Fridays and we were already totally drunk—I mean totally, we all were, especially me cuz he was buying me these

tequila shots, you know, I think he was trying
to get me drunk. Like, he hadn't gotten any
for a while and I think he was trying to hit on
me so we could go back to his place. Which
would have been okay, but you know. We
were all drunk and I started dancing to this
song . . .

Jeremy namechecks this particular trashy pop song I
only half recognize but I nod my head and make this
little *mmm* sound and he continues.

Jeremy: I hate the city. They're always playing trash like that, but I always dance to it.
Especially when I'm drunk, you know, so I'm
dancing and Joe's dancing really close to me
and sort of feeling me up a bit, which is okay,
but I wasn't really sure if I was in the mood
to fuck him or not, you know, it was all a bit
weird and I didn't really feel like it, so I was
sort of hinting for him to get away from me,
and I think he was getting the picture—he
was kind of pissed off, I mean, because he'd
been buying me tequila shots all night . . .

Should you fuck a guy because he's been buying you
drinks all night? Is it, like, polite or whatever? That's
the reason I let Adam do me.

Jeremy: . . . and we sort of drift off to the side a bit, out onto the balcony, you know, because you can see the river and all the buildings in the city and everything and it was a totally beautiful night so I figured we could just go out there and get some fresh air, so we were sitting out there down on one of those bench things and we spotted this one particular guy. He was pretty hot, just standing near the bar out there by himself, and . . . well, okay, imagine a cross between Billy Idol and that guy from, oh, you know, Buffy . . . my sister used to pin pictures of him up, and he was, like, English, with the cheekbones and everything—and anyway . . . Where was I going with this?

Jeremy's acting as though he's on speed. I hope it's not just the coffee doing this to him. I couldn't do anything to fuck up the flow of the conversation even if I wanted to.

Stephen is back with our coffees. He sets them down on the table in front of us, carefully so he won't spill any. Some of mine spills over the rim of the cup, leaves a mark down the side. I stare at it, hypnotized, as it slides down over the cafe's logo—some kind of stylized fish—cutting it in two.

Jeremy picks up his cup, blows on it. Drinks some. Stephen asks if we're right. We are. He walks away, slowly. Looks back over his shoulder, like he's trying to confirm something, then he keeps walking. Fucking . . . weird.

Me: So you saw a guy by the bar.
Jeremy: Oh yeah. So Joe was *fully* checking him out, and I was like, Joe, you can't pick up here, dude, it's fucking *Fridays* . . . It's like, a *city club . . . jocks* come here, they'll fucking *beat you up,* and he was all, yeah, I think I'll go and talk to the guy and I was just like, fucking, Joe, you *don't* pick up guys in the city, it's just not *done,* and I think he was doing it half to get back at me because I was refusing to give it up for him, you know, which is just typical of Joe, so he goes up to talk to this guy and I follow him, I guess just to keep an eye on him or whatever . . .
Me: So what was the guy like?
Jeremy: The guy? Like, okay. This is where the night got really interesting. Joe went up to him and I was following pretty close behind, so we start talking to him, and he was like . . . Okay. His name was Søren, you know, with that thing through the "o"—he explained that to us about three times—and

he was a backpacker or something, didn't say where he was from, might have been Sweden; I mean, he looked Swedish, like really *sleazy* though, and he said, I mean, he and Joe had moved away from the bar by this point, off by themselves, and I just sort of followed but I felt pretty, you know, excess to requirements or whatever . . .

There are two women sitting at a table near us. They look like mother and daughter and they are both blonde; the younger looking one has this scarf tied in her hair and the older one is wearing sunglasses, and they're both looking at us in what might be disbelief. I don't know whether they can even hear us. Something seems to have offended them anyway. I stare at them until they look away.

Jeremy: . . . but the guy kept shooting me these looks like he might be interested and I thought, why let Joe have this guy if I can? Fucking, just to prove a point or something. I'm screwed up like that. So I went over with them, and he was talking to us, he had this full-on *accent,* and he was explaining about his country and stuff, and that thing with the "o" in his name, and then he tells us, cuz he's bought Joe this cocktail and I don't know what was in it but it was really fucking strong, and Joe was very *very* drunk, and the guy was telling us he was an inmate in one of the European Big Brother houses . . .

Me: What the *fuck?*

Jeremy: I *know*. Like, *seriously*. And I'm thinking, that can't be true, I mean, there's no *way* we can tell for a fact if that's true or not, but he has this *really* serious look on his face, and I wonder if it actually might be true, but then I started to think *no way,* he's just trying to get Joe to fuck him, and Joe was all, "Oh, why would they evict *you?*," like this Søren dude was just the most attractive human being in the universe and why would anyone toss *him* out of the Big Brother house, and he's totally flirting with the guy, and it's like . . .

Me: That's really gross.

Jeremy: It's disturbing, I *know!* But then, the thing is, he keeps looking at me, and then he sort of moves around so he's almost touching both of us, Joe and me, and he's telling us he made all this money after they evicted him from the house, from doing ads and stuff in Sweden or whatever country he was from, and he told us he was on a world trip, and like, this was his first night in Australia and he loved it except he was all alone and didn't have anybody to stay with and it was like, *hint hint*, seriously, he was fully *cracking onto* the both of us, he could *not* have made it any more obvious, and I actually thought, you know, this might be kind of all right. I mean we didn't know if he was bullshitting or not, but he bought us another round of drinks, and I was almost too drunk to care by that point, I just wanted to see what would happen, and then the Søren guy asked us back to his hotel room.

Me: Did you go?

Jeremy: Well . . . Yeah. I thought, what the fuck? I just wanted to see if it was true or not. So we leave Fridays and we're getting all these stares from all the fucking jock types who hang out there, and their girl-friends, you know, that was pretty funny, and then we're walking back up towards Elizabeth Street, his arm around both of us, and I realize, you know, maybe he's not kid-ding, and so yeah, he takes us to the Hilton, and we're going through the lobby and everything, up in this elevator, and he's kiss-ing Joe and then me and the whole thing suddenly becomes hilariously funny, and I'm laughing and laughing and we eventually get up to his room, and I mean, whether or not he was telling the truth about the Big Brother thing, he certainly had, you know, the means to obtain a room at the Hilton, which isn't exactly the most obvious back-packer place to stay, so Joe was asking him all these really stupid questions about what it's like to be famous and stuff like that, and he told us he'd been in this ad campaign for energy drinks or something, and he was thinking about making an album or what-ever, "cutting a single," he said . . . "cotting eh seengle," *whatever,* and Joe was totally eating it up, you know, and then he asked us if we wanted to get stoned . . .

Me: So you did, I'm assuming?

Jeremy's gaze slides away from me for a second. I fol-low his eyes and see that the man in the charcoal suit is walking past again. In the second that he allows himself to look at us, I give him this menacing look. I'm not sure why. He probably assumes Jeremy and I are together. I don't know why I want him to assume that, any more than I know why I give him the look. I'm not really into Jeremy. I don't care about Jeremy one way or the other, but suddenly I want it to *appear* as though I do. The man walks away, embarrassed. Or something. Good.

Jeremy looks back at me.

Jeremy: Well, yeah, totally. We got fucking *smashed.* We had to use a pipe or we would have set off the smoke alarms. And he had this really good pot, like total bodyfuck pot, I was *really* stoned after just a couple of cones, and whenever I'm fucked I get really, you know, touchy-feely and stuff, and then Søren starts kissing me, like, full-on kissing me and he drags me towards the bed, Joe's sort of following, and we all collapsed on one another, and you know . . . Let's just say, I've never fucked two guys at once before but it was a totally amazing experience. I mean, seriously . . . It was really fucking cool, you know. We were all *so* wasted. It was fucking unbelievable . . . It lasted for hours. Totally. I think we finally fell asleep at about four or something. Fucking exhausted.

He looks right at me. Smiles at me.

Jeremy: I'm glad we met, Calvin. You're cool.
Me: Thanks.
Jeremy: Hungry?
Me: I guess.
Jeremy: Sushi?
Me: Okay.

196

We agree on Sushi Central. Jeremy says he once got food poisoning at Omekaido Avenue. As we're walking back towards the center of the city, it starts to rain. We duck into the entranceway of a building and wait for it to pass. He stands close to me. He feels warm. I don't know where this is heading.

> **Jeremy:** My dad works in there.
> **Me:** Oh, cool.

I look inside.

> **Lobby of the building:** High ceiling. Walls painted deep red, and a painting hanging over by the elevators, like an art deco approximation of an octopus. There are lights, globes, hanging on long, thin cords from the ceiling. A table in the center, a glass vase, thick, almost overgrown, with some kind of water plant.
> **Jeremy:** Hope he doesn't see us.

He looks at me like he's going to kiss me but then he doesn't. I'm kind of relieved.

Observations of Jeremy now I've met him in the flesh: Jeremy is young and dumb and hot and he knows it and you know he knows it because of the way he carries himself, and the look on his face which says *I can make guys do whatever I want— including you,* and he's so cocky and so sure of his good looks and his power over guys that it would be sickening if he weren't good-looking. Older faggots go absolutely nuts for guys like Jeremy. Because guys like Jeremy are young, cocky, available, and that gives them power. I have that power. I had that power over Adam. I've had that power over all the other guys who've sucked me off. They don't do it for me, they do it for what I am, which is to say, I'm young. That's the ultimate attraction. In this particular world, *that's* the ultimate power, and you can say whatever you want and make whatever excuses you want, but it's true. Being young and pretty means having power. And it's the kind of power that we have to exploit while we can.

Every time Jeremy's with a guy, I'm sure he feels it slipping. When there's an older guy frantically sucking his dick, Jeremy must look down and almost *pity* him—I mean because of how desperate the guy must seem. I mean. Desperate for *something*. An idea. Something from the past that he's trying to recapture, or at least remember. Whatever. Whenever Jeremy's with an older guy I'm sure he must look down at the guy and think, one day I'll *be* that guy. Maybe that fear is what motivates him. Maybe under the swagger and the perfect hair and the cool shirts and the come-hither glances, there's someone who's terrified because he knows one day it's all going to end. I guess Jeremy must feel this, because I feel exactly the same way.

198

We talk for a while as we're standing in the entrance-way of that building. I can't even remember about what. The point is that eventually the rain starts to ease off, and we keep going, head to Sushi Central.

Jeremy: I fucking love sushi trains.
Me: Yeah. I'm thinking of having one installed in my bedroom.
Jeremy: Are you . . . serious dude?

Oh my god.

There is a woman sitting at the sushi train, with these two small children, one sitting either side of her. She is eating a piece of what looks like tofu. Little brother leans around and hits little sister, who starts to cry. The woman turns and says something to little brother, but I can't hear what it is. She shakes her head at him and then turns away. Little brother goes back to playing with this little plastic dog that's sitting on the counter in front of him. Little sister stabs a big piece of avocado right through with a chopstick.

It's lunchtime and the whole restaurant is packed. There is music playing over the sound system, and I think I might recognize the song, but it's difficult to hear over the noises of conversation, shouting, plates being set down, the noise of rain outside.

199

> **Me:** There's like . . . A friend of mine. This guy I met . . . At a party.
> **Jeremy:** Sounds wonderful.
> **Me:** Thing is, I recognized him. I'd seen him before.
> **Jeremy:** You had.

This is not phrased as a question.

Me: Look, forget about it.
Jeremy: Okay.

He's staring at me, waiting for me to say something.

Me: Those photos of you that were on the website. The ones you showed me . . .
Jeremy: What did you think of them?
Me: They were cool.
Jeremy: I looked kind of weird in some of them. Sort of pale, or like, I don't know, too young or something. I didn't really like all of them.

I don't know whether he's fishing for compliments or whether he's actually serious, but I indulge him anyway.

Me: You looked good.
Jeremy: You think so?
Me: Yeah, you looked hot.

He leans in closer.

Jeremy: You're making me blush.
Me: So, you know . . . Where were they taken?

Jeremy gives me this weird and fairly suspicious look that is halfway between a smile and an "I promise to rip you to shreds if you so much as fuck with me!". It takes him a second to launch into his explanation.

Jeremy: Those photos were . . . Look. It was just this guy I know through my dad. He took them.

Me: Who was the guy?

Jeremy: Are you really so interested?

Me: I guess.

Jeremy: Okay, well, the guy . . . He's in his fifties. Like I said, he works with my dad. He's a lawyer too, and he has this *thing* for teenage guys. He got all obsessed with me, came to my parents' house one night for a dinner party thing, and he was, like, *staring* at me whenever I came in the room, asking me all sorts of questions about how I was going at school, my interests, really painful stuff. Anyway, later in the night he, like, *cornered* me in the hallway outside my room, and he was acting all pathetic, like, you know, I'd never normally do this kind of thing but you're so young and so beautifully put together and, you know, fucking, blah blah blah. You can imagine how it went.

Me: I guess I can.

Jeremy: So we . . . I don't know why I'm telling you this story . . .

When people say "I don't know why I'm telling you this story," they're always lying.

Jeremy: I let the old guy suck me off a few times, and eventually, this was months later, he asked me if I'd like to pose for some photos, like, for his collection. So, you know, I *indulged* him. I thought, whatever, cool.

Me: So that was when you did it?

Jeremy: Yeah. He gave me his address, his apartment, and told me to come on such and such a day, which ended up being a Friday night, after school, and he told me if I wanted I could bring a friend. Like, the emphasis he put on *bring a friend* . . . You fucking had to be there. It was funny. So yeah.

Me: Is that the guy who was with you, in the photos?

Jeremy gives me a look. He's wondering where this extremely subtle line of questioning is leading.

200

The woman with the two little children is staring at me. The little boy is still playing with the plastic dog. The dog menaces a half-eaten plate of paradise rolls and then makes a suicidal leap off the edge of the counter. The woman looks back at the little boy. The little boy reaches down for the plastic dog.

201

>**Jeremy:** The guy who was with me . . . That was just a friend of mine.
>**Me:** Like, your boyfriend or something?
>**Jeremy:** Ex.
>**Me:** Did you . . . His name. Was it Anthony?

Jeremy smiles at me.

>**Jeremy:** Fuck . . . Yeah, it was. Do you . . . Like, are you a friend of his or something?
>**Me:** I know him, yeah.
>**Jeremy:** Fuck!

Jeremy laughs.

>**Jeremy:** Small world. Seriously. Six degrees and all that.

I give him my best "blank" look.

Jeremy: You've heard that saying before. You're always hearing of guys who, you know . . . It doesn't matter . . . So were you . . . you know . . . going out with him or what?
Me: With Anthony?
Jeremy: . . . *Duh.*
Me: I guess.
Jeremy: Hahha. How fucking funny is that? You were with Anthony. God. *Small* fucking world.
Me: Yeah.
Jeremy: I haven't seen him in so long.
Me: How long were you guys going out?
Jeremy: I don't know. Few months I think.

This Britney Spears song begins playing over the sound system. Britney is requesting that we hit her, baby, one more time. Jeremy looks up.

Jeremy: Hahha, this song. Fuck. We were listening to this on that afternoon.
Me: That afternoon. Before, like . . .
Jeremy: It's *so* fucking tacky. I love it.
Me: You and Anthony, you mean? Like, the afternoon before the photos and stuff?
Jeremy: Yeah.

Me: What was it like?

Jeremy: The . . . Calvin, what's with all these questions?

Me: I don't know. Just interested.

202

Jeremy grabs this piece of tuna and avocado with his chopsticks; puts it in his mouth, chews very slowly, staring at me the whole time. I don't know if the look in his eyes is sexy or scary, I think it's possibly both, but the whole time he's doing this, with the sushi, he never breaks eye contact.

Jeremy: You want to know what it's like.

He has this totally evil look on his face.

Me: What do you mean?

Jeremy: That's why . . . That's why all the questions. You're asking me because you want to know what it feels like to do something like that.

Me: What? Don't be weird, Jeremy.

Jeremy: Tell me I'm wrong.

Me: What?

Jeremy: Tell me I'm wrong. Tell me you *don't* want to know. Tell me that and I'll drop it.

Me: I *don't* care.

Jeremy: You're *totally* lying, Calvin.

He stares at me. Says nothing.

Me: So what if I am?

Jeremy: You want to know?

Me: I do. Fine. I guess I would like to know. What it's like.

Jeremy: Why Calvin?

Me: I don't know. Why the fuck not?

Jeremy: That's not a reasonable answer.

Me: I don't know.

Jeremy: You're not the type, Calvin.

Me: What does that mean? What's the type?

Jeremy: You think too much.

Me: No I don't. I don't have to.

Jeremy: It's not a bad thing. You're really fucking smart, Calvin. I don't doubt that. But you're totally, like, neurotic about it. About sex, I mean.

Me: What?

Jeremy: Look, I know the type. There's this whole . . . *elaborate* facade, and you try to make out that sex is all a game to you, but it isn't . . .

I wonder where he learned the word *facade.*

Jeremy: You can't fuck a guy without *thinking* really hard about it, can you Calvin? It's never just about the sex. You always have to put something more in there. To make it seem significant or worth the effort or whatever. That's you, isn't it?

Me: How can you come to that conclusion? We've only just *met.*

Jeremy: I know. I can tell.

He smiles at me. Actually, no, that's the wrong word. He sneers at me.

Jeremy: You can't *think* about things, Calvin. That takes all the fun out of it. You just have to do them.

Me: You're *being* really fucking *weird* Jeremy.

He ignores this.

Jeremy: I can help you.

Me: Help me what?

Jeremy: You want to know what it felt like. For Anthony.

Me: Why would I?

Jeremy: That's the reason you're asking me all of this, right? Anthony? The two of you *are* going out?

Me: I guess.

Jeremy: You want to know what it felt like for him. What it feels like to *totally* let yourself go.

I don't say anything. I let him interpret my silence however he wants.

Jeremy: I can introduce you to this guy.

Me: This *guy* . . .

Jeremy: If you really want to know what it's like. Like I said . . . This guy. He's not dangerous or anything. Okay. Man, I don't know if I should tell you this.

Me: What?

A plate comes by, six little avocado rolls on it. Jeremy grabs it as it goes. I stare, transfixed at these six perfect little avocado rolls. He picks one up with his chopsticks; the pattern is broken and I stop staring.

Me: Tell me what?

Jeremy looks up. Eats the avocado roll in one motion, then picks up another and offers it to me. I don't know if I'm meant to open my mouth or what. I don't want to play right now. I leave my mouth shut,

stare at him with an expression that's about forty percent bored and sixty percent contemptuous.

Jeremy shrugs. Sets the avocado roll back down on
his plate.

>**Me:** What do I have to do?
>**Jeremy:** You don't *have* to do anything. Not
>exactly.
>**Me:** I'm just asking.
>**Jeremy:** This guy . . . I mean, okay. He likes
>to take photos.
>**Me:** Obviously. Like . . . Photos of me, I assume?
>**Jeremy:** Yeah. Well. I mean. He's basically
>pretty harmless.
>**Me:**
>**Jeremy:** Look. This guy . . . He gets off on
>seeing teenage boys in uniform. Like, school
>uniform, or sports, basketball or whatever.
>That's his thing. So all you have to do is dress
>up for him, and then he takes photos of you
>for a while, and then that's it.
>**Me:** You *know* this guy?

Whatever part of me it is that registers discomfort
registers discomfort at this.

>**Jeremy:** Yeah. Like I said. He's not dangerous.
>**Me:** And I don't have to do anything else?

Jeremy: Not if you don't want to.

Me: If I don't *want* to? What does *that* mean?

Jeremy: Look. You can just play it by ear, okay. Like I said, he's harmless. Seriously.

Me: How well do you know this guy?

Jeremy: I mean . . . Okay, look. He has this website, and he sometimes puts the photos up.

Me: Are you sure about this guy?

Jeremy: I can give you the address of the site if you want. It's all . . . I mean, it's basically harmless. He won't try anything on with you.

Me: Fine. Okay.

Jeremy: Might teach you how to let yourself go.

I take the guy's name from Jeremy. That's all I do. I mean, I don't think I'll actually go to *see* this guy. I mean, I probably won't. I mean, if that's what it takes to understand Anthony . . .

I don't know. It's all too weird.

It's still raining when Jeremy and I leave the sushi train.

203

Anthony's house: The next day. We're watching *Muff: The Vampire Slaves, Part IV.* He's watching it. I'm just kind of sitting there. He tells me it will be fucking funny. He tells me he *knows* one of the guys who's in it and I have to figure out who. I don't know whether he's kidding or not. But then, he's extremely stoned.

Watching it is riveting, in the car crash sense of the word, when you don't quite have it in you to look away. A wide-eyed brunette who looks to be in his late teens is kidnapped and gang-banged by a group of vampires, and they menace him for a while until a striking blonde transvestite (who I can only assume to be Muff) comes to save the day, then has her way with the brunette.

One of the vamps looks vaguely familiar, looks like one of the guys I've seen out, around the place, like someone's boyfriend or someone I've encountered at a party or a club, but it's probably just coincidental. We all start to look alike after a while. His only line in the movie is, "Put that boy down."

Anthony is lying on the couch watching the movie; there is a bong on the floor beside him which he occasionally takes hits from. He never looks up at me, as if he doesn't know I'm here, or if he does, he's making an effort not to care. I guess it wouldn't matter to him either way. He offers me the bong and I pack it again and take an extremely big hit, which makes this whole thing more bearable. No less surreal, but more bearable.

I hope he'll get bored of this soon so we can mess

around or something. He keeps rewinding it to the part where the taller of the vamps, the one I'm, like, sure I know from somewhere, is menacing the brunette with a switchblade, and he keeps saying, "Put that boy down."

"Put that boy down."

Click. Whirr.

"Put that boy down."

Click. Whirrr.

"Put that boy down."

PART 3

THEY ONLY WANT YOU

WHEN YOU'RE SEVENTEEN

204

There is something on the floor, one of those stress toy things that drug companies give out to doctors. My father has about six hundred of these things lying around the house. Anthony's must too. I pick it up to take a look—an unpronounceable word with a lot of d's and x's is written on the clear plastic. It's full of a blue liquid that just kind of sits at the bottom in a big, goopy mess, but when you flip it upside down, it all drips in a spiraling pattern towards the other end. It's the kind of thing that amuses you greatly when you're a little kid, or when you're bored, or when you're incredibly high and close to tripping out of your mind at your boyfriend's house at one in the afternoon on a school day.

A lot of the events leading up to this are a blur, but in sequential order, the day so far has progressed as follows:

> 1. Morning. I'm supposed to be going to school, but it's too depressing a prospect at this point. Walk to the bus stop. I stop in a grove of trees not far from home and I suddenly remember a summer night about a million years ago when my little brother and I were playing somewhere just like this. He was wearing this shirt he used

to have with a picture of Astro Boy on the front. I don't know why I remember this, but I wish I hadn't, because for some reason the memory gets such a tight grip on me that it hurts and I can't even think, and I have to shut my eyes tightly for a second to make it go away. I walk home, hoping the place will be empty, which it is. Get stoned and spend most of the morning re-reading *Less Than Zero,* playing *Yoshi's Island* on my old Super Nintendo and wishing I was with Anthony.

2. Anthony calls; he has this incredibly noncommittal tone. Says we can meet up if we want, whatever. I try not to let on how excited I am by this. I catch the bus into the city and the whole time I'm so on edge it's like there are bugs crawling under my skin or something, because of how badly I want to see him. It's cold. The bus keeps stopping, and people get on at every single stop. I can hardly sit still.

3. I meet Anthony. We walk to the Valley; duck up to the top floor of this parking lot, kiss for quite a while. The sky is overcast, a silvery gray. I can see Chinatown, the tops of a lot of the older buildings; an ocean of glass and corrugated iron. Anthony has a joint already rolled, and he says he really needs to smoke it before he can face out there again. I'm not a hundred

percent sure what he means by "out there," but whatever, I smoke it with him, and the whole time there's this abstract feeling I have that keeps bugging me, and I realize it's fear, fear that someone might come up here and we might get caught, but I manage to put it out of my mind. We kiss some more, smoke another joint and I kind of drift away into the moment.

4. We're in a shop looking for clothes or whatever. The girl behind the counter has strange, sharp features and her hair is cropped very short and bleached. Anthony tries on a pair of sunglasses—which make him look really hot, predatory almost, but he doesn't buy them—and a shirt, with blue checks, which he buys even though it's two hundred dollars or something. I wonder where he gets the cash but after a while I forget to worry about it.

5. This coffee shop at New Farm. An older woman dressed all in black, sitting at one of the front tables smoking a cigarette. Her hair is dyed a very severe shade of red; a pair of Gucci sunglasses are sitting on the table in front of her, next to a tiny espresso. She stares at me, gives me this hungry look and she doesn't stop even when I look right back at her and make eye contact; she continues to look at me and she then licks her lips, which freaks me out a

lot, and suddenly I can't deal with it at all and when Anthony finally chooses a table, I sit with my back to her. I can still feel her eyes on me and it gets to me more than it should.

6. Our waiter is also dressed in black. He is also cut and dyed to the point of perfection, and his nametag says "Sean." He and Anthony keep trading sneakily meaningful looks and whenever Sean comes past the table he lingers for a few seconds longer than he should. As he is taking our menus away, he touches Anthony's finger with his, and lets it slide all the way up. Anthony does not seem to be bothered by this. I hate to think what kind of history they have, if they know and/or have fucked or if this is just a random event or what, and the possibilities kind of split off from one another like fractals, but I don't want to say anything, mostly because:

   a) Things are going well with Anthony and I don't want to fuck them up.

   b) If I said anything it would probably come out wrong anyway.

7. We're both drinking our long blacks. Mine helps ground me a little, but not a great deal. Anthony and I don't talk. There's a strange, intricate ballet going on with our eyes; he will stare right into mine, hard enough and long

enough that it seems he's trying to see right inside me, and then suddenly he'll look away and stare off into the distance for a while, then back to me, then back out again, etc.

8. Wondering if Anthony likes me as much as I like him.

9. Wondering if it isn't stupid of me to be getting like this over him.

10. Deciding that, yes, it's definitely stupid, but I don't care, because he's so hot and that's all that really matters.

11. Sitting in the passenger seat of his mother's Audi, which is in that big parking lot where we were getting high before, and there's this faux new-wave music on the stereo, a French or possibly Swiss woman moans lyrics about how *everyone wants to be Hollywood* above this loud and sinewy and sexy bass line, and I'm totally lost in Anthony, and he begins to play with the gear stick, moving it around and around, into neutral and back into park, running his fingers around the ball of it and staring straight into me the whole time, and I think I'm blushing but I'm not entirely sure, and I'm only catching vague threads of the conversation we're having, and he asks me if I want to and I ask him do I want to what? and he leans over the shift and kisses me, a cold

afternoon front seat of a very warm expensive car, hope we don't get caught but then again who gives a fuck if we do? kind of a kiss, and the French woman on the stereo is saying that maybe one day I can visit her in her condo *on a big hill, you know, like 90210,* and Anthony reaches over, takes my hand and sets it down on his leg, and I can feel his cock through the fabric of his pants, and I notice it's becoming extremely hard as we sink deeper into the kiss and he pushes me back into the leather seat with as much force as he can and he moans a little and I can feel his hand in the small of my back, and he makes me press down harder on his cock, which elicits a series of incredibly, like, guttural noises from him, and we break the kiss off but I stay close enough to him that we're still breathing on one another, and he's into it, I can tell, but the expression on his face is still a little, like, *other,* like it was at the cafe, and it's like . . .

12. Somehow arriving at the decision that we should drive back to his house and continue getting high, and there's an implicit promise of something else in there, though I couldn't say for sure, but something in the tone of his voice . . . I don't know, but at that point, going back to his house seems like the best

idea in the world. I'm still very high and everything is passing me by in a blur. We're stopped at a set of traffic lights when I suddenly get the urge to lean over and give him this mad/passionate kiss. His hand moves to the small of my back and we sink right into it and we only start moving again when the car behind blows its horn at us.

13. Arriving at Anthony's house in Windsor. Tripping out. Confused. But happy.

205

When we were walking up to Anthony's, I saw his neighbor, a woman, standing in the driveway of a big, new-looking house. Hurrying on the way to something, or maybe back from something. She was wearing a black cocktail dress, stepping out of a sleek four-wheel drive and slipping a high-heeled shoe on her foot. She looked up and saw me; we stared at one another for a second. She had the strangest expression on her face when she saw me; it felt as though there was a connection between us. An "I won't tell anyone if you don't" kind of a connection. We were joined by our secrets, or whatever. I don't know. But it was a very grown-up look she gave me. Sardonic, kind of. Hard to explain, but it made me feel part of something bigger, a secret world of desires and things unspoken.

206

I am now sitting on the floor of the living room; big, and kind of airy, with glass windows that stretch right up to the ceiling. The executive toy is sitting in front of me and for second I'm trancing out on it. Everything in the room is immaculate, sterile almost. There are prints of some kind of Japanese scene hanging by the window. The sofas are huge and white, the kind you'd be afraid to sit on unless they were covered in plastic. Anthony is flopped down on one, his legs crossed underneath him, and giving me this "I want to rip you open" look that is extremely sexy. He tilts his head back, moves it to the side a little, as though he's appraising me.

Certain secret things connect in my mind, and suddenly I'm seeing him as he was in that photo. The one where he's standing on his own, his head cocked to one side and his hands behind his back. The product in his hair, the tightness of the shirt, the expression on his face, was the look just an accident or was it all contrived?

The look in his eyes. I mean, on the surface, it's all "come on, I dare you," really sexy, but there's something underneath that. It's weird. Like the way he's sitting now. That "rip you open" posture; the look in his eyes. Is it real or is it a carefully contrived fake? As far as Anthony goes, is anything real?

This is the time. Now. I have to do it. Ask him.

The photos. All of it.
Hey Anthony?

207

Me: Anthony?
Anthony: Yeah?
Me: I need to . . . Okay. This is going to sound weird.
Anthony: What?

As he's talking he's pulling a pre-rolled joint from his pocket. Lighting it up.

Me: I saw these . . . Like. Okay. You're going to think I'm crazy when I tell you this, but I'm not. I'm being completely serious.
Anthony: What is it?

He takes a huge drag from the joint. Holds it in for a long time, then passes it to me. I take it.

Me: I saw some photos. On this guy's web page.
Anthony: . . . Photos.
Me: Yeah.

I take a drag. Make sure I keep the smoke in for as long as possible, to fortify myself or whatever.

Prepare for what's coming. I hand the joint back to Anthony.

Me: I saw some photos. But the thing is, the guy in them . . . He looked kind of like . . . you.
Anthony: What were they like?
Me: The photos? What did they look like?
Anthony: Yeah. What did they look like?
Me: Normally this would be the part of the conversation where you tell me I'm crazy. Ask me what I'm talking about.
Anthony: Would it help if I did?
Me: I don't know.
Anthony: Seriously. What did they look like?

Anthony takes a drag. He's hot when he's smoking.

Me: I don't know, you were . . . No. It was a guy who *looked* like you . . . Just with this other guy. A couple of other guys.
Anthony: Where did you find it? Where did you see it, I mean.
Me: There's . . . A friend of mine showed me the page. His name's Jeremy.
Anthony: Jeremy, as in . . . ? Wow. Okay.
Me: You know him?

He passes the joint back to me.

Anthony: If it's the same . . . Yeah, look, I know the photos you mean. Fuck. Dude. I can't believe you saw those. Oh wow . . .

Me: So . . . that . . . was you?

Anthony: It was. Fuck. That was such a long time ago. I can't *believe* he put those up on his site.

Me: It wasn't Jeremy's page. It was just some guy's. I guess it must have been the guy who took them.

Anthony: Oh. Right.

Me: Who was he?

Anthony: The guy who took the photos?

Me: Yeah, who was he? Did you know him? Was he just . . . ?

Anthony: Just . . . a friend of Jeremy's.

Me: Why did you? I mean . . . Why did you let yourself . . . ?

Anthony: Calvin . . . Are you okay?

Me: Yeah.

Anthony: You're not acting like you're okay.

Me: I'm . . . Like, I'm just . . . It's just . . . This seems . . . like a really big deal.

Anthony: It's not. Not really.

Me: It doesn't bother you that there are photos of you . . . ?

Anthony: Not really. I don't know.

Me: How did you do it?

Anthony: How did I do it?

Me: I mean, didn't it get to you or anything? Didn't you feel, like, I don't know. Weird or whatever when you were doing it?

Anthony: Not really. Why would I have felt weird?

We have somehow between us smoked the joint right down to the end. I don't recall exactly how this happened. I watch as Anthony puts it out.

Me: The . . . Some of the photos on the page, I mean, some of them weren't just you. Not just you and Jeremy. Some of them had, like . . . *other guys* in them. And they were . . . You . . . Didn't you feel . . . like . . . ? Did you know those guys?

Anthony: No. They were just some friends of . . . Well, whoever. I don't remember his name. The guy who was taking the photos.

Me: So . . . What were you thinking?

Anthony: I wasn't really thinking anything.

Me: You were thinking about nothing at all?

Anthony: I was just thinking it felt good.

Me: It felt good?

Anthony: Calvin, it was just something I did, okay? Just something I did for fun. Because I could do it. You know? I did it because I could.

Me: Because you could? That's the only reason?

Anthony: Calvin, we . . . Well, you have to enjoy it while you can, you know? Being young . . . good-looking. It doesn't last forever. You should have as much fun with it as you can.

Me: I don't get how you could . . .

Anthony: Calvin, fucking . . . It was nothing to me, okay? I did it because it was easy.

Me: How could you not think . . . ?

208

"I want to show you something," he says. There is an edge to his tone, something, I don't know, *weighty.*

"What is it?" I ask.

"Just . . . I don't want to explain it because I'll fuck it up. You need to see it first." He's looking right at me, with that unknowable expression on his face.

"Anthony, you're being weird. Don't."

"Come on," he tells me. He stands, raises an eyebrow in a way that half intriguing, half disturbing. I can't help but follow him; over the course of the day he seems to have become even hotter. I mean, even that conversation we just had, confusing as it was, only made me more attracted to him. I follow him, watch him—the way his hair sort of stands up at the front, the angle of his nose, the impossible way his shirt hangs from his shoulders—and I want him so much it's almost, like, overwhelming.

209

Kind of a sideline issue: It's probably wrong to get so wrapped up in a person's looks, but, like, what else is there really? I think about what he said. About being young and good-looking. Making the most of it. It doesn't last forever. It sort of made sense. Anthony's young and pretty, I'm young and pretty, and maybe nothing really matters beyond that.

210

He leads me into what must be his parents' room. There is a big four-poster bed in there, and the carpet is white, like, immaculate. There is a huge flatscreen TV set at the end of the bed and the room is so perfect it's almost too perfect, and it's virtually impossible to believe that people actually *live* here, that this is where Anthony's parents sleep. The only sign of life in the room is in the corner; there is a shoji screen, one that looks as though it's made out of real silk, and on it, on a coathanger, there is a red dress. A cocktail dress, I guess. It's a burst of violent color, of passion; it looks as though it's a chance happening; its placement there is accidental in a room where everything else is deliberate. Seeing it there makes me feel good; makes me feel as though not everything in here is hostile.

"Sit down" Anthony tells me. "Sit on the bed."

"Anthony, you're being really weird. What is this?"

"Just sit," he tells me. "Please." I've never heard him say please before, and something about it is so sudden, so *strange* that it knocks the defiance right out of me.

I kick off my shoes, sit down cross-legged on the bedspread. For a second I see myself reflected in the screen of the TV set, this blank, twisted, like *other* Calvin; his features are blurry, and his eyes are two infinite black hollows.

Anthony flicks the TV set on and for a second there is nothing but angry static. It startles me, and out of it as I am at this point, it still makes me jump a little. The static shuts off as Anthony slips a videotape into the machine and the screen reverts to black. There's a hissing noise now. Something like a warning. Or whatever. I don't know.

The video begins to play.

211

The videotape: There's static and fuzz for a second, then the picture comes in halfway through a scene. The whole thing is awash with gray, and there are shots of council estates and hospitals and for a second I have no idea what's going on or what it's meant to mean, but eventually, after a few seconds in limbo, I realize it's a documentary. The narrator is a man; he speaks with a foreign accent, it might be German or something, I don't know, I think it's probably German, but his voice is extremely deep and he sounds very serious. It cuts to another shot, inside a nightclub, two boys—one of them highly pierced and both kind of slutty look-ing—are kissing underneath a strobe light, with crunchy nouveau electropop playing on the soundtrack, then the music suddenly stops and it cuts to a shot of this boy who looks to be, I guess, in his early twenties, and he's lying in a hospital bed and I realize that he's sick with something; with what, I can't quite work out, even though I do have very definite suspicions. (I mean . . . What's *everyone* worried about nowadays? Why is it you can't even go out, meet a boy, without this vague worry that the drinks and the pills can never quite push away, this worry that you might be about to . . .) It's still showing the boy in his hospital bed and the narrator is explaining all sorts of AIDS statistics in his deep, solemn voice, then some still photos come up on the screen, one of the boy, the patient (whose name is Benni or something), as a little boy, then one of him with his arm around this other guy, who is poking out his tongue, pierced, at the camera, then back to a shot of Benni in the hospital bed, and he looks incredibly weak, his arms are thin and he's covered in purple blotches, and he's having difficulty speaking, though when he does it's subtitled, obviously, because he doesn't speak English, and the subtitles are this incredibly bright shade of yellow, and Benni is talking about how we live in a world where "even the things you'd never expect can kill you, where you can die from love," and the fact that he's so young and so good-looking, especially in the still photos, and he looks like he could be one of my friends, one of my exes, a guy I've *slept* with, really gets to me, and suddenly the skin on the back of my neck is starting to prickle, then there's a shot of a funeral—I guess it must be Benni's—shots of snow, because it's winter, and crying relatives who are all wearing black, and this extremely mournful string soundtrack, then it cuts back to a scene inside a nightclub, same crunchy electronic music playing, but this time the two boys are different (or they might be the same two boys—it's difficult to tell, but it doesn't matter, because ultimately we're all the same two boys), and the final shot is this grainy shot of Benni as a little boy, walking in the snow, in this hooded parka or whatever, carrying around a huge sled, or I think it's a sled, then looking up at the camera and smiling, this totally innocent smile, and all of this played in slow motion, then finally it fades into the credits, white text on a black screen, silence, and it's like . . .

212

Anthony stops the tape. I look across at him and for a second he says nothing.

Calvin: Oh my god.

Anthony: Mmm.

Calvin: That's really . . . That's . . .

Anthony: You see what I'm getting at?

Calvin: . . . I don't. I really don't. What were you trying to . . . ?

Anthony: Nothing lasts forever.

Calvin: What do you mean?

Anthony: Nothing. I mean . . . Look. One night about a year ago I was up late watching TV. I'd just broken up with this guy and I was in a pretty bad way, and I happened to come across this documentary on SBS. And I stopped it there for a second, mainly because the guy in it was pretty cute, and they were showing all these close-ups of him, like, photos from when he was younger and stuff, then suddenly it cut to that shot of him in a hospital bed.

Calvin: Okay.

Anthony: Then I realized what it was actually about. That the kid was dying of AIDS or whatever. And I mean, it really got to me. I grabbed this videotape and stuck it in there because I felt I just kind of *had* to videotape it so I could see it again, or keep a record of it or something. Because I mean, the kid . . . That Benni kid. He was so cute. Seriously. He could have been me. Or any of my friends. Or even a guy I've dated.

I make this little throat noise at this point. It's not loud, but it's enough for Anthony to look up at me and realize I've made the same connection, and he gives me this strange little smile . . . I guess you'd call it a smile because, in context, I really don't know what else you'd call it.

Anthony: He was only, like, eighteen when it happened, which isn't even that much older than we are.
Calvin: I know what you mean.
Anthony: And it really started to get to me. I mean, really. It got to me that this boy, through no fault of his own, just by living, by going out and partying like we all do, that suddenly he had this death sentence on him. And I was all hung up after that. I mean, you know, if someone as cute as that can be dying, if someone whose only crime was being good-looking, going out and having fun, has to die in such a shitty fucking hospital room like that, then what hope is there for anyone?
Calvin: So why did you . . . ?
Anthony: It got to me, that's all. It made me

think. You might as well live, or whatever. You might as well have fun. I don't know. Fucking . . . I don't know. We're all going to die Calvin. Why shouldn't we have fun while we still can?

Calvin: I understand.

Anthony: Do you?

Calvin: I want to hear you say it. I want to hear someone else say it.

Anthony: Because I want to give myself to as many people as possible before I'm old and ugly and nobody wants me anymore. You know, Calvin, seriously, after a certain point, when we're not as young as this anymore, our lives will pretty much be over. There'll be nothing left. A new group of kids will come up to replace us and that will be that. Is there going to be anything left of us? No. Not even a memory. So why the fuck shouldn't I sleep around? Why shouldn't I have fun while I still can? Because there are guys out there who *want me.* That's power.

213

Hungry: I don't know what this was. Insight into Anthony or something. Some sign of weakness, a crack in the facade. I don't know, but it was enough. I mean, I was thinking about Benni, thinking that, yes, the world was an extremely horrible place and I could totally see Anthony's point, but the whole time I was thinking how incredibly hot I was for Anthony. How wrong is that? We fucked just after that. Desperate. Hungry. Or I was. It felt like Anthony was holding back. I think it did anyway. I'm starting to wonder if I know anything anymore.

It was raining outside the whole time.

214

Cut ahead to Friday night: Cold. Whale are playing on my headphones, and the singer is telling me about her habit of crying at airports. I'm meeting Anthony later, but right now I'm in the city waiting for Margot. She and I haven't been out in ages, like, in *forever*, so we're meeting for sushi. My friends and I always seem to meet for sushi; it's not like it's deliberate or anything, someone always says "let's get sushi" and we all agree.

215

There's this necklace thing that I used to wear around all the time and I thought I'd lost it; it had been gone for,

like, a year or more until the other day when I was digging around in my room and I found it again. Patrick
gave it to me—remember him? This is one of those
things I forgot to mention earlier. It's silver. A chain.
Reminds me of a time when everything was less complicated, which is probably the main reason I'm wearing it.

216

I'm standing by that fountain thing on the mall, arms
crossed. Feeling strange. Kind of edgy. I'm still thinking
about Anthony. Thinking about the two of us last
night. What he said.

> **Anthony:** Because I want to give myself to as
> many people as possible before I'm old and ugly
> and nobody wants me anymore. You know,
> Calvin, seriously, after a certain point, when
> we're not as young as this any more, our lives will
> pretty much be over. There'll be nothing left.

If that's true, then what purpose do either of us
have? Anthony, or me, or Mykal or Jamie, or any of
my friends? Once we're old, once we've outlived our
usefulness, is there going to be anything left of us?

> **Anthony:** Is there going to be anything left
> of us?

217

The Queen Street Mall is full of people:

1. **Boy in a brown corduroy jacket:** With his arm around a girl. They're both carrying books, like they're uni students or something. But he has his arm around her and he's protecting her from the cold.

2. **Girl in an Elmo shirt:** With a belt buckle that looks like it's meant to be a pair of apples or something. I guess she's waiting for someone. Tapping her foot, looks kind of impatient.

3. **Boy in a chef's uniform:** Or what is probably a chef's uniform, hurrying past in the other direction. He is tall and has bleached hair and a nose ring, and I wonder if they mind—wherever he works, I mean—I wonder if they mind about the nose ring.

4. **Woman in a suit:** Who looks like she might be a lawyer or something. Carries herself like a lawyer anyway. She looks kind of like that actress, whoever it is. She's talking to someone on a slim silver mobile which looks exactly like mine. Laughing.

All of these people seem to have a purpose. A reason for doing what they're doing. I don't know if I have a purpose. I don't even care.

218

Purpose: Up to this point in my life and in everything I've done, my only purpose seems to be drifting around picking up random sensory information and occasionally providing pleasure to others. I think that's the main one. Pleasure. I've never done anything worthwhile. Nothing I've done is ever conceivably going to change the world. The only reason I'm here, it seems, is to stand around in clubs and at parties taking drugs and looking attractive. To fuck/be fucked. To take people out of themselves and occasionally take myself out of things in the process. I struggle to think of what meaning there is in any of this. But I can't. I think about it for a long time and I can't come up with anything at all. I'm a cipher. All the boys I've been with I've treated as conduits for fantasies too complex and, ultimately, too boring to explain. They've probably treated me exactly the same way. So maybe *that's* my only purpose. As a cipher for other people's pleasure. I mean . . .

219

I suddenly realize where I am—which is to say, standing in the middle of a crowd—and try to snap myself out of that particular thought process. I only partially succeed. It suddenly seems like everybody is looking at me, and I need to escape, get away from people for a few minutes.

There's a random stupid stuff shop nearby. The kind that sells imported crap that you won't need, ever, but it's all pretty, shiny, you know, distracting, so I head in there. I walk through the shop, searching for something, past a giant teddy bear—it's more of a panda, fat, with huge eyes and a red tongue that sort of pokes out, and it freaks me out, though I really can't say why exactly, so I head for a stack of manga.

I have no idea what I'm doing but I don't really care. I just want to pick up something, to read it, to distract myself. Even if I can't understand it. I pull one at random from the stack. I guess I pick it because the boy on the cover is cute and mysterious looking. I don't know. Whatever.

220

The manga is in Japanese, so it's difficult to work out exactly what's going on. The characters are all these beautiful, angular creatures, too serene/ethereal to be human, but I don't know what else you'd call them. I flip through it, sometimes looking at all the panels on a page, sometimes skipping ahead three or four pages. Just to get a feeling for the story, to work out what's going on.

Panel: The main character is a beautiful, glassy-eyed, spiky-haired boy who I think is meant to he a famous rock singer. He is onstage, pouring his heart into a microphone, performing in some huge auditorium in front of an ocean of people. Floodlit. Spectacular.

Panel: Close-up of some girls in the crowd. Also glassy eyed and spiky-haired, screaming the singer's name, or what I can only assume to be the singer's name—or maybe they're screaming declarations of eternal love or swear words or whatever, I don't know.

Panel: A plain brown envelope slipped under a door. Sealed so you can't see what's in it.

Panel: Close-up of the rock singer boy. Still on stage, but now he is looking down. An unguarded moment. His glassy eyes are watery and he could almost be crying. I don't know what could make someone like this cry, someone too beautiful to even be on earth.

Panel: A whole page—a city skyline at night. Neon, Coca Cola, a blur; a woman's face on a billboard, twisted weirdly out of proportion, although this only makes her more beautiful; a busy street, far below, and towers, and office buildings, and thousands upon thousands upon thousands of lights, disappearing up into the darkness.

Panel: The beautiful rock singer boy standing at a window, looking out at this floating world. He himself is half reflected in the glass, so you almost can't tell which version of him is real.

Panel: Close-up of a bottle of pills sitting on a dresser, next to a bottle of what might be champagne.

Panel: Hotel room. The beautiful rock singer boy is lying dead—or he appears to be dead—on the floor. He is flat on his stomach. You can sort of see his profile. One arm is extended, and a thin strip of leather is tied around his wrist. A charm is attached to the strip of leather. Tiny. Silver. Might even be a raccoon. He is lying in a pool of vomit.

Panel: Paparazzi. Cameras—flash/flash/flash. Close-up of girls in a crowd. Might be the same girls from the auditorium. Might not. Doesn't really matter that much. They are crying. Screaming. In mourning. Everyone is in mourning for the beautiful dead rock singer boy.

Panel: Close-up of another boy. Feathery blond hair. Wide eyes. Nervous/sad/something, it's difficult to say. He is staring off into the middle distance. Impossible to tell what he's thinking.

Panel: Close-up of the blond boy's wrist. There is a thin strip of leather tied around it. A charm attached. Small. Silver. Looks like it might be a raccoon or something.

Panel: A plain brown envelope slipped under a door. Part of the corner is ripped up, almost enough that you can see inside, but . . .

221

That's the last page. It's obviously meant to be continued. I can't see the next issue anywhere and I'm kind of upset, but not really, a) because, courtesy of the language barrier, I wasn't really following the plot anyway, b) because I can now make up my own ending. This fantasy spins off in my head wherein

Anthony—no wait, I am, no Anthony—is beautiful dead rock singer boy, and it's his last performance, and I'm standing backstage watching him, no, wait, I'm discovering his body, maybe I'm the feathery blond boy—yeah, that would work—so I'm the feathery blond boy and I'm discovering dead rock singer/Anthony's body, and discovering the envelope, and it's like . . .

222

Someone taps me on the shoulder.

> **Margot:** Hey Calvin, whatcha doing in here?
> **Me:** Couldn't handle waiting around on the street. It was kind of getting to me.
> **Margot:** Tell me about it. So how are ya?
> **Me:** I'm ail right.
> **Margot:** Porno. Totally. So come on, let's get going. I need some sushi before I, like, fucking *die*.

I'm feeling kind of sick and I don't overly feel like eating anything. Still I say:

> **Me:** Cool. Sushi. Immediately.
> **Margot:** Definitely . . . What's that thing you were reading?

Me: Just this manga I found.

Margot: Cool. The guy in it's pretty cute.

Me: I guess.

Margot: I'd fuck him.

Me: He's a fictional character.

Margot: I'll bet you'd fuck him too.

Me: Probably. Come on, should we go?

Margot: Okay.

223

Margot is making some kind of punk rock fashion statement tonight. She's wearing this polka-dot dress—black on white—and on anyone else it would just look like a polka-dot dress but it fits the curves of her body perfectly and it made her look . . . I don't know, kind of like Siouxsie Sioux if she were younger and a fag hag. Margot also has on about a dozen of these little bracelets with brightly colored beads on them. They're in deep, semitransparent blues and reds and they look almost like candy, almost like you could eat them, which is maybe the intention.

224

On the way to sushi Margot tells me that Mykal and Jamie are meeting us there. I don't want to see them again, though I can't exactly say why.

Maybe it's the thought of Mykal and Anthony. I wonder what Anthony is doing right now. I wonder if it's going to be awkward with Mykal.

I don't communicate any of these things to Margot. On the way to sushi, we are talking:

Margot: No, I didn't see it.

Me: I think it was on a while ago. On SBS or something.

Margot: And it was a documentary?

Me: Yeah.

Margot: What was it about?

Me: AIDS. Like, this boy with AIDS, I mean.

Margot: Oh. Sounds depressing.

Me: It was. I mean, he was so young, and he was pretty cute. But that wasn't even it. It was like . . .

Margot: Where did you see this documentary?

Me: Anthony showed it to me.

Margot: Anthony. As in that guy you were telling me about?

Me: Yeah.

Margot: So . . . why did he show you an AIDS documentary? As, like, a *public service announcement* or something?

225

When we get to the sushi train, Mykal is already waiting for us. He is sitting at a booth near the back, with a half-eaten plate of tempura vegetables in front of him. He looks up; sees the two of us. Smiles.

> **Mykal:** Hey you guys!
> **Me:** Hey Mykal.
> **Margot:** Dude! How was the party the other night? Did you guys end up going?

Mykal laughs. We all sit down.

> **Mykal:** We went . . .
> **Margot:** Yeah, and . . . ?
> **Mykal:** It was fucking *bizarre*. That ex of mine . . . Simon, the doctor. *Total* fucking sleaze. He got us both really drunk and tried to crack onto the two of us. And I was like . . .

At this point we are interrupted as Jamie walks in.

> **Mykal:** Jamie!
> **Margot:** Heey baby!

Jamie walks over. Hugs Mykal, sort of. Doesn't kiss him.

Jamie: Hey guys.
Margot: *Love* the shirt.

Jamie is wearing this faux-cowboy shirt with red checks on it.

Jamie: Thanks. You like it?
Mykal: Totally.
Jamie: Urbane cowboy.

We all laugh, but I'm suddenly thinking about something else.

226

Home, home on the range: I only think of it now because of the way Jamie is dressed. A cowboy shirt, with red checks and little pearl buttons. I've seen them around, in the Valley; the shirts, I mean. "Urbane cowboy," the kind of off the cuff remark that it probably took him all day to come up with. Before Jamie sits down, Mykal lands this very aggressive kiss right on his lips. People are looking at them but it doesn't seem as though they could care less. The two disentangle.

Mykal asks Jamie if they're going out tonight and Jamie says he has a plan, and

Jamie asks Mykal if he has anything, and Mykal says of course he does, and I know that in about four hours both of them will be tripping out of their minds, and by the end of the night they'll probably be tearing one another to shreds before they even make it back to whoever's house they go to. The thought of that worries me a lot.

Worries me because despite how vulnerable and I guess boyish they both look, what's underneath is quite different: boys who can *deal with* taking eccies and dancing all night, who've been with lots of guys between them, felt strange hands all over their bodies; although they're so young, they've somehow had the kind of lives that have equipped them to deal with all of this.

I used to have a cowboy shirt like Jamie's, when I was a kid. Like, even down to the little pearl buttons, although mine had a little horse, though I guess you'd call it a pony or whatever, sewn onto the front pocket. I used to wear it all the time and my parents used to sing that song, "Home on the Range." Where the deer and the antelope play. Where seldom is heard a discouraging word and the sky is not cloudy all day. That one. They used to sing it to me all the time. It used to make me happy. I remember a time when it only took something like that to make me happy. The memory of it, in all its retrospective perfection, washes over me and for a second I can't breathe, can't stay balanced. Six years old. It was only ten years ago but it seems a lot longer. Like, way longer. I look at Jamie to see if there's a little pony sewn onto the pocket of his shirt. There isn't, and that somehow calms me down.

227

Mykal: . . . and she *almost* would have gone home with him again, just, like, out of *boredom,* but she came to her senses and thought, you know, it's not worth it.

I have been at the fridge in the corner getting myself one of those energy drinks—the ones that taste *green* and have about six billion units of caffeine in them—and I come back to the counter just in time to catch the tail end of this particular conversation.

Jamie: Totally. The guy was a *sleaze.*

Margot takes a plate of California rolls from the sushi train. Mykal turns to look at me.

Mykal: So Calvin, are you still seeing that guy? What was his name . . . ?

Oh yeah. Sorry Mykal. Like, you *totally* wouldn't remember.

Me: Anthony. And yeah, I am. I'm seeing him tonight.
Mykal: Oh, cool. How's that working out?
Me: Pretty well.

228

The conversation drags on for about half an hour longer, mostly about uninteresting stuff. As we're standing outside and we're all about to go our separate ways, I realize something that really bothers me.

I'm looking at Mykal and Jamie. They're standing very close; every now and then one will look across at the other and they will smile, both of them. In spite of their tough/sarcastic exteriors, you can tell that they really . . . you know . . . *like* one another. They've both been sluts in the past and they're probably still sluts, but they probably *will* be together this time next month/year. Mykal and Jamie have the closest thing to a functional relationship I've seen in a long time. That really gets to me.

229

Margot and I walk to the Valley after that. We're making small talk about music—which member of the Strokes is the most attractive, that kind of stuff—and this new French movie that's just come out and the government are trying to ban, and, you know, the usual boring stuff, and that's when I get the urge to tell her about Anthony. Like, maybe if I talk about this with another person then that will make it real. I don't know. But anyway:

230

Me: I saw these . . . photos of him.
Margot: Where?
Me: On the net.
Margot: On the net? Doing what?
Me: Well, like, what do people . . . What are young guys usually doing when photos of them show up on the net?
Margot: Nofuckingway . . . Are you serious?
Me: Yeah. Totally.
Margot: And you're . . . *Going out* with this person?

Me: I don't know if we're going out or not. It's weird.

Margot: Okay, yeah, but my point remains. You're, like, *seeing* this person . . . this *porn* person. From the *net*.

Me: I guess.

Margot: How . . . I mean, what were they like?

Me: The photos?

Margot: Yeah.

Me: I don't know. Just Anthony and this other guy.

Margot: Doing . . . ?

Me: You know.

Margot: Oh wow. I mean . . . Isn't it weird?

Me: What weird?

Margot: Going out with him . . . After you've seen him . . . Like . . .

Me: Not really.

Margot: I mean, you don't know how many other people have seen these photos. It could be hundreds. Thousands.

Me: I didn't know it was him at first. I mean, I met him at that party and I wasn't really sure, but I . . .

Margot: It's weird, isn't it?

Me: Me seeing him?

Margot: No, the whole situation. I mean, you

think of . . . You see photos on the internet or wherever. Sex photos, and you never think of those people as being real, do you? I mean, you don't think of them as existing in any context outside of, you know, the photos, I guess.

Me: That's what I thought.

Margot: It's so weird. I mean, to think that the people in porn have lives outside of it. That they're just, you know, normal people. Walking around.

Me: It's the age of the internet. Anyone can be a porn star.

Margot: I guess.

Margot laughs. Leans across to tickle my cheek.

Margot: *You* could be a porn star.

I hesitate.

Me: No way.

Margot: You could. You totally could. Calvin the porn star! Calvin the double penetration slut!

Margot's laughing very hard now.

Me: Stop it. Come on, seriously, it's not fuck-ing funny.

Margot: Ahh, you're sensitive, Calvin. I wouldn't get so upset. Hell. I think *I'd* make a great porn star.

Me: The best.

Margot: Thanks.

Me: Anytime.

Margot: . . . So what's he like?

Me: Anthony?

Margot: Yeah.

Me: . . . I don't know.

Margot: You don't know?

Me: Not really. He hasn't told me anything about himself. He doesn't give anything away. It's hard to even know who he is. Whenever we're together, all we do is . . .

I freeze, because in this context, I suddenly find it impossible to say the word "fuck." I don't know why. Weird.

Me: I mean, it's like we've only known each other one night. Still. It's like he doesn't *want* to get more involved than that.

Margot: Doesn't that bother you?

Me: Yeah, but what am I supposed to do about it?

Margot: Fuck.
Me: Exactly.
Margot: . . . Porno.
Me: Totally.

231

Words: There is no word for Anthony. He's a gap in the English language. Margot picked "porn star" because that's the most convenient reference point, but it doesn't really describe him. Anthony is just a screwed-up teenage guy who let himself be photographed with other screwed-up teenage guys. I guess his situation is not really unique. But there's no word to describe it. And if it can't be described, then how can it be understood, or tied down?

232

I'm meeting Anthony in front of Ric's Café at nine-thirty. He's ten minutes late. I've been standing here for a long time; I suddenly get the feeling that he might be approaching, just a feeling, so I turn around, but instead the person coming towards me is a boy/girl with long black hair and too much make-up, wearing one of those "Fuck Me I'm Famous" shirts, and he/she, seeing the look on my face, sashays up to me swinging his/her hips and kind of sizes me up for a second before he/she says something I can't make out, and when I fail to respond, he/she blows smoke in my face and then walks off. It's the Valley. You know. Whatever.

Anthony arrives fifteen minutes late, and he doesn't apologize, but I don't care. As usual he is the very definition of "young and hot" and as usual he is completely blank. We kiss once. Hard. We're getting looks from the people around us but I don't care. I don't really know if I care about anything at all except for Anthony.

233

We're at The Beat again. Sitting out on the terrace. It's dark and noisy and there are lots of guys around us, and one of the bartenders was checking Anthony out before and Anthony didn't respond, didn't seem to care, which I took to be a good sign, except for the fact that Anthony doesn't seem to care about anything tonight. He's kind of, I don't know, *out of it* or whatever. He's slumped on his chair with a vodka tonic in front of him. He's not really drinking it. He's not really making eye contact with me.

I'm drunk already. I can feel the pull from the music inside.

female voice: love you/love you/love you/
love you

I want to go in there and dance. Not even dance. I just want to stand on the dance floor and feel the people in there moving around me. Absorb some of their heat, or energy, or, like, youthful abandon or whatever. Try and feel more . . . alive.

I look directly at Anthony. He seems to be staring off into space.

Me: You want to go in and dance?
Anthony: Not really.
Me: Come on, why not?
Anthony: Fucking . . . I don't know. I just don't. Get over it.
Me: What do you want to do?
Anthony: I don't know.

He pauses, for effect or whatever. I know what's coming.

Anthony: I wish we had some weed.
Me: I guess.
Anthony: I have some at my house.

I know what this means by now. Anthony's "I have some at my house" generally means "I'm bored and I want to fuck you and I know you're going to let me so why bother with the pretense?".

234

My reaction is divided. Anthony knows he can have me whenever he wants me. Part of me resents that. Part of me doesn't care. Fuck it. He's really hot.

> **Me:** Okay. Your house.
> **Anthony:** Good.

Good. That kills me. Oh well. Whatever. Porno.

235

Cut to Anthony's house. Living room. I am lying on the couch—white, expensive, impeccable—and he is sitting on the floor nearby, holding the control pad and staring up at the tv. The room is dark except for the glow of the screen, which casts this ghostly kind of light on Anthony's face as he stares up at it. The central character of the game is a skater—he's tall, with short darkish hair and this blank but weirdly inviting look on his face. Actually very realistic looking. I'd fuck him; if he were a real person I mean. You know. Basically, the idea is to maneuver him around a series of jumps, sliding down these rails and staircases, and, well, you probably understand. It's pointless but compelling. The way a lot of things are.

Anthony's arms and his body move every now and then; occasionally, if he makes a mistake or the character falls off his board, a small spasm will run through him and he'll grimace a little, but his eyes remain still, focused on the screen. Anthony watches the skater and I watch Anthony and we're both sort of drifting, I think, and it stays this way for an indeterminate length of time.

Finally, he speaks.

"Do you want to pretend we're not ourselves anymore?"

"What?" I ask him.

He doesn't look up from the screen. "Do you want to pretend we're not ourselves? Like, we're both different people, or we're not even people anymore? Like we're characters in a movie or this game or something."

I don't know what this means. It gives me a feeling of unease. I wish he'd look at me but he doesn't. He barely even moves.

"Continue," I tell him.

"What I mean is, wouldn't you like it if we could strip away all the stuff that makes up 'us'? If we could just get rid of it, forget about it."

I sit up. "Are you aware of how stoned you sound?"

"I guess. But do you understand me?" His body shifts a little; the character on the screen is in the midst of an extremely complicated jump. Anthony remains focused on that for a second, and when it's finished, he keeps talking. "Wouldn't you be happier if you didn't have to be you? Would you rather be 'Calvin,' as in, like, an accumulation of all the meaningless detail that makes up who you are, or would you rather just shed that stuff? Get rid of it?" He still hasn't looked away from the screen.

I'm struggling to follow, but . . .
He continues. "When we're together, like, in bed, we wouldn't have to be Tony and Calvin anymore. We could just be, like, two bodies. I mean, if we could just forget who we are and lose ourselves in the moment, we wouldn't have any kind of, like, guilt or conscience attached. We could go totally crazy on one another."

"Why would we . . . ?"

The character is advancing to the next level. Anthony keeps the control pad in one hand and rubs his eyes with the other. "It's better. I think that's the ultimate goal of, you know, sex. To forget who you are. Totally. To leave yourself behind. Because otherwise it can break you."

"What can?"

The next level loads. He's maneuvering the skater around a more difficult course now. It's this kind of wasteland, industrial desolation. Dead grass and concrete walls that are alive with graffiti, an overcast sky, random pieces of rusted metal jutting upwards at crazy angles, and all of it rendered in seamless polygon graphics.

"It's hard to explain," Anthony says.

I'm silent.

236

Anthony: I realized it with the first guy I ever slept with. Back when I was fourteen and I was really *really* stoned, drunk, and just generally, like . . . I didn't know him at all. I mean, it's hard to explain. Not really that hard. I hadn't been stoned much before and it was still kind of a new experience, you know. I'd been over at some girl's house, I think she liked me, I don't know, some private school girl I knew through one of my dad's friends, and we were sitting in her room that afternoon and she kept sort of pressing up close to me, trying to kiss me or whatever, and I just totally wasn't into it, and eventually she told me she had some pot, which seemed like a really big, exciting thing at the time, like something really bad, so we smoked it and suddenly I was all relaxed, and I just thought, okay, why not?

The character on the screen falls off his skateboard. Anthony flinches, taps the control pad as he waits for the level to reload. The whole time, his eyes never leave the screen.

Anthony: You know, it wasn't bad, it was pretty good, but it felt kind of weird afterwards, you know, because it was my first time with a girl and I knew it was probably going to be the last. But then we smoked some more, a lot more, and it was pretty late so we went downstairs and she asked her mum if she could drop me off in the city, and I remember wondering if her mum could, like, smell it on us, smell weed or sex or whatever, or if she was, you know, wondering what had been going on, but she seemed distracted, or out of it maybe, or something, and she said sure, and we're in her BMW and suddenly we're in the city, and Francesca— that was the girl—sort of kisses me goodbye, and I'm there all by myself, and I don't really feel like going home so I call my friends to see a movie or something and that's when it happened. I was waiting in front of the Hilton, looking at the people who are walking past, waiting for my friends to show, still really stoned and feeling kind of jittery or whatever, you know, and anyway, there was a guy sitting at one of those cafes nearby, like an older guy, sitting by himself, and he was dressed in a suit, and I mean, it was a *really* nice suit, and I was just standing there waiting for my friends and he kept looking over at me, like he was cruising me or something, I mean, you know what it's like, everyone's had it happen, and I didn't really look back at him, but I didn't really move either, and the old guy kept looking over at me, and eventually, like by accident, we made eye contact, and he stared at me for a really long time, and I kept staring back and he kind of touched his wallet, which was sitting there on the table and I was just kind of lost in the look he was giving me and I couldn't quite believe what was happening, like if it was real, or I was imagining it, but . . .

Suddenly he's concentrating hard on the screen as the guy on the skateboard gets entangled in a difficult jump. He spins around, once, twice in the air, makes a perfect landing, keeps going. If Anthony's pleased or impressed, or, like, moved at all by this, he doesn't let on. His concentration on the screen is more intense than ever.

Anthony: . . . but I wanted to go along with it just to see what would happen, so I kind of nodded at him, I mean, I don't know if I nodded or not, but the next minute he's motioning me over to the table, like he wants me to join him or something, so I went over there, sort of cautious, slow, and he's looking at me the whole time and he's not exactly smiling but he's just sort of, like, hungry, and it's a look I'd never seen on anyone's face before, and I sit, and he doesn't even move, just looks at me, and I don't know whether to be scared or not, and he speaks and he has a foreign accent, German, I think, and he asks me my name, and I tell him Anthony—I mean, I could have lied, made something up, but at the time I couldn't, I mean I didn't know what was happening, I was so freaked out, confused, I didn't have it in me to lie—and he asks me my interests, and I sort of rattle them off, I mean, I don't remember what I said, and he's listening with this look on his face like he's really interested in the things I like, then when I'm finished he asks me if I'd like to make some money, and I don't know why I said it, I mean, I think a part of me just *wanted* to do it, wanted to know what it was like, what it felt like, because it seemed so dangerous, like, the most dangerous thing in the world, and if I did it I'd have something on everyone else, I'd have, like, done the ultimate, I'd have fucked someone, a guy—a man—because at the time that seemed like such a big deal, that I'd be capable of doing something like that, so I asked him how much money, and he told me four hundred dollars, and I thought, you know, I didn't know what to think, and I asked him what I had to do and he said nothing you don't want to, and I was so stoned it was kind of a blur after that, but he told me if I wanted to I could come up to his room with him, and I told him okay, because, well, I wanted to know what it would feel like, I really wanted

to know, that was all at that stage, so I followed him, he stands up from the table,
leaves, like, a *fifty* lying under the ashtray
even though he'd only been drinking this
one cup of coffee, and he doesn't say anything, just walks towards the hotel, and I follow him, and we're both in the elevator, and
it's cool in the air conditioning but I remember I'm feeling really hot all over, and it
wasn't just the pot anymore, it was the feeling that this was really happening, that I
couldn't turn back, and that I liked it . . .

He finishes the level, slumps back, breathes a sigh of
relief. Then he looks up at me for about an eighth of a
second. The expression on his face is indecipherable. I
don't say anything. The next level is in the process of
loading, and Anthony turns back to the screen. I'm not
sure what that moment was about. Was he sizing me
up? Did he want to know what I thought? My mind is
racing through the possibilities, but I'm too stunned to
construct a rational opinion of anything at this point.
His attention is on the screen again. The next level
begins. He continues.

Anthony: . . . So he was standing there looking down at me, and I remember thinking
how handsome he looked, how normal, like

someone's father or something, like my own father even, and we're up very high all of a sudden and he's unlocking the door to his room, and I've stayed in hotels with my parents heaps of times before and it's just like that, that feeling, but it's not, and we're in his room, which is bigger than any of the hotel rooms I've been in before, and there's a smell in there, new car smell, you know, clean like the kind of smell that's meant to make you feel safe and comfortable, which is funny, and I can see the view, the city, all the lights and whatever, and he tells me to sit down on the bed, asks me if I want a drink or something, and he pours me one anyway, I can't see what but when he hands it to me it's vodka, and it's really good vodka, and I just sort of down it, and he touches the back of my neck, asks me if I want to take off my shirt for him, so I tell him yeah, okay, and I sort of slip it off and he stands there looking at me, like, amazed, and touching me, my body, and saying, "Look at your chest . . . your young chest" and it sounds weird with the accent and whatever, but he kisses my chest, then he gets up to pour me another drink and it's more vodka and I drink it and I start to feel really weird, I mean, because I was stoned anyway and now I'm drunk too and he asks me if I'll take off my shoes—if I want to is what he actually says, I mean, it's like, do you want to do this or that or whatever, like it's something I've chosen to do, because I mean, I've followed him up there, he didn't force me, so I slip them off and he, like, picks one of them up and he's sniffing it or whatever, and it's kind of funny, I mean, if you think above it, and then he asks me if I want to take off my pants and I don't know if I should but the vodka's really starting to kick in, really sudden, and I take them off, because it feels like there's nothing else I can do, and I slide out of them, and he's still fully dressed, like in his tie and everything, and I'm feeling really blurry by this point, like I'm really out of it, sort of swaying on the bed, and he starts touching me all over, like, kissing me and whatever, and his face is rough, and he just keeps saying, "Such a perfect young body . . . a young . . . young body . . . so perfect" and it was freaking me out a bit but thanks to the pot and the vodka I was kind of into it, I mean, I probably would have been into anything, and I'm still in my socks, which seems kind of weird to me, but anyway, he comes forward and slips my boxers off, and he's rubbing himself against me and everything, touching me, and I'm suddenly hard, like, almost against my will, and then he asks if he can suck me off—that's exactly the way he puts it—and he's almost begging, and like, what else am I supposed to say? so I let him, I mean, he gets down on his knees and makes this big ceremony of it, like, he takes my cock in his hands and kind of feels it for a while, kissing it, and it feels pretty good; he's just kind of licking it at first, like these doggy licks or whatever, slurping at it, and then he sort of moves further down onto it and starts sucking me off really hard, like, he's totally into it and he's using a lot of tongue, like, sucking it and I mean, he's growling, it's like these animal noises he's making, and he's digging his fingers into my back and it kind of hurts but at the same time it feels good because he's sucking me off, and I have no idea how long it goes on for because I'm really drunk at this point and sort of drifting away, but I remember thinking, I'm just about to cum and should I warn him or something . . . I'm sure you know what I mean, Calvin . . .

He breaks his concentration on the screen, flashes me this look—quickly, like we're in the middle of a shared secret or something—and then he returns to the game.

Anthony: . . . And I make this noise, but he starts sucking harder and he won't stop and then I cum, like, really hard, into his mouth and he moans like he's so grateful and he's licking it all off and saying, like, thank you, thank you, and I don't even know how to deal with it, because this is the second time I've ever been sucked off by anyone, and I'm feeling really hot and flushed and I start to realize what I'm doing—like, my cock has just been, *inside* this guy's fucking *mouth*— but I have no control over it now and he asks me if I want to lie down on the bed, and I do, because I mean, I actually do, I just want to curl up and go to sleep or something, like really, and I kind of take my time because I'm pretty nervous, even though the vodka and the pot are starting to erase all that, but I lie down for him, and I still have my socks on, which seems really weird to me, and I can hear him saying over and over, "Such a perfect young body . . . such a young body" and I can't see what he's doing anymore, but then I can feel him, like this weight on the bed, either side of me, and I feel his hands on me, and I feel him putting this lube on and then, all of a sudden he sticks it in me, and it's kind of unexpected and it really hurts, and I have to bite my lip to keep from shouting or something, but I think I start to cry at this point, and then he starts fucking me, like, really hard, and it hurts and I want him to stop, and that's when it happens, I mean, that's when I become someone else. I couldn't deal with what was happening as "Anthony," I mean, it was all too much, so I let that part of me go, and "Anthony" just kind of ceased to be there, like, my personality, my worries, conscience, all that stuff was just, like, gone, and I was just a body on the bed with this old guy on top of me, fucking me and breathing, like, these noises, and it wasn't even bothering me because I wasn't there, I was gone, and that's what I mean Calvin. That's why it's better not to be there. Because it can break you. Sex can break you. That's what I realized, but if you take yourself out of the equation, if you're not there anymore, then suddenly it's no big deal. That's all you have to do, take yourself out of the equation. You just think to yourself: I'm young, I'm good-looking, someone wants me, and that's all that matters. And it is. And the man keeps going, but it's fine, because I realize I don't feel anything anymore. Not a thing. I'm lost in the moment, just a physical presence, and it's fine. And he goes on fucking me forever, and when he's done, it really hurts really, a lot, even through all the drugs it's this incredible kind of pain, and he lies next to me for a while, asks me if I want another drink, and I tell him okay, then I see him disappear, like, into the shower I guess, and I look over and see he's left these fifties on the nightstand. Crisp ones. There are nine of them. Four hundred and fifty. And I left. I couldn't stay around, but that was the night I realized . . . that's all you have to do. Take yourself out of the equation.

When he doesn't talk for a while, I realize the story is finished. I'm silent. He doesn't look up from the screen.

237

A very long time has passed. I don't know how long.

I don't know whether I'm shocked or not. It's difficult to adequately describe my reaction. I look over at Anthony again, to see if he's moved, to see if there's any hint of an expression on his face. I'm thinking, as I look across at him, so maybe that's Anthony. We all have something horrible we carry around inside us. The story he's just told me, that's the thing he's been carrying around inside of him.

238

Me: That's really . . . Oh my god.

Anthony: I don't know. It's not really anything.

Me: Is that how you do it?

Anthony: How I do what?

Me: Take yourself . . . Like you were saying. Make yourself disappear. Take yourself out of the equation.

Anthony: That's what I said.

Me: Is that how you did it? I mean, when that guy . . . When he took those photos of you, is that what you did? Is that what you were thinking? Take yourself out of the equation?

Anthony: I don't know. I wasn't thinking very much.

Me: I want to know . . . I don't . . . I mean . . .

Anthony: What?

Me: I don't understand. How you can "take yourself out of the equation." You must have . . . You must have *felt* something.

Anthony: I don't know. It didn't feel like anything.

Me: I can't understand that . . . That it didn't feel like anything. You must have . . .

Anthony: I didn't.

Me: How can that . . .

Anthony: I don't know. I . . . Fucking . . . It was just something I did.

Me: Can we . . . ?

Anthony: Calvin, I don't feel like talking about this any more.

Me: What do you . . . ?

Anthony: I don't. Look. Are we going to fuck now or what?

Me: I guess.

Anthony: Thank god.

239

Out of the equation. Something larger and scarier than I'm capable of understanding.

240

Dream: A room. Huge, it seems to stretch on farther than I can see, but there don't seem to be any exits. This doesn't really bother me.

Blue lightbulbs. At the very center I can see tiny points of red. Blue light. Fills the room. Anthony is there. Or maybe it's me and I look like Anthony. Maybe Anthony looks like me. Maybe it's someone else. It probably doesn't matter who it is. We all start to look the same after a while. All I'm really interested in is the lightbulbs. Blue. Red.

241

Saturday morning. Early. Overcast. I'm meeting Anthony in the Valley today. He wants to go shopping for a shirt or something. Told me I should meet him in there, that we'd have coffee or something, just hang out.

Out of the equation.

I'm standing at the kitchen counter, fuzzy and incoherent. Coffee's in the pot. Black. I want strong black coffee this morning. The coffee machine matches all the other appliances. Everything matches everything else. Everything is blank and sterile. Trendily vacant. Empty spaces.

242

The only points of color in the kitchen are:

1. A vase, glass, which sits by the window. There are two flowers in it. They're both red, and their stems are crossed over, pointing in opposite directions. That vase always has two flowers in it. Different flowers, of course, and usually different colors, but ever since I can remember, that vase has been sitting near the window, and always with two flowers in it. In the morning the water breaks up the light and you can see the patterns it makes on the far wall. This morning, though, it's too gray for any light to be refracted through it.

2. A Polaroid on the fridge, stuck there with a magnet. It shows the three of us in New York. I look really young, though the trip was barely two years ago. I'm smiling. Mum has her sunglasses on. Dad's looking out of the shot. I don't know what he's looking at. We're at the World Trade Center, which is really weird when you think about it. To think that it's not there anymore, I mean. Maybe if we'd known it was going to be destroyed we would have taken more photos. Maybe we wouldn't have taken any at all. I don't know.

3. A copy of French *Vogue* sitting on the counter. Mum doesn't speak French but I suppose that's beside the point.

243

My bare feet are cold on the tiles. I pour myself a cup of coffee, but by the time I get to the counter, I don't feel like drinking it. I'm in a weird kind of limbo. I don't know *what* I feel like.

Mum is sitting close by, looks as though she's reading. There is a glass of what looks like orange juice on the bench in front of her, but it doesn't look as though she has drunk any of it. She looks up at me. "Black coffee," she says. Smiles. "Calvin. At your age." I try to smile back at her and I think I succeed.

I'm really into dealing with the real world this morning.

Mum asks me if I feel like anything for breakfast, and I tell her I don't. She tells me that I'm starting to look too thin. I don't say anything. I think maybe I am, but I *like* being too thin. It makes me, I don't know, cuter, or more unique or something.

244

I sit at the counter, slick, vaguely interested, through the French *Vogue.* There is a boy standing in a tunnel. A model. I guess he's a model. He seems to have the attitude down anyway. His black sweater is ripped, and there is a jacket tied around his waist. He's wearing what look like bondage trousers, his hands behind his back, and I suppose he fits the criteria of good-looking, full lips and an attractively disproportionate nose, but expressionwise, he's a total blank. It's impossible to know what he's thinking, if he's thinking anything much at all. I guess when you're that good-looking and you're being photographed for French *Vogue,* you don't have to worry too much about details like that.

I wonder if this boy is still in the equation. Maybe he's not. Maybe that's the preferable option. If I stare at the boy, blur my eyes and then unfocus them a little, I can see Anthony in his place.

245

Dad comes into the kitchen, fully dressed. Clean blue shirt and a tie I think I may have given him several birthdays ago. He sees me and pats me on the back, pours himself a coffee and asks me if I have any plans for today.

I tell him I'm meeting a friend in the Valley, for coffee or something.

He tells me he's going into the city this morning, that he has to go to the Mater. Some work thing. Dad's always vague about his work. But he asks me if I want a lift into the city with him.

I hesitate. I can already hear the conversation, and it's already bugging me. I suspect he's going to want to talk, about me, about how things are at school, my future, whether there's anyone special—any special *girl*—and I don't know what I'll say to him. I'm not really prepared to answer those questions. But then I think of getting the bus into the city and the idea of that is something I totally can't deal with. Dad's Saab is comfortable. Leather seats. I can pretend to be asleep, or at the very least turn the stereo up to nip any attempts at serious conversation in the bud.

It's not that I don't want to talk to Dad. I can't tell him the truth and I don't particularly want to lie, so we always end up in awkward silences. But he'll give me a lift to the city. Comfortable seats. Nice stereo. I guess it's going to be fairly painless.

246

My dad's Saab. City in the distance. Heavy traffic.

> **My Father:** It's been a while . . . since we've had a chance to talk.
> **Me:** I guess.
> **My Father:** Just the two of us.
> **Me:** It's been a while.
> **My Father:** So . . . What's new in the world?
> **Me:** I don't know. Not a lot.
> **My Father:** School?
> **Me:** It's okay.

My Father: What are you studying this semester?

Me: I don't know. Stuff.

My Father: What kind of stuff?

Me: I don't know. Physics. Fluid dynamics. Fellatio. (I say this under my breath).

Beat of silence.

My Father: *Hamlet*?

Me: Yeah, that's the one.

My Father: What do you think of it? Of *Hamlet*? What do you think?

Me: I don't know. It's okay.

My Father: It's *okay*? It's a classic.

Me: It's great.

My dad decides to abandon this line of questioning and goes in search of another. He reaches down; fumbles around with some CD cases in the side pocket. Picks one and slips it into the machine. Vivaldi's *Four Seasons* fills the car.

My Father: Remember you used to play the violin?

Me: Yeah.

My Father: You used to play this. I remember . . .

Me: "Spring."

My Father: Pardon?

Me: The movement. That I used to play. It was "Spring."

My Father: That's right. Wow. That was a long time ago. Do you still play your violin?

Me: I guess.

My Father: I haven't heard you play it in a long time.

Me: I don't really play it that much.

My Father: You were good.

Me: I guess.

My Father: Your teacher always used to say you could have played professionally.

Me: I don't know.

My Father: You could. If you'd practiced.

Me: I used to practice.

My Father: You . . .

Dad can sense that this is getting him nowhere. He's silent again. I hate that I'm doing this to him. He's making an effort. He really is. I don't know why I'm behaving this way. Spoiled brat is as spoiled brat does, I guess.

My Father: What *do* you want to do?

I know exactly where he's going with this. I wish he wouldn't. I wish he'd change the subject. I wish he'd crash the car right now or a four-wheel drive would plow into us and kill us both so I won't have to answer that question. I'm serious. I'm not even kidding.

Me: What do you mean?
My Father: After you leave school. Do you have a plan?
Me: I don't know. Not specifically. Nothing yet. I'm thinking about it.
My Father: You're thinking about it.
Me: I really am.
My Father: You need to have a plan, Calvin. Life's not going to wait until you're ready. I mean, if you don't step up and take your place in the world, there's always someone waiting in the line behind you and that person's only too eager to take it for you.
Me: I know, Dad.
My Father: You have to start planning for your future. You need to start now. I mean . . . I mean, where do you see, yourself, say, ten years from now?

I don't know. Death. Gaping void. All of the above. I wish I wasn't in one of these moods.

Me: I don't know, Dad.
My Father: You need to have a plan. You

need a *direction.* What are you thinking about? For university? What do you *enjoy*?

Can I do a BA maybe? Double major in spliff-toking and oral sex? Media production: gay porn; several units dealing with obsessional neurosis.

Me: I don't know. I . . . Seriously . . . University's a long way off.
My Father: It's never too early. To start thinking about these things, I mean. You have to consider making a future for yourself.
Me: I know.
My Father: Think of it as . . . I mean. Your brother never had a chance at a future. Think of your future as though you're doing it for him.
Me: Don't bring Jonathan into this, Dad.
My Father: I'm sorry.
Me: Doesn't matter.
My Father: Have a think about it?
Me: I will.
My Father: Will you?
Me: I absolutely will.

Silence in the car for a few minutes. The future. Whatever. Maybe I'll write a novel or something, although thanks to all the drugs it probably won't make any sense.

My Father: So who are you meeting today?

Me: Just a friend.

I stumble over Anthony's name and I almost don't say it, but then I realize I can't be bothered to lie, because whether or not I'm meeting a "friend" called Anthony, Dad won't really care. He'll probably forget about it straightaway. It won't matter. It won't be important. I don't lie.

Me: Anthony. My friend Anthony.

My Father: . . . Anthony.

Dad coughs.

My Father: I don't think I've met this Anthony. Is he a friend from school?

Me: Just from around.

My Father: Oh. That's good. It's good you're making friends.

Me: Thanks.

My Father: Calvin. Is there anything you want to . . . ?

Me: Anything I want to . . . ?

My Father: Never mind.

Me: What was it?

My Father: Don't worry about it. Do you have enough money for today?

Me: I'm good.

My Father: Would you like me to give you twenty?

Me: I'm good.

My Father: Just twenty. Come on. I'm sure you can use it.

He fumbles around in his pocket. Pulls out his wallet while he's still driving. Fishes around in there for the money I don't particularly want.

Me: Dad, don't worry about it. I don't need it.

My Father: Here, take it. It's just twenty.

Me: I'm fine Dad.

He takes my hand. Lays the money in there and then closes my fingers around it.

I'm thinking: *Out of the equation.*

247

Street press magazine: There are some newspapers piled up by the door of a cafe, several of them promoting the underground music scene, several about the local dance culture, one or two gay magazines. I always find it easy to distract myself with the lurid, bite-size pieces of information you find in those street-press magazines. Waiting for Anthony, I need some kind of distraction. I pick up one of the gay ones, purely because the boy on the cover has something vaguely compelling about him, or maybe he looks like someone I've slept with. Admittedly this possibility is fairly remote, but you know, taking into account the six degrees theory, trace it back one or two steps.

The boys who are draped all over the pages and each other are different in appearance, but they all have the same sad, faraway and drugged-up look in their eyes. One advertisement in particular: a quarter page promoting some new website. The ad itself is innocuous enough: small white print on a black background. "Sick Puppies," it says, along with the address of a website. It promises "All Hardcore Kid's . . ."—it makes sense that whoever is responsible for this would have a shitty grasp of basic grammar—". . . and Young Stud Action." All of this in plain black and white, and a photograph of a boy down the bottom. Not really a boy, just a chest and a pair of shoulders, a face in three-quarter profile. Looking off to the side; that terrible kind of defeated look about him, a smile you can tell is intended to hide something, his eyes so dark they seem almost smudges of pure black.

Just like it was with that model in French *Vogue*. I unfocus my eyes, blur them a little, and suddenly I'm looking at Anthony.

Sick Puppies.

All Hardcore Kids.
Out of the equation.
It's suddenly way more than I can deal with.
How does it feel to lose yourself?

248

He looks . . . studied. He's doing whatever he can to maintain that cool/aloof poseur air. And I guess it's working. He sees me but doesn't approach. Waits for me to approach him. We don't kiss cuz we're standing right there on the street but I can totally tell he wants to. Or maybe I want him to want to and some of that is transferring across to him, or my perception of him, or . . .

Up close, I notice that Anthony is wearing a tiny silver cross. I wonder what this could mean. Probably means nothing. Anyway, who cares; Catholic boys are the coolest.

249

A familiar house anthem is playing on the stereo, playing in all corners of the cafe. A man's voice, high and androgynous, put through a computer and digitally edited; thumping, cold and beautiful beats. Anonymous. Icy. This one sample that fades in and out, the singer talking about what he'd do if he had another chance.

We're in one of those cafes along the Brunswick Street Mall, below ground level. We just kind of drifted down here. I don't know. Anthony led and I followed.

There are various interchangeable Valley types in here. A girl with too much eyeshadow and severe black bangs is sitting at the next table playing with a cigarette. She looks a lot like Jodie, the Hello Kitty girl, who looked a lot like something out of a Japanese cartoon. These two boys in black, I guess they must work here, waiting by the door. Waiting for their shift to start or something. They're both pretty, bleached, pierced, aloof, etc, like every other boy in the Valley, and I'd fuck both of them and thanks to six degrees of fornication I probably have and Anthony probably has too and the girl with the black bangs who looks like Jodie probably has as well.

250

We're waiting for our coffees. Long blacks, of course. I shouldn't drink so much black coffee, but my system is probably thankful for the break I'm giving it. Caffeine is the *least* dangerous thing I've consumed with any kind of regularity over the last few months.

Our table is actually an old Pac Man machine, reclaimed or whatever, with a thick sheet of plastic over the top so people don't spill coffee on it. I am leaning back, watching Anthony, who has just fed a coin into the machine and is maneuvering Pac Man through the maze.

251

Anthony: This is stuffed.
Me: What do you mean?
Anthony: This game. The Pac Man machine. It's not fucking working properly.
Me: What do you mean?
Anthony: The joystick's all fucked up. Half the time Pac Man's not even moving in the right direction.
Me: What do you mean?
Anthony: Well, okay, look at this.

He taps the joystick three times, pushing it to the left. He taps it quite hard, but Pac Man only moves on the third one.

Me: I getcha.
Anthony: Of course you do. It's fucked.
Me: Maybe you're not doing it right?
Anthony: I *know* how to do it.
Me: I just mean . . .
Anthony: I mean, like, I've been playing video games since I was four years old. I know how a joystick's meant to work.

Me: Whatever. Forget about it.
Anthony: What's up with you this morning, Calvin?
Me: Nothing.

Anthony is distracted. His Pac Man is moving blindly upwards, and in that space of a few seconds is consumed by the red ghost. Flashing. Then the screen goes blank.

Pac Man Machine: Game Over.
Anthony: Fuck.

Several beats of silence.

Anthony: You want to play?
Me: I'm fine.
Anthony: You sure.
Me: Yeah, I'm okay. I suck at Pac Man anyway.

Silence.

Anthony: What's up?
Me: What do you mean?
Anthony: You're acting weird this morning, and it's fucked. Seriously, what's up?
Me: Nothing. I don't know.

Anthony: Seems like something.

Me: It's really not.

Anthony: What is it, Calvin?

Me: Nothing. I saw this photo.

Anthony: What?

Me: I mean, in this street press thing. A photo, in, like, this ad. For a website, I guess it was.

Anthony: . . . And?

Me: And nothing. It sort of looked like you, but it wasn't. It wasn't you, I mean. It was just a photo of some boy.

Anthony: But he looked like me?

Me: . . . Kind of.

Anthony: So . . . Why did you bring it up then? What makes this boy who *kind of* looked like me so significant?

Me: I don't know. Nothing. I was just thinking about him.

Anthony: Right.

Me: I don't understand.

Anthony: Don't understand what?

The waitress arrives with our coffees and sets them down on the Pac Man machine. I smile, thank her in a distracted sort of a way. Anthony says nothing. He's staring at me, waiting for the waitress to go away so I can explain what the hell I'm talking about. Which might be difficult, because I don't *know* what the hell I'm talking about.

As soon as she leaves, Anthony asks again:

Anthony: Don't understand what?
Me: The ad was for this website. This website that was called Sick Puppies, and it was like . . .

The expression on Anthony's face changes.

Me: What, you've heard of it?
Anthony: I know of its existence, yeah.
Me: So then you can probably appreciate what this ad was like.
Anthony: I probably can, yeah. I'm still struggling to see what you're getting at.
Me: Anthony, look. This is weird for me. Being with you, I mean. I really . . . I'm trying to understand what it was like . . . for you, with the photographs and everything. What it felt like . . . Why you did it. I mean, why you would . . .
Anthony: Why I did it?
Me: This thing, with the photos. I don't understand. I mean, because, I really like you, and I possibly even love you, and it's like . . .
Anthony: Calvin, no you don't.
Me: I do.

Anthony: You don't, Calvin.

Me: This is weird for me as well, Anthony.

Anthony: Calvin, you don't love me. You . . . I know you better than you suspect.

Me: I don't think you do.

Anthony: Calvin, you're a mess. You don't know what you want . . . You love an *idea*. And, like, at *best,* I happen to slot into that particular idea.

Me: That's not true.

Anthony: Well it's pointless, Calvin. Being in love is pointless.

Me: At, like, at our age?

Anthony: At *any* age, Calvin. Where does love get you?

Me: I don't know, I'm just *saying* . . .

Anthony: Fucking, at . . . at *best* you're fucking obsessed with me. With this. It's scary. I liked you at the start, Calvin. It was fun, because we *didn't* have to think about it. Because we didn't have "love" or whatever you want to call it as a complicating factor. We were just two guys having fun. I should have known. I should have *realized.* You're the obsessive type, Calvin. You're fucking scary and obsessive and I don't need that, and this *thing* . . .

Me: What thing?

Anthony: This *thing* with the photos. With

Jeremy. With *all* the photos. It's just something I did, Calvin. You don't understand it. You're trying to analyze it on every fucking level imaginable and that's why you *won't* understand it. This . . . This *analysis* thing you do. It's fucking boring. And I don't care. I don't *expect* you to understand any of this, but . . .

252

The machine is playing by itself now. All of Anthony's goes are up. Even though nobody's playing with him, Pac Man refuses to die. The game lights up again, a demo game. The same every time. Pac Man races through the maze, trying to eat all the little pills. The red ghost gains on him. Eats him. Game over. Play again. This cycle repeats itself over and over. I stare at it in dumb fascination, thinking that eventually, maybe, it might be different. It's not impossible.

253

Several beats of silence.

Anthony looks right at me. "I know what this is really about. You want to know what it feels like."

Several more beats.

"I do. I mean, I don't know. I think I do."

He looks at me. Says nothing.

On the screen: A tiny, darkened room. Pac Man sits, blinking and yellow, just near the center. The music starts; chunky, electronic, hypnotic. He begins to move, and he really goes. So many little pills to munch up, so little time. The smaller ones are worth ten points, the bigger ones a hundred, and when he eats the bigger ones, the ghosts become vulnerable. Until then, he's easy prey. And the ghosts are out to get him. As he starts out, Mocky, the red ghost is pursuing him. Micky, Mucky and Macky are still locked inside that tiny little box eager as fuck to get out. Those three want to get Pac Man. They want him really fucking bad.

"Okay, I do. I want to know what it feels like."

"That makes sense."

"Why does it make sense?"

"Because you've never felt anything. You've never had to."

On the screen: Pac Man moves to the left, chomping up the first of the smaller pills. He turns a corner in the maze, continues chomping them down. Mocky is swerving blindly around the maze. The look in his eyes is totally blank, empty. He has one mission: Find Pac Man. And he will. He'll get the little fucker. No matter how much mindless swerving it takes to get there. His tentacles, always moving. Pac Man swerves to the left, then the right, misses a big row of pills. He'll have to go back. He has to eat them all. He has to. Micky, the yellow ghost, is free. Now Macky, green ghost. One of the big flashing pills is in sight.

"What does that mean?"

"Calvin. I like you a lot. You're really cute. I mean that. You're fucking gorgeous, but you don't know anything. You're basically just a bored teenage fag who's all hung up about the fact that he has *nothing* to be hung up about. It's all a mind game. I mean it Calvin. It's all *you*. You're good-looking and you've always had everything you've ever wanted, and those are really the most complicated things you've ever had to deal with . . . and it kills you."

On the screen: Micky is closing in on Pac Man. The two will almost connect, and then Micky will fall back. Mucky is free. Blue ghost. All of them begin to swarm Pac Man, gliding down to the lower left-hand corner of the maze. They swarm. Swarm. Pac Man is in danger now. The big flashing pill is in sight. Connect. Fall back. Connect. Fall back. If Pac Man can only get to it . . .

Maybe he's expecting me to say something at this point, but I don't. I let him continue.

"We're not nihilistic and stupid because the world made us this way. We're nihilistic and stupid because we can be. Because it's fucking *fun.* It's a *distraction.* That's the only reason. The fact that we're faggots doesn't make us any different from anyone else. The truth is, we're just as fucking boring as our parents and all of our parents' friends, we have basically the same preoccupations; and we go out of our way to try and be different because we know that ultimately our lives amount to just as little. We need something to distract us. Everyone does. You need something to distract you. Fine. So you just *happen* to do it by sleeping with a fuckload of guys."

"Way to fucking rationalize things, Anthony."

"I'm not rationalizing, I'm just *saying.* The thing is, you don't just want to be a slut, you want to be a victim too. You're hoping that being knocked about by all sorts of guys will give you something to be truly upset about. That's really all it is, Calvin. You're a slut because you think this beautiful/damaged act it allows you to perform will make you stand out, make it seem like you're the one with *real* problems. You really are special. All this gives you a feeling of *legitimacy*. Am I wrong?"

On the screen: Pac Man has eaten the big flashing pill. The ghosts all change from their respective colors into black; begin to flee. Now Pac Man has the power. He chases them, munching up pills as he goes. He is invincible. Nothing can touch him. Mucky is eaten. He's just a pair of eyes now; they float back to the center, back where the game began. Back where it's always going to begin. Pac Man continues to pursue. Chomping pills. But their effects are wearing off. The ghosts stop flashing. Mocky is the red ghost again. He has the power now. Pac Man turns a corner.

"You're just the same."
  "I know."
  "You know?"
  "The difference is, I don't try to make it

seem more profound than it is. I suck lots of cock because it makes me *feel good.* I let guys take my picture because it makes me feel good. *Really* fucking good. That's all. That's the extent of it. I don't pretend I'm being exploited. Nobody ever fucked me in the ass as a little kid. Nobody ever interfered with me. I don't pretend that any of it's deep and meaningful. I let guys fuck me because I can. Because I *like* to. Because I want to do it before I'm old and ugly and nobody wants to fucking sleep with me anymore. That's the *only reason.* And I don't pretend it's anyone's doing but mine."

On the screen: A line of little pills in front of Pac Man. He can make it. There's a big flashing one just up and to the right. He can get to it. If he just turns this next corner. But he doesn't turn. The corner is right there, right beside him, but he doesn't turn it. He keeps going, chomping at nothing. Chomping at the air. Mocky is gaining on him. The red ghost. He's angry. Pac Man could turn here. He doesn't. He doesn't turn, he just continues. Mucky doesn't even have to work; there's no fun in this anymore.

I say nothing.

On the screen: Mocky consumes Pac Man.
Game over. The whole cycle starts again.

254

Cold wind on the street. The sky is still gray and I don't
know quite what I'm doing. I still have that street press
folded up in my hand but I've twisted and folded it so
much that it's probably unreadable now. Doesn't matter anyway.

Chinese Opera is drifting out of the restaurant
behind me, delicate—a woman's voice, high, and she
could be singing about anything at all but because I
don't understand it, it seems somehow sinister. Every
time someone opens the door the music becomes
louder, and a blast of cold air follows it. Everyone
seems to have a purpose. Everyone is walking to something, or from something.

Out of the equation.

Behind me there is a fish tank built into a wall. I
guess it's the wall of a restaurant. There are actually
about six tanks built in, all facing out onto the street,
and all filled with crayfish and eels and weeds and
pebbles and green scum. They all float around lazily, as
if in a trance, and this one tank near the top has way
too many lobsters in it—there must be at least twelve

of them in there, in a small tank—and they're all swimming around helplessly, though they don't have a great deal of room to move, and their feelers are getting tangled and they swim into one another and some of them are clawing at one another, probably clawing for space, but who knows, and it's way too crowded in there and the thought of it troubles me so much I can't even begin to deal with it.

There is another fish tank, right down the bottom, which seems to be empty until I look closely. The water is green, thick with weeds and mold, and a single fish floats down near the bottom, languid, not even really moving, just there. I look at it for ages, but it hardly moves the whole time, just floats there, and it's difficult to tell whether it's even alive or not, or whether it's just floating there, dead, and nobody has noticed it yet. I'm not sure what worries me more, the idea that it's dead or the idea that it's not. I wonder how long it's been there. Weeks? Months? Couldn't be, but it's possible. Anything's possible. I look at the fish for a bit longer and I realize the same green mold that covers the glass has started to grow on the fish itself, all over its scales, which look like they might once have been shiny and iridescent and beautiful but are now gray and murky, and I peer in there and realize that some of the green mold has even started to grow over the fish's eye. Its eye.

This is something I absolutely can't deal with. I mean, I fucking lose it. I don't know how to describe it exactly, but the idea of the fish just floating there, not moving, the idea that the mold has started to grow over its *eye,* is way more than my fragile composure can cope with. I kneel down on the pavement and put my face right up to the tank and I start tapping on the glass. Gently at first, just to try and wake the fish up or whatever, to try and get it to move, to blink or something. My forehead is pressed right up to the glass and I'm knocking on it now and there are people walking past me and staring, I can tell, I think I'm starting to draw a crowd, but I don't even care because suddenly my life *depends* on getting this fish to wake up.

Mold. On its eye. *Its eye.* I can see through the tank into the restaurant, and some of the diners at a corner table—their figures are all distorted and green through the glass—have stopped eating and are staring at me as I knock on the glass. I keep going. I keep knocking. I have to wake this fish up. I have to make it move. It can't be so far gone that it doesn't care enough to move anymore. It can't be. The idea that anything, even a fish, could be that far gone—really troubles me. I have to believe that it's not possible. That it's not possible to let the mold grow over your *eye* and still not move. It can't be possible.

I'm really losing it. Knocking on the glass. Yelling at it. The fish doesn't move. It floats there, doesn't blink, not even a ripple in the water. The tendrils of weed so long they could probably strangle you. I can't believe the fish won't move. It has to. It has to fight back. It has to *blink*. It has to just blink and I'll be happy. I'll be satisfied.

"Blink!" I tell it. "Blink!" And I've really started to draw a crowd now. I can hear hushed noises from behind me, a woman's voice, I can't hear what she's saying but she sounds concerned, and the fish just floats there with the green mold covering its eye.

Out of the equation.

"Blink!" I tell it. "Blink!"

And it blinks. Just then, and just once. When its eye opens again, the clump of mold is shaken loose and begins to float away. Slowly. Twisting upwards. Almost like a ballet dancer in the murky water.

I don't know how I feel now. I probably don't feel anything.

A man has come out of the restaurant. He is Asian and he's wearing a business suit, and I guess he's the owner of the place. He looks down at me, uncomprehending, like, "what's this stupid white boy doing?" He looks at me like he totally doesn't understand, which is not surprising because I don't either.

I stand. The crowd draws back a little, and there's one woman, blonde and holding a camera, whose expression is a mix of fascination and terror, like I might be planning to attack or something, like I'm one of those children they bring back from the wilderness, who've been raised by wolves or, like, baboons or whatever.

The owner says nothing at all, just stares at me.

"I'm sorry," I tell him. Which I am.

I begin to move away, and he just stands there, staring at me. And the weird thing is, he doesn't yell. I look at him and he starts to cry.

He cries in that way men have of crying, in that way my father has of crying with shoulders hunched a little, choked but silent, like someone trying to stifle a yawn.

He cries. The owner of the restaurant cries, and the moment becomes big, like, bigger than I can even quantify, and I realize I'm just a very small part of it. The man stands there. Says nothing. Just cries. This is probably just the final act of some much greater personal tragedy for him. Whatever that might happen to be I feel bad about the fact that I've somehow been a participant. Whatever emotion has overwhelmed the man, whatever I've somehow triggered by being a part or a representative of some much greater sorrow . . . it's a lot more than I can cope with.

"I'm sorry," I tell him, backing away. I don't understand this, and it frightens me a lot.

He doesn't say anything.

"I'm sorry."

I don't run away or anything. I just walk. I walk away. What else am I *supposed* to do?

I don't look back at the crowd. I guess they're starting to scatter.

Out of the equation.

255

Earlier, at the cafe: Anthony put another coin into the Pac Man machine and I left. He told me to call him when I'd got over this fucking attitude thing that I have.

256

I am at Sushi Central. I don't know why I came here, except that this is the place I always seem to drift to, and I feel most at home here. I feel like sushi, though I don't really feel like sushi as much as I feel like the *idea* of sushi. It will calm me down. Something familiar. Anthony has just told me to get over this fucking attitude thing that I have and I am thinking. I am thinking about losing myself, wondering if I am capable of doing this, and I think about it until it is all I'm thinking about, losing myself, letting myself go, wondering if it's *possible* for me to let myself go, to be like Jeremy, like *Anthony* for that matter, to be the kind of person who doesn't think, who just *does*. I am wondering if this is possible.

I am sitting at one of those stools with the red vinyl covering. Fast and candy-sweet pop music with lyrics I don't understand is blasting out of the sound system. There are couples all around me. They seem happy. There is a man sitting two seats down from me, by himself. The waitress asks if I would like some green tea. I tell her I would. Yeah. That would be cool. I take a plate of the tuna salad from the sushi train. Eat it without even tasting it. I'm cold. I am thinking. Anthony. I am thinking.

257

My system is crashing: At home Saturday afternoon. It's raining outside. Sitting at my computer. Nobody is online. I bring up that one photo of Anthony, the profile shot. Leaning into the glass. His reflection; two Anthonys.

258

From: Calvin <hearts_filthy_lesson@hotmail.com>
To: Jeremy <jezza99@i-accelerate.com.au>
Subject: kind of urgent

Hey Jeremy, how are things?

I need to talk to you again. Will you be online soon?

Stay cool,
Calvin.

259

Saturday night. Living room, sitting over my old Nintendo. The sounds of rain outside.

Super Mario Brothers 3: Mario is in his raccoon suit; gliding through the level, spinning around and knocking out the little turtle things with his tail. Mario's jumping up into this secret area in the clouds. You can tell you're meant to be looking at "clouds" because the area is rendered in deceptively simple white and blue pixels. That faux-naïve way they had of representing things like that in old video games. Huge globs of white, they take up the whole screen, and every now and then a patch of blue will emerge from behind. So you can tell it's meant to be clouds. Mario is running through the area collecting the little coin things. White. Puffy clouds. Blue sky. This is the first blue sky, or even representation of a blue sky that I've seen in as long as I can remember. I want to make Mario fall off the cloud but there are no gaps for him to fall through.

260

Sunday. IRC chat.

sweet*Prince: hey jeremy

ŠaÇ©hå®™inë/RELIGÍºùs: hey hey calvin! how r things?

sweet*Prince: all right. you?

ŠaÇ©hå®™inë/RELIGÍºùs: hahhahha. pretty sweet, you know

ŠaÇ©hå®™inë/RELIGÍºùs: there was this fuckin kick *asssssssssssss* rave at southport friday night.

sweet*Prince: sounds cool

ŠaÇ©hå®™inë/RELIGÍºùs: ahha, it was kuhl!!! we were pilling and dancing around and it was a fuckin blast. I wuz *so* tired by the time we crashed the next morning but it was totally worth it.

sweet*Prince: sweet

ŠaÇ©hå®™inë/RELIGÍºùs: so what did u need to talk to me about?

sweet*Prince: um, nothing much, it's just

ŠaÇ©hå®™inë/RELIGÍºùs: ahha!

ŠaÇ©hå®™inë/RELIGᶥᵒ̀ùs: I knew u couldn't resist me!

sweet*Prince: okay, um . . .

sweet*Prince: do you remember that guy you were telling me about?

ŠaÇ©hå®™inë/RELIGᶥᵒ̀ùs: the big brother guy?

sweet*Prince: no, not him. I mean the guy with the photos. the uniform guy.

ŠaÇ©hå®™inë/RELIGᶥᵒ̀ùs: . . . yeah.   I remember that.

sweet*Prince: I've changed my mind.

ŠaÇ©hå®™inë/RELIGᶥᵒ̀ùs: changed your mind?

sweet*Prince: yeah. about the guy, I mean. I want to meet him.

ŠaÇ©hå®™inë/RELIGᶥᵒ̀ùs: u want to meet him?

ŠaÇ©hå®™inë/RELIGᶥᵒ̀ùs: =)P

sweet*Prince: yeah, I guess

ŠaÇ©hå®™inë/RELIGᶥᵒ̀ùs: are u serious about this?

sweet*Prince: I need the money

sweet*Prince: it's a long story. I can't even explain, but I'm really short, and like . . .

sweet*Prince: I need the money in kind of a hurry

sweet*Prince: and since u told me about this guy, I thought, you know . . .

ŠaÇ©hå®™inë/RELIGⁱ⁰ùs: hahhahhahha, I *knew* u would.

sweet*Prince: what does that mean?

ŠaÇ©hå®™inë/RELIGⁱ⁰ùs: I don't know. whatever

ŠaÇ©hå®™inë/RELIGⁱ⁰ùs: all I mean is I know u can do this. you're hot enough.

sweet*Prince: you think so?

ŠaÇ©hå®™inë/RELIGⁱ⁰ùs: sure, yur hot. totally.

ŠaÇ©hå®™inë/RELIGⁱ⁰ùs: =)

sweet*Prince: so . . . what's the deal with this guy exactly?

ŠaÇ©hå®™inë/RELIGⁱ⁰ùs: nothing too extreme. He's basically pretty harmless, you know.

sweet*Prince: how much can he give me?

ŠaÇ©hå®™inë/RELIGⁱ⁰ùs: how much do u need?

sweet*Prince: . . . would how much I need change things? I mean, do I have to . . .

sweet*Prince: . . . like . . .

ŠaÇ©hå®™inë/RELIGⁱ⁰ùs: look, just to take the photos, this guy will give you like, a hundred bucks, maybe two hundred if you play your cards right.

ŠaÇ©hå®™inë/RELIGͺùs: anything over that and you can negotiate . . . you know, play it by ear.

sweet*Prince: okay

ŠaÇ©hå®™inë/RELIGͺùs: u sure?

sweet*Prince: yeah

ŠaÇ©hå®™inë/RELIGͺùs: kay then. I can hook you guys up. I'll have to get in touch with him first. organize when and where, u know.

sweet*Prince: cool

261

He's basically harmless. I let this information sink in; I wonder what *basically* harmless actually means; like, if it's possible to quantify harmlessness on a scale of, say, one to ten, where would this guy, this *basically* harmless guy, fit in?

Harmless, like, "it doesn't bite, you know, unless you put your hand in the cage"?

262

At this stage I'm taking a number of factors into consideration:

    a) I don't have to do this.

b) I'm choosing to do this. A lot of guys are actually forced into these kinds of situations. I'm doing it because . . . Why, because I want to? That doesn't make sense. But I'm doing it anyway. Because:

c) I have to know how it feels. How Anthony felt. Therefore, it's okay lying to Jeremy about needing the money. I want to know how it feels to disappear completely.

And thinking about it, the whole thing can't last more than about two hours anyway. All I need to do is dress up for the guy and then stand there. That doesn't require a great deal of effort on my part. I mean, in a weird way I should probably be *flattered* if the guy finds me good-looking enough to take photos of in the first place.

Everyone's good-looking at my age.

No. Push those thoughts away.

Take yourself out of the equation.

Would that be possible?

263

Kitchen: Still the same two red flowers in the vase. The Polaroid on the fridge. Cold day. One of those moments that seem suspended in time, when the half-light of the overcast afternoon fills the room; when there is nothing around you but silence; when you find yourself barely able to move, or even breathe. There is a lemon lying on the bench in front of me. The bright color seems incongruous; it's sarcastically bright. So I cut it. I cut it in half, then half again, then half again. I pick up one of the smaller pieces—an eighth of the lemon—and drop it into a tall glass. I know that if I lick my fingers, the taste of lemon juice will be on them, but I don't lick my fingers. I stare at the glass for a while, at the glass with the eighth of a lemon in the bottom of it. I stare into the glass and try not to think about Anthony. I pour some water in—four cubes of ice, even though it's such a cold day—four cubes of ice, leaving just one in the ice tray, and sit it back down in front of me.

264

I've become totally neurotic about that Placebo album, especially that one song. You know the one. I was at HMV in the city; there's a guy there who I used to totally want to fuck, and I was always devising, like, these little scenarios wherein someone introduced me to him and we hit it off and he told me how hot I was and blah blah, you know exactly the kind of thing I mean, but anyway, yeah.

I was in there the other day and I happened to pick the album up, just to look at it again, and this particular guy happened to be walking past, and he told me "This is a killer cool album" and I smiled and told him "Yeah" and then he sort of looked away or something and we didn't really talk much after that, and as I was leaving I was wondering if it was kind of, you know, crazy of me to get all bent out of shape about a stranger from HMV, and possibly it was, but it seems like such a long time ago now, a more innocent time. I miss stupid crushes. When did everything get so serious?

265

Porno: Anyway. As I was saying. I've taken to sitting in my room listening to that album over and over again, like, sometimes six or seven times in a row. I'm playing it now. One in the afternoon. I'm about to head into the city, so I can meet Jeremy. So he can give me directions. That guy. I don't know why I have to meet Jeremy. I don't know why I'm meeting him in the first place. It's stupid. I'm stupid for doing it. I'm stupid. I'm fucking stupid. But I have to know.

Trying to decide what to wear. What do you wear?

You know. I mean, it's not like I'm freaking out about this or anything. I can totally handle it. It's just, like, an equation. A transaction. Whatever. Totally not a big deal.

I continue looking through my clothes, hunting through them, trying to find something I want to wear. There's a blue T-shirt with "King Of Cool!" and a big picture of a polar bear on the front. It's, like, postmodern, or ironic or whatever. There's that red "Brain Dead Body Still Rockin'" one. I consider them both.

I put the red one on and take it off again. I choose the blue one, mostly because of the picture of the polar bear.

266

I printed out this email that Jeremy sent me and blu-tacked it to my wall. It seemed kind of significant or whatever. I don't know. I worried about the position-ing of it for ages and ages. I put on a CD and kept try-ing to sit down, trying to make myself concentrate on the music or something, but every few seconds I looked up and it seemed to be in the wrong place, and I kept having to get up and move it around. It never seemed to look right anywhere. In the end I took it down.

267

From: Jeremy <jezza99@i-accelerate.com.au>
To: Calvin <hearts_filthy_lesson@hotmail.com>
Subject: all set up

Hey Calvin

How r u?

Talked to the guy and it should be fine. If yur interested, call me. U have my number

Talk to ya soon
Luv yur work,
Jeremy

268

I'm standing on the terrace. There is a coffee mug in my hands, white, with the logo of some drug company on the front, along with the name of some prescription drug or other, I don't know. There are coffee stains in the bottom and around the rim. It feels cold in my hands. I walk to the railing, hold it out and then let it drop all the way down to the tiles by the pool, just to hear what it sounds like when it smashes.

The noise is not as satisfying as I expected it to be.

269

This one particular song I used to listen to all the time is on the stereo. The final track from this particular album, which is kind of fitting. The singer is being taken over. She's practically ready to kill herself. All fucked up over a boy and only because he looks so fine. It kills me that the lyrics of some sticky pop song can so totally reflect my exact thoughts and feelings. I mean it. It's really fucking annoying.

270

I almost stop myself on the way out of the house. I don't know why I'm doing this. It's fucking insane. Every so often things get like this. It's hard to explain, but it's like my mind detaches from my body. I'm outside myself, and I'm doing something and I don't even know if I *want* to be doing it or not, but it's as though my body is on autopilot so my mind can be elsewhere. A warmer place, or a safer place. When I'm like that, I'm almost happy. Almost. But my mind always has to go back. Even when I've managed to kid myself that I'm happy, even when I've almost managed to disconnect myself from the real world, there's still a part of me that knows I will have to go back.

As I'm opening the door, I have this moment of

weird clarity. I want to know what it feels like to lose myself totally. *I want to know.*

How stupid is that?

271

Bus to the city: Placebo are playing on my discman although I can't even hear them properly, and I'm sure this is partly because of the noise of the bus but mostly because of the noise in my own head. The day is a negative image of itself and everything is strange and everyone is staring at me and I close my eyes and suddenly I'm not there anymore; it's early in the morning, and I'm sitting in the window seat and we're *flying*, somewhere over the Pacific ocean, and I'm looking out of the plane and seeing nothing but a mass of clouds, as far as I can see, stretching on forever, and up here, the world as such doesn't exist, it's a different world, where the morning sun reflects off the clouds, beautiful, calm, and there's nothing around you but sky, and you feel almost like you're at peace, like everything is different up here and nothing matters, and if the plane would never land, you wouldn't care, and you would stay up here in this world forever, because . . .

272

I'm at Sushi Central. Can of extremely sticky-sweet energy cola sitting in front of me. I feel good. Maybe not good, but different. I'm waiting for Jeremy, who said he'd meet me here later. I pulled a plate of tuna salad from the sushi train, but I'm not eating it. The music on the stereo is this loud and saccharine and incredibly highNRG electro-punk. One of the waitresses is dancing, swaying, but not to the music; she's dancing to something else. I am thinking. Anthony. I don't know how I feel. My notebook is in front of me. That picture of Stefan Olsdal is staring at me.

273

Picture of Stef: Even though this picture was taken not so long ago, he probably looks nothing like this anymore. People change in so many minor ways. This is a picture of a version of him that probably doesn't exist anymore. But still, the picture exists, and it's here, on the front of my notebook, and in a bunch of magazines all around the world, and on the net, preserved in some version of cold, digital eternity. This picture *is* Stef. He will change, he'll get older, but this picture won't. This picture will always be a record of a time when he was young and beautiful. This picture will preserve him. The *real* Stef won't even matter. People don't know him for who he is. *I* don't know him for who he is. I know him from his music and, more importantly, from his pictures. Pictures like this are all Stefan is to me. As far as I'm concerned, they make up the whole of his identity. He will be remembered from his photographs.

So if that's the case, then . . .

274

Writing in my notebook: I've been trying since I was fourteen to turn all of this despair and hatred inside me into wild sexual abandon. I thought that if I could, I could defuse their effects. Give it all a context to make it seem worthwhile. I don't know. I've been fucking around and giving myself to any old body for god knows how long and I wanted just once for sex to happen in the right place and at the right time and with the right boy and it would all be cool and it would all be beautiful and it would be stronger than the effect of any drug I could take, and it would be my salvation. A way out. So I hooked up with Anthony. It felt good, and it felt interesting, but in the end it didn't mean shit. It meant nothing.

So yeah. Big deal. People are what you want them to be. I guess you shut out a lot of the things you don't want to see. I wanted someone to cling to, someone to save me, so I found that in Anthony. The real Anthony and the Anthony who existed in my head were two entirely different people. I don't know how much was invented and how much was real. Maybe it doesn't even matter.

I wanted to stop being me and start being someone else's toy, but I didn't think I'd have it in me. But these photos once they get taken, they'll still be there. They'll still be there on the net or whatever, like, a record of me. A record of a time when I was young and hot and people wanted me.

The real me won't even matter. The real me will be taken out of the equation. And it will probably be a lot better that way. That's really all that matters, isn't it? Those pictures of me will always exist. Keeping a record of myself. That way at least there'll be something. One day soon I'll be old. I'll probably be dead or something. I don't know.

My whole identity will be tied up in them.

275

I feel a hand on my shoulder. It's Jeremy.

276

Jeremy: You sure?
Me: I'm sure.

He picks at a plate of salmon and avocado rolls, and I take another sip of that fizzy green hyperactive energy cola caffeine drink thing.

Jeremy: Okay. This is where you can meet him.

277

When I open the door, I can't see him at first, and the entryway is extremely narrow, and when I turn my head I see a brownhaired boy, a little too thin but basically pretty cute and with this worried look on his face, and I realize it's me, because there's a mirror set into the wall, and I turn back quickly, move into the main part of the apartment, and when I look around I see him sitting there, in this lounge chair, new and expensive-looking, though the others in the set don't seem to be here, and he's older than I expected, bigger, and better dressed—he's wearing a *tie,* like he's just come from a meeting or something—his hair is silvery and very neat, and when he sees me come in, he looks up and says, "Hello there," speaking in slightly accented English, and I sort of give him this nod that could be interpreted as hello, and he can tell I'm nervous and I can tell he's getting off on it, which is not, like, unexpected, but it's disturbing nonetheless, and he says to me, "You must be Calvin," and I tell him yes, I am, as far as I know, anyway, and he smiles at me and says, "Well, just like Calvin Klein," and I'm not sure if he's making a joke or not but I force this little laugh out anyway, like, trying to be cute or whatever, like I need to win his approval or something, which is just pathetic but let's not even think about it, and he sort of motions me over, gives me a smile and then he says, "Come a little closer so I can see you, Calvin Klein," and I do, I mean, I feel myself moving closer to him, sort of taking these tentative little steps, checking out the decor of the apartment, but not really, because I'm nervous, although there are some blinds that are drawn, and I guess that if they were open you might be able to see the river, and there really isn't much in the room, like, for a place that's so new and seems so nice, it's oddly bare, like someone's only just moving in, or moving out, or something, I don't know, but there aren't even any boxes sitting around, just this armchair, a tiled white floor leading onto cream-colored carpet, and he's nodding at me, I'm treading cautiously, stepping onto the carpet in the main part of the room, and once I get there, I'm standing more or less in front of the sofa, and he says nothing at all, but after a while, what seems like an incredibly long time, he stands, and he's a lot taller than I am, and he puts his hand on my chest, leaves it there for a long time, and the feel of it, the weight of it, and the heat, like he's feeling for a heartbeat or something, and it's a gesture that in any other context could be interpreted as compassion, like, a *tender* gesture, but here it's twisted out of context and horrible, and my heart's beating, like, incredibly fast and he can feel this and all he does is smile at me, this incredibly warm smile, like a family doctor kind of a smile, like a smile the doctor would give to a four year old before giving him his shots, and he asks me after a while, "You nervous there, Calvin Klein?" and I really wish he'd stop calling me Calvin Klein, like, really, more than anything, it just seems so familiar and every time he says it it's like being slapped and I just wish he'd, like, STOP IT already, but he just keeps smiling at me, then he runs his fingers through my hair and asks me if I'm ready, and I find it in me, somehow, to speak, and I ask him, you know, am I ready for what specifically, and he asks me if I'm ready to have my picture taken, and I sort of stall, and I'm not really sure what to say, I mean, because, it's the reason I came up here, and I don't say anything, just look at him, and he's still giving me this warm, genuine-looking smile, although now it has the faintest edge to it, like, maybe because of what he's doing with his eyes or whatever, and he pretends to be confused, and he asks me, you know, "You *did* come up here so I could take your picture, didn't you, Calvin Klein?" and I suddenly wonder about running away, just, like, running, as fast as I can, and I wonder about the door behind me, whether it's locked or not, because I heard it click when I came in, I think, and, and oh god, god, I'm really doing this, I've got myself into this and it's something I can't get out of, and I can't call my dad or Anthony or anyone else to come rescue me, I'm all alone with this guy who keeps, like, smiling at me and calling me Calvin Klein and he could pretty much do anything he wants to me, and I realize the only way to get out of this is to just go with it, it's a transaction, remember, just take myself out of the equation and it will be like nothing's happening at all, so I look the man in the eyes and tell him, "Sure, okay, I'm ready," and just like that his expression loses that edge, like he's really pleased with me or whatever, and I'm thinking, you know, if he patted me on the head and told me "good boy" that really wouldn't surprise me at this point, and thinking about that I suddenly almost choke with laughter and he asks me what's wrong and I tell him nothing, and he asks me if maybe I want to smoke a joint or something to calm me down before we get started, and I think it seems like a really good idea, so I give him this pathetic/cute little smile and scrunch my eyes up a bit and nod at him, and his hand is in the small of my back and he's leading me through another door, into the next room, a bedroom, which is darker, and there are several things in here, like, a rack, a big silver one, with all kinds of clothes hanging from it, and I realize they're all uniforms, like sports uniforms etc, which makes sense considering what Jeremy has already told me, and an umbrella, to reflect the light, I guess, I never know what photographers use them for exactly, and on the far wall, a poster for the movie *Last Tango In Paris*, and something about the word *Paris* gets me, because I remember when I was young, when I was eleven or something, my parents took me to Europe, and we travelled all over, for weeks and weeks, but the place that really sticks in my mind is Paris, because to me, at the time, Paris was magic, like, genuine, magic, the way magic can only be when you're a little kid, when you're impressionable and optimistic and the possibility of magic is still real, and the word *Paris* sends me into a trance for a second as everything it represents to me begins to come back, and if I can put myself there when what's obviously now about to happen starts happening, then I won't feel a thing, and as for the rest of the room, the space in front of the camera, it's like a set, I mean, it's a bedroom, but it's obviously not the bedroom of the person who lives here, it's designed, contrived, to look like of a teenager's bedroom, I guess—a bed, with this quilted bedspread, a desk nearby with some trophies and I guess they must be textbooks lying around on the desk, and all these other insane little touches, and the end result actually looks pretty genuine, like it could *actually* be some kid's bedroom if you don't look at it too hard, but I guess whoever's looking at these photos will be looking at me most of all, and I can't tell whether that thought comforts me or not, and I'm sort of wondering how the hell it's possible for something this, like, *elaborate,* to be here in the city without anyone *noticing,* but the man's hand is still on the small of my back, and soon I forget all about it, because from a table that also has sitting on it some camera equipment and various other things I try not to look at, he grabs a joint, already rolled, and lights it for me, and it's really strong weed, which is good because I need something to knock me out at this point, and I sort of offer it to him at one point but he declines and I end up smoking the whole thing, and I can already feel it starting to take hold, the seasick feeling of it, when he walks over to the rack and pulls off what I realize is a basketball uniform—a red singlet top with a big number sixteen on it, an extremely loose pair of shorts—and he looks at me and says, "I think so, yes," mostly to himself, and then when I don't do anything, just stand there, he starts to look impatient, and I realize he wants me to undress, and the pot has loosened me up a bit so I start, I sort of kick off my shoes, slip my T-shirt off, ball it up, then my pants follow, and I'm left standing there in my underwear, and he looks at me and tells me, "Take those off too," and his tone of voice suggests that it would not be a good move to do anything else, so I do, I sort of nervously hook my fingers into the band and slide my boxers down, kick them off, and I'm standing there naked now, and he can see all of me, everything (. . . and I'm eleven years old and in Paris and my father is buying me this really big ice-cream cone, which is vanilla I think, and it's cold, on such a hot day, and it's the best ice-cream cone ever . . .) and he walks over to me with the uniform, tells me to put it on and it's cold to the touch, and I sort of shiver as I'm slipping on the oversized pair of shorts—Nikes— and the singlet with the number sixteen, and when I'm done I just sort of stand there, not sure what to do, and he messes with my hair a little, and I let him, and when he's satisfied—he tells me to pose—don't remember exactly what he says because my heart is beating so fast and the pot has made its way to my brain now so I'm feeling kind of fuzzy as well, but I walk over to the set and position myself on the bed, sit there, my hands behind me, trying to assume a pose that could be considered, like, "cocky" or something, which is probably what he's looking for, and the whole time I'm thinking of Anthony's words, *out of the equation,* and I realize, yeah, this is only a transaction, and the look on my face, what I'm wearing—the costume—none of it means anything, because it's not really me, it's all part of the transaction, and that's a thought I can deal with, I'm happy with that, and I don't even notice that he's walked up to the camera or that it's started flashing: click, whoosh, *bright light,* click, whoosh, *bright light* (. . . and it's night-time, a cool breeze, and we're standing on the balcony of our hotel room looking out across the city, at the rooftops, and the lights, millions of them, the whole city lit up as brightly as I've ever seen, and I can't even speak, because to me it seems like magic, for something as beautiful as this to be possible . . .) and the man tells me to move around; stand up; go over to the desk; lean against it; touch myself; and I give him this look, which is my best approximation of "bedroom eyes" and I'm not even there anymore, I'm playing a character, and he's loving it, and I'm giving him what he wants, and it's great, because I realize, I don't care, I don't feel anything (. . . and we're at the zoo, staring at this big polar bear, and I'm, like, amazed, because I've never seen one before and when it slides into the water and I can't see it anymore I get really upset because I want it to come back out again, but it won't, and . . .) he tells me to get back on the bed; lie down; slip my shorts down a little; I slip them down just past

my hipbones with, like an inch of smooth flesh showing there, and I'm looking right into the camera the
whole time, eyes half closed, flash, flash, and he's fucking loving it, I can tell, he's getting off, I'm getting him
off and it feels fucking great, I'm young and I'm hot
and he fucking wants me and he tells me to jerk off so
I sort of sneer at him, dare him to ask me again, and he
does, like he's pleading now, "Jerk off," and I do, and I
close my eyes and throw my head back, this wholly calculated gesture that I'm sure will get the message
across, and it does, and I keep jerking off, sort of
writhing around on the bed, the covers getting all
twisted, and I don't hear the camera anymore, and I
don't care, and when I open my eyes he's standing by
the bed, just watching me, and I stop, he looks into my
eyes, like, right into them, and I nod (. . . and later on,
in a big toy store, I think, my father is buying me a big,
plush polar bear . . .) and I try not to feel anything
when he's inside me, and after a while I don't, I'm
somewhere else.

I'm gone.

Acknowledgments

Madonna Duffy and Nick Earls for their endless support and encouragement, Kristy Springer for always being there, and my parents for consistently going above and beyond the call of duty.

ALASDAIR DUNCAN is twenty-two years old and lives in Brisbane, Australia, where he is studying journalism at the University of Queensland. He won his first writing award, the State Library of Queensland Young Writers' Award, when he was eighteen. Visit his website at www.alasdairduncan.com.

Don't even pretend you won't read more.

The Whole
John Reed
It all began with a small boy and a large hole. Where will the whole thing end?

Generation S.L.U.T.
Marty Beckerman
A brutal feel-up session with today's sex-crazed teens.

Lit Riffs
What happens when your favorite writers write stories inspired by your favorite songs? You're about to find out...includes riffs by: Tom Perrotta, Jonathan Lethem, Aimee Bender, Neal Pollack, Amanda Davis, JT LeRoy, Lisa Tucker, and many more!

Door to Door
Tobi Tobin
She controls who does and doesn't get in. But when's she going to get in herself?

A Hip-Hop Story
Heru Ptah
Words become powerful weapons as two MCs fight to be #1.

The Perks of Being a Wallflower
Stephen Chbosky
Standing on the fringes offers a unique perspective on life. But sometimes you've got to see what it looks like from the dance floor.

More from the young, the hip, and the up-and-coming.
Brought to you by MTV Books

MTV: Music Television and MTV Books are trademarks of
MTV Networks, a Divison of Viacom International, Inc.

POCKET BOOKS
A Division of Simon & Schuster
A VIACOM COMPANY

11227

As many as 1 in 3 Americans
have HIV and don't know it.

TAKE CONTROL.
KNOW YOUR STATUS.
GET TESTED.

To learn more about HIV testing,
or get a free guide to HIV and
other sexually transmitted diseases.

www.knowhivaids.org
1-866-344-KNOW